God Bless the Child

Books by Anne Shaw Heinrich

The Women of Paradise County Series
Book One: *God Bless the Child*

Coming Soon!
The Women of Paradise County Series
Book Two: *Violet is Blue*
Book Three: *House of Teeth*

For more information
visit: www.SpeakingVolumes.us

God Bless the Child

Anne Shaw Heinrich

SPEAKING VOLUMES, LLC
NAPLES, FLORIDA
2024

God Bless the Child

Copyright © 2024 by Anne Shaw Heinrich

All rights reserved. No part of this book may be reproduced or transmitted in any form or by any means without written permission.

ISBN 979-8-89022-143-8

*To Jane Reed and Constance Moore,
my first writing champions and dream weavers . . .*

Acknowledgments

Every good thing happens when we have the space and grace to consider possibilities. My fortunate path has been forged by my loving parents, Patrick and Ramona, my soulmate and husband, Bret, and our three children, Eleanor, Harrison and Charlotte, who have my heart.

I'd also like to thank some of the best friends in the world a person could have. Fortunately, there are too many to list here.

I'm forever thankful to my editor and friend, David Tabatsky, and to my literary agent, Nancy Rosenfeld. Thanks, too, to Erica and Kurt Mueller at Speaking Volumes.

Chapter One

Mary Kline

I like to keep a dish of bridge mix nearby so I can nibble while I sew. I usually do my best work with a mouth full of milk chocolate.

My dear Johnson gave me a clever pincushion I can wear on my wrist, like a gaudy bracelet. I keep a few extra needles stabbed into it, along with my pins. I only use long pins with pearl tops. They're hard to find, but Johnson always gets me what I need.

I keep a tape measure handy around my neck, and my good scissors are never out of reach. You can't cut worth a darn without a good pair of shears. They are a godsend. No one touches them either except for my dear Johnson.

I've pieced together enough quilts in my time to know that it's best to follow a pattern when you start a big project. It's advantageous to have all your material selected and cut before you break out the needles and thread.

For me, the best part is selecting fabric. There's nothing more delicious than running my hands along rows and rows of textile bolts, grazing over each colorful surface with the tips of my fingers. Choosing the right bolt is almost as agonizing as selecting the best goody at the bakery. The attendant always gets irritated because I want a particular éclair wedged between two others. For some reason, that treat always calls to me.

"Mary Kline! I'm yours!"

Selecting the goody that's easiest to retrieve will never do. It's the same when I buy material. I insist that the clerk spread out a bolt on the counter so I can smooth it over with my fingers and inspect the veneer for flaws. I even catch myself pressing the softest part of my palms onto the surface. This sensation is erotic for me, and I often lose my breath for a minute. It's almost as good as when my Johnson nibbles the back of my neck.

"Mary, Honey, I've got to have a taste of that gorgeous, sweet neck of yours."

Then he growls and pushes my graying hair to one side and sends me straight to Heaven.

Johnson offered to take me up to his fabric shop to get what I needed to make a quilt for my Elizabeth, but I told him no.

"Not this time, Johnson. This quilt is going to be different."

He looked almost insulted. You'd think I'd just refused to have sex with him. As if. I'm probably the only woman in the world with a man who loves sewing as much as I do. Some couples travel. Others dance or play cards. Some go to the movies. Johnson and I love nothing better than sitting together in the living room on a Saturday night to sew.

Sometimes, we work on our own projects, or we do one together. I've always struggled with buttonholes, and Johnson saves me every time. My sweet man knows fabric like most men know baseball and engines. He drives his sewing machine like a skilled, daring drag racer, navigating curves and putting on the brakes in just the nick of time.

He's a problem-solver, too, always figuring out how to get the most out of a piece of fabric. I love watching him concentrate on difficult hand-stitching, like the time I had him attach tiny snaps to the backs of Barbie dresses for my darling granddaughter. We call her Little Mary.

Johnson stood there with his hands on his hips, looking bewildered.

"But Honey, selecting material is the best part. That's what we do. I'll take you out for dinner first. We'll hit the fish fry down at church and then I'll unlock the store. We'll have the whole place to ourselves."

"Sweets, that's not what we're doing this time. But I *do* have a job for you."

Johnson Kuhlman, my girlishly wonderful male companion, will do anything for me. I love him for it.

When I gave him that look, he rolled his eyes, but stood at attention, awaiting his marching orders. He followed me as I made my way slowly up the stairs to Elizabeth's old room. After I caught my breath for a minute at the top of the stairs, we entered the room and I threw open the door to her closet, pulled out every dress that hung there, and heaved them into an enormous, colorful mountain on her bed. Then we went into the back bedroom, where Mother and I used to sleep, and Daddy, too, long ago. From that closet, I pulled out all the dresses Mother had sewn for me, dating back to when I was a chubby little girl.

"There, Johnson. We're using these. And Elizabeth's dresses. And Pearl's too."

Johnson shook his head and folded his arms over his chest.

"Mary, why? Why use this old stuff? Nothing even matches. You've got plaids here, and calicoes and corduroys. All of Elizabeth's stuff is light dotted Swiss, and taffeta and satin and silk. Nothing will coordinate. God, some of this is even rotted in spots. Moth-eaten, too. Don't you want to make something *nice* for Elizabeth? Look at this, Honey. It's awful."

"Johnson, I love you, but I know what I'm doing."

I pulled a few dresses off hangers and motioned for him to help me.

"Don't try to talk me out of this, because I know exactly what I'm going to do. Go get the scissors and help me cut these up."

My darling headed down the stairs, pouting just a little. Once he saw the finished product, I knew he'd understand.

The quilt for Elizabeth was going to be like nothing she'd ever seen, better than anything I'd ever made for her. Ever.

The life I've given Elizabeth hasn't been perfect. How could it be? I started taking care of her and her birth mother, Pearl, without a reasonable role model and before I had a good pattern to follow. I started piecing the three of us together before I had the right tools on hand, long before I knew what the finished product was going to look and feel like.

The three of us weren't made from the same cloth, that's for sure. We didn't belong together in the beginning. Not at all. Elizabeth was just a baby. Pearl was sweet, but slow. And me? Well, I was nothing but a great big kid myself, looking for anything, anyone, to fill an enormous, gaping void that just about swallowed all three of us whole.

Elizabeth, Pearl and I have been patched together, rough and ragged, with nightmares, secrets, shared lies and the sad truth, and even a measure of complicated love.

We are bound.

Chapter Two

Elizabeth

We needed Mary Kline. My mother and I could not take care of ourselves, or each other, without her. Mary Kline was ever present for the occasions that were supposed to be festive, such as holidays, birthdays, my first day of school, and graduations. Pearl was there, too, but only as an observer. It was Mary, not Pearl, who made special dresses for the Christmas pageants at church and in school. She stayed up all night to put finishing touches on my elaborate Halloween costumes.

"My Elizabeth will be the prettiest one there, won't she?"

I watched her work for hours at a time, sewing tiny, clear sequins on the skirt of a princess gown I wore one year. The dress, one of a long line of hand-sewn confections Mary created for me, was the most elegant thing I'd ever seen. She made a larger version of the dress for Pearl. I felt prettier in that shimmering costume than I did in my wedding dress, which took Mary nearly four months to make.

She took care of the daily essentials, too. She cooked our suppers, all of them as delicious for the eyes as they were on the tongue. She'd eat with us, herd me into the tub, then dry my hair with a clean, white towel. Next, she'd slip a nightgown over my head and tuck me in, gently rubbing my back with the tips of her fingernails until I drifted off to sleep. When I didn't fall asleep right away, I could hear Mary doing all of those things for my mother, too.

"Silly, Pearl!" she cooed. "You're not going to go down the drain, Honey. Wait a minute, Darling, while Mary gets a towel. There now, let's dry you off. Where did we put your old nightgown, Pearl? Oh, that's better, isn't it? Nice and warm. You two girls are going to wear

Mary out. Yes, you are. That's just what my girls are going to do. Let's get that hair dried a bit and we'll getcha tucked in. I'm going to check on Elizabeth, and then Mary will leave. See you in the morning, Honey. That's right. Mary Kline will be right here when you wake up."

Soon after that, the front door would close with a click. For the longest time, Mary Kline went to her own house each night to sleep, leaving me and Pearl alone in the dark.

Even after we moved back into the Kline's house for good with Mary and her parents, she was the one who signed all my permission slips for field trips, and helped me memorize the multiplication tables, flashing cards at me in the kitchen while a pot roast, potatoes and carrots bubbled in the oven.

From a distance, our bizarre little scene looked and sounded and smelled normal, but we were an odd, mismatched crew. Two mothers and one child, you might say, or one mother with two children, with Edward and Louise Kline standing on the sidelines, watching, fielding questions from curious onlookers, and offering answers that must have left folks stumped.

Years later, the wording on my wedding invitations reflected the truth that Mary Kline preferred.

Miss Mary Kline and Mr. and Mrs. Eugene Garner request the honor of your presence at the wedding of their children, Elizabeth Grace and David Eugene.

There was no formal mention of Pearl, who sat next to Mary during the ceremony, fumbling with a corsage on her wrist and staring at her hands. The two women had exchanged roles. Mary Kline stood in as the mother of the bride while Pearl was honored as some kind of special guest, a mercy project some might call a consolation prize.

Mary surely nursed resentment for the energy she dedicated to raising a child who wasn't hers. But the job had its perks. She was the recipient of all the hugs and wispy kisses that only little girls can deliver. I was her excuse to buy crayons and paper dolls and dye for Easter eggs. But Mary and Pearl (in her own way) would tell you that life at home was not all sugar and spice, with everything nice.

Filling in the enormous blanks of my day–to–day care, Mary was privy to snips and snails, too. I screeched and bellowed at her for each injustice I suffered. I wailed as she dragged a comb through my stringy hair before school and minutes before we left for church. I was ashamed of her if she wore something silly to my school, and like a true daughter, I sassed her relentlessly, unable to recognize that she had feelings, too.

She bore it all, Mary Kline did—my love and frequent tirades—with a mixture of patience and exasperation, not unlike most mothers. I'm certain that I hurt her feelings on many occasions, and sometimes she cried. When she did, I was unmoved, irritated that her tears would slow down our next transaction.

She gave. I took.

I started my period at age 13. It was one of many things Mary Kline let fall through the cracks—telling me that one day I'd find a pool of blood in my underpants. That initial, inconvenient confirmation of my fertility caught us both by surprise. She was flustered, babbling on about how this meant I was no longer a child, but a woman, and that I could become a mother. At that point, my "real" mother needed help getting dressed. And Mary, Pearl's stand-in, was an embarrassment.

About two cycles into my womanhood, we were waiting in the checkout line at the grocery store when Mary Kline remembered I was running low on pads.

"Elizabeth, we forgot something."

She said it in that singsong voice I found annoying and inconsistent with her huge body. "You stay here."

She waddled down one of the aisles, making a gigantic fuss. In the meantime, the clerk had rung up all our other items. I stood there with the clerk and the bag boy, all of us uncomfortably silent as we waited for Mary to bring that last, essential item, the one we couldn't leave the store without. Was it a pound of ground beef for the spaghetti, or flour for piecrusts? Pickle relish for the egg salad?

Mary Kline finally returned, panting, waving a giant box of super absorbent, unscented pads for everyone to see.

"Is this the kind you like, Elizabeth?"

She knew full well that she had the kind I liked. It was the economy box, with 75 pads packed inside, ready to absorb my blood. The clerk pecked the price into the cash register and gave Mary the total. She always insisted on jotting down the amount right there in her register. She wrote a check with a pudgy hand in what seemed like slow motion, while the rest of us eyeballed the gigantic supply of napkins that were clearly not for a Sunday picnic.

I knew the bag boy, Les Wolff, an attractive ninth–grader who sat across from us in church every Sunday with his parents. Now, Les knew I was menstruating. He had probably surmised this at the very moment I stood there with a colossal, super absorbent surfboard between my legs, riding the waves of a red ocean.

Les discerned, together with the clerk and Mary, and everyone else in the store, it seemed, that the box of super absorbent, unscented pads was too big to fit into one grocery bag. This realization came after much handling and jostling of the box and two bags. Together, the committed group determined that Les would just carry my box of pads under his arm out to Mary Kline's car, so I could take them home, remove one immediately, and put it right inside my underpants.

I left the store and waited in the hot car with an even hotter face for Les to place our bags in the back seat next to Pearl. We'd left her there because it was such a hassle bringing her into the store and making sure she didn't wander away. She was hot and cranky, too.

Finally, Mary Kline heaved herself into the driver's seat. The three of us sat there in the car, stewing. I was angry and embarrassed at the scene that had just unfolded in front of a boy I knew. I waffled between giving Mary the silent treatment or letting her have it. Just because I could, I guess, I chose the latter.

"I will never, never go into that store or to church, or anywhere with you again! Are you happy, now that the entire town knows that I'm having my period? Are you happy that Les Wolff knows I'm bleeding like a stuck pig?"

Mary Kline was stunned into silence. Pearl whimpered. I needed to go home as fast as possible to change my bloody diaper.

"Why do you buy this kind of thing for me, anyway? It's not like you're my mother! I don't need you to buy my pads. Don't ask me if I'm having a period anymore either. It's not your business! I'll let you know what I want you to know. And you can stop asking me if I've had a bowel movement lately! That's something that mothers do! You are *not* my mother!"

Mary Kline looked so startled. The words I'd spat at her buzzed between us like flies. She didn't look at me as she started the car, and we headed home. Tears pooled in the corner of her eyes as she hustled Pearl into the house and carried the groceries in by herself. She left my lifetime supply of pads on the front seat.

I waited until dark, after she'd fixed our supper and while she was bathing Pearl, to slip outside and carry the box into my room. Mary never inquired about my periods or my bowel movements again. Every once in a while, she'd leave some money on my dresser with a note:

For the things you need.
Love, Mary.

Chapter Three

Mary Kline

As a teen, Elizabeth never brought friends home. She was ashamed of our house and the state to which I'd let it slide. Mother and Daddy would have been so disappointed. The clutter was not offensive on its own, nor was the filth. But combined, the two were repulsive.

It was obvious as soon as anyone entered the living room that the grand piano my parents purchased for me was unusable as a musical instrument. It had a surface, but to unearth it, one would have had to disturb a mountain range of newspaper clippings, photographs, Elizabeth's artwork and report cards, along with notes home about events that came and went. Magazines, brochures and outdated coupons and calendars were stacked precariously among hundreds of sympathy cards I received when Mother and Daddy passed away a year earlier. Deep in the bowels of that pile were my high school diploma and Pearl's "certificate of completion." Somewhere between Elizabeth's birth certificate and the sewing patterns for her Halloween costumes were the patterns Mother had sketched like blueprints to cover her house of a daughter.

The sheet music gave way one afternoon, unable to bear the burden of yet another grocery receipt. An avalanche spilled several years of documents onto the carpet. Bending over to pick up the pieces was dangerous for someone my size, so there it all remained. I started a new pile on the bed in Daddy's room.

Pearl was another potential source of embarrassment for Elizabeth. By the time I moved them back into the house with us, she had slipped even further. She said almost nothing and cowered to communicate.

She even drooled sometimes when she was anxious. Elizabeth showed little compassion for her birth mother.

"Pearl looks like a science project, Mary. Look at her! God, get her a bib or something! It's embarrassing. If you think for a minute that I'm bringing any of my friends over to this dump, you're wrong. And don't think she's coming to my chorale concert with you either. No. No way are you bringing Pearl to that."

I would object and remind Elizabeth that she was speaking about her own mother.

"Oh, she's my mother, is she? Oh, now *she's* my mother? I thought *you* were my mother, Mary. Aren't *you* the mother here? Who's the *mother* in this house, Mary?"

Then, she'd just walk away from me and Pearl.

I often felt as resentful about Pearl as Elizabeth did.

"Pearl, stop that drooling," I'd say. "Just stop that right now. What's happened to Mary's big girl? Where's that girl, Honey?"

I was also probable cause for Elizabeth's ire. One day, I dropped one of my good needles on the floor underneath Mother's sewing machine. I simply could not bend down to get it, so I left it there. The sluggish way I was forced to lurch through my days was just as unappealing as my inadequate housekeeping and Pearl's occasional slobber.

I wondered if Elizabeth's friends would notice the smells of delicious meals permeating from our kitchen. I wondered what they would think if they saw me hunched over Mother's sewing machine, making a vest or a diaphanous fairy costume or an Easter frock with matching purse and cape. Would her friends forgive the rest if they stayed long enough to notice what stood at the creamy center of our threesome?

Elizabeth never could. None of it satisfied her.

Chapter Four

Elizabeth

Mary Kline tried so hard to anticipate my desires. It often seemed like she was waiting with bated breath for my next request, ready to smother me with her response.

I once made the mistake of mentioning that I liked chocolate milk. Mary Kline came home from the grocery store with four large jugs of milk, more than the three of us could consume in a month. In another bag, she had collected all the ingredients to make enough chocolate milk for my entire fourth grade class. Our kitchen became a laboratory and Mary the mad scientist, determined to concoct the best chocolate milk possible, something perfect enough for my spoiled palate. She had purchased two types of dry cocoa mix, three kinds of syrup and even a bag of semi-sweet chocolate chips, which she melted in a double boiler, all in a furious effort to unlock the secret to my happiness.

All I wanted was a glass of chocolate milk. Mary turned everything into an elaborate, sticky-sweet, big fucking production.

When I was about 11 years old, I had a brief infatuation with cats, especially kittens. In the beginning, I liked all the knick-knacks and posters of kittens Mary found for me. She even sewed a nightgown out of fabric with kittens all over it, and a matching housecoat.

Encouraged by my rare display of enthusiasm, Mary Kline went further, determined to keep my love flowing toward her. She brought home a kitten. The infatuation lasted two days before we figured out I was so allergic to the thing that my eyes swelled shut and my arms and neck were covered with hives. We ended up giving the cat to someone down the street.

Once I could see and breathe again, the allure of cute kitties was over. But Mary Kline clung to the cat thing for quite some time. She was always bringing me books about cats, clothes with cats on them and figurines of cats doing the rumba, having tea and riding little cat bicycles. She was convinced that cats would keep us together. One day, at least two years after the allergy fiasco, I blew her cat bullshit out of the litter box.

"Mary, I don't want another stupid cat thing, okay? I don't even like cats anymore. God! Haven't you figured that out yet?"

I was rude and unkind.

Mary took the little cat bride and groom figurine out of its packaging and placed it on one of the crowded shelves in my room. I said nothing and she shuffled away.

If Mary could have just loved me like a normal person we would have been fine. But she did everything to excess, embellished with her suffocating, exasperating Mary Kline goo, which obliterated all her good intentions.

I always shut down her attempts to mother me. Mary was so needy. Her zealous desire to surrender herself frightened me, and I rebuked her like a cruel and ruthless daughter.

All along, I'd never given her the courtesy of calling her "Mama" or "Mom" or even "Mother." To me, she was always Mary, or Mary Kline, or under my breath, "Fat Mary."

I never called Pearl any of those names, either. They were just Mary and Pearl to me. It must have hurt Mary Kline deeply. I didn't realize just how deep until many years later, as she wept and fussed when I told her that David and I had named our baby girl after her.

"You've really named her Mary?"

Her lip quivered. She couldn't believe I would do such a thing. Me being me, and Mary Kline being Mary Kline, we turned the gesture into a quarrel.

"Yes, Mary! David and I have chosen the name Mary for our daughter. Is that so surprising to you?"

She was thrilled, but she couldn't allow the honor to have legs of its own. She had to let me know (more than once) how shocked she was that I would do something so kind and nice. After all, Elizabeth wasn't kind. She was stingy with her love. If she did something nice, it was because she felt obligated or forced or manipulated. Elizabeth wasn't capable of a genuine good deed.

"Listen, Elizabeth. You don't have to name this baby after me. I'm not really the child's grandmother. You should name her Pearl."

This was classic Mary Kline bullshit.

"No, Mary. You are her grandmother. You know that."

I was exhausted after hours of excruciating labor.

"Well, if you say so."

Mary Kline actually cooed the words out of her big wide mouth.

"If you say so, Elizabeth. Whatever you say goes."

Jesus Christ. Mary was going to suck me dry. The woman was going to suck up every ounce of sweetness I could muster. If anyone could do it, Mary Kline was the one for the job. I just wanted to kick her right in her fat butt.

"Mary, can't you just take what I'm offering you? Can't you just be happy and smile or something? I've just named my daughter after you and you're trying to get something bigger, aren't you? It's pretty damn big, Mary. Take it."

"Thank you, Elizabeth. I'm honored."

"You should be, Mary Kline, and you're welcome."

It was a typical exchange between us. Love needed to be delivered like the punchline of a joke, or on a silver platter. And when those funny or formal moments presented themselves, neither one of us could just let things happen. It made us both uncomfortable. We preferred to hack each loving gesture we made into something we could divvy up for ourselves and hoard away to enjoy later.

Chapter Five

Mary Kline

My little namesake loved French toast. I was more than pleased to hear the little imp compare my breakfast efforts to those of her mama. Sometimes, I got the feeling Elizabeth didn't appreciate that little girl of hers enough.

"May I have some more powdered sugar, Gramma Mary?"

Little Mary's sugary little mouth was already coated with the stuff, but she craved more.

"Of course, Sugar. You like my French toast, don't you, Baby?"

Little Mary could only nod her approval. Her mouth was crammed with a third helping.

"You'd think by the way you're stuffing yourself, that you'd never had French toast, but your Mama makes this sometimes, doesn't she?"

The child considered her response, and then swallowed a mouthful.

"Mama doesn't know how."

"Well! She does so! Who do you think showed her?"

After all, I *had* shown Elizabeth how to make French toast and a number of other dishes.

Little Mary pointed her sticky forefinger right into my giant chest and smiled at me.

"Why doesn't your mama make French toast, or a stack of pancakes or waffles?"

"I guess she doesn't know how much I like them, Silly!"

Little Mary laughed as she licked sugar and syrup from her plate.

"Look at me. I'm a puppy!"

I laughed.

"Okay, little Pup. Here's a drink for you."

I poured the remainder of the milk from her cup into a shallow bowl and put it on the floor. This beautiful little girl smiled, and instead of making me happy, like it should have, I wanted to cry. Something so simple and fun, like letting the child pretend for a few moments that she was a dog, made her face light up. I knew that kind of play never happened when she was with her mother.

Elizabeth didn't have the patience for make-believe, and I searched my heart to understand why. I'd played with her. I know I did. Pearl demanded more and more of my attention, but whatever happened to the child who once smiled and swirled around in that same kitchen in her pink fairy princess gown?

"I love it, Mary Kline!" Elizabeth had shouted. "I love it! I love, love, love it!"

I hadn't forgotten the way she sang those words, squealing with unconscious rapture. Where did that little girl go? My Elizabeth grew up. And she grew bitter. She stayed with me only as long as required and then she left me, holding the princess gown and hundreds of dresses I'd made for her. On top of my artificial attempts at mothering, my presence repulsed her.

Pearl loved the identical princess gown I'd made for her. She never grew tired of wearing it. I used to watch her walk shyly down the hallway, trying to suppress the little girl smile on her big girl face.

In that instant, it felt like I'd finally done something right. At least my questionable status as the guardian and all-knowing grownup had some transient value. Pearl was just another child, and she needed me. *Some* of what I was doing was okay. I was mother enough to recognize that my Pearl deserved a fairy princess gown, too.

"Look at Pearl!" I cooed, clapping my hands as my poor, childish friend ran her hands over her gown.

Elizabeth came running to greet her mother. The two held hands and swirled around and around in their matching gowns. Yet again, I was left outside the family circle, looking in. I'd never had a princess gown. I was always the frumpy stepsister or the evil stepmother. But who was I, in this little family that Mother and Daddy created for me?

Chapter Six

Mary Kline

A fortress of fat. That's what I built around myself. I would never be kissed, never be approached, not even with unwanted advances. I'd never love a man or feel my love returned. To find me, my prince would have to fight his way through layers and layers of lonely flab.

I returned from my grandparents' home that summer larger than ever, which sent my poor, devoted seamstress of a mother into a sewing frenzy. My proportions had become so unwieldy that she was forced to expand her understanding of geometry and conventional theories of mathematics. Fabric arrived in bolts, and I soon had a closet full of tents to cover the freak show my body had become.

As my mother measured my bulky waist and gargantuan upper arms, taping and pinning in silence, she must have known that the hulk before her represented the end of our bloodline. There would be no grandchildren coming her way. This could only happen if we recruited a benevolent Eskimo to plunge a harpoon into my side.

My mother's hands brushed against my skin as she smoothed and adjusted enormous swaths of fabric over my body. This was the only physical contact I received, aside from the occasional slap on my backside from an uncle or my father.

I was ready for market.

My prospects were slim to none, but it wasn't the dearth of romantic possibilities that saddened me so much. What bothered me more was the probability that I would never have a child, a suckling piglet of my very own. This hog could not bear the notion of a life without children. Little humans liked people like me, and I was drawn to them. Whenever

I had the chance to get my fat hands on a toddler or baby, I did, often making a pest of myself.

Mother and Daddy knew that they would one day leave their precious whale stranded on the beach, unless they did something about it. When they learned that Pearl Davis, my simple and *only* real friend, was expecting, they saw an opportunity and pounced.

While ringing up bottles of perfume, sweater sets, nightgowns, shoes, hats, and coats, anything, really, that people were willing to pay for in his store, my father took stock. It was time to invest and expand.

My parents indulged their only child. Despite my grotesque appearance and the whispers that followed the three of us everywhere we went, my mother and father were determined to appease me. They wanted, more than anything, for their gigantic girl to have some small measure of happiness.

If a steaming bowl of mashed potatoes looked good to me, even after I'd wolfed down enough for a grown man, Daddy made sure I was given more scoops, with extra gravy. When I was nine, I longed for piano lessons, and after asking only once, I was rewarded with a grand piano, delivered right to our door. The finest music teacher in the county was charged with teaching an elephant how to play chopsticks.

Mother was reluctant at first to take on Pearl, but when she saw how thrilled I was at the notion of having my own baby, she jumped on board. Pearl's pregnancy represented an opportunity none of us could pass up. The life growing inside her, that sweet idiot Davis girl, a slender slip of a thing I had befriended, was a chance for my parents to push our dirty little secret a bit deeper into the ground. Providing resources to people in need would be charitable and good for business and at church. They'd be saving three lost souls: Pearl, the baby and me.

"Just look at that tummy of yours! It's almost as big as Mary's! We're going to get a baby, Pearl. A real, live baby and we're going to keep it right here at our house. Mother and Daddy said we can keep our baby, Pearl. And you're going to stay right here with Mary Kline! Isn't that the best news ever?"

Daddy arranged for the proper papers to be drawn up with Pearl's two brothers. They signed. I felt a little guilty, knowing my father essentially paid them to leave town, and I felt even more ashamed when Pearl's brothers came to our house to say a final goodbye. Dean stayed in the truck, but Frank came into our front parlor. He leaned down to his sister and his voice changed as he spoke to Pearl.

"This is going to be so good, Pearl," he said. "You're a good girl, Pearl. A real good girl. I'll call you sometimes, and you better answer, okay? Pearl, you better pick up that phone and talk to your brother."

Pearl nodded and smiled, but when she saw Frank tear up, she did, too. I was irritated with them both for spoiling my treat. Daddy cleared his throat to move the exchange along. Pearl and Frank hugged. He kissed her quickly on the cheek and headed for the door, sniffling and wiping his face with his jacket.

I tried to distract Pearl. I pulled her from the window and coaxed her into the kitchen with the prospect of hot cocoa. I didn't want her to see Frank climb into their beat-up old truck and drive away.

As I plopped marshmallows into Pearl's cocoa and crammed a handful in my mouth, I comforted myself with self-righteous thoughts.

Pearl Davis was one lucky girl to have the Klines take over like we did. That baby she housed in her ignorant belly would want for nothing, and neither would she. All we wanted in exchange was for Fat Mary to play Mama.

What none of us could anticipate was how seriously I would demand my due. Pearl's inadequacies were bountiful indeed, but I was all too ready to fill in the gaps and satisfy my own needs at the same time.

I took over because I was good. I took over because I was huge and not to be denied. I took over because I could not resist that baby any more than I could turn down seconds and thirds at dinner. If that baby had been edible, I would have devoured her, and Pearl, too.

Chapter Seven

June Essex

I wouldn't attend high school again if you paid me. No, thank you. Nobody leaves those four years unscathed.

The cheerleaders and jocks have their problems. So do the honor students, the class clowns and the smokers. But my heart always goes out to the outcasts, students who get rejected at every turn.

I'm soft-hearted like that. My dad always asks me why Bill and I don't have children of our own. It's an exhausting question he poses almost every time we talk, and I always give him the same answer.

"Dad, Dad, Dad," I sigh. "I don't need kids of my own. The kids at school are mine. They keep me plenty busy, and plenty worried, okay?"

He doesn't like my answer, but my father doesn't understand all that comes across my desk each day. I feel like I'm a mother and father to all of them, and like any good parent, I keep those worries tucked into my heart to take home each night. Bill and I sit on the couch, watching the television, and I tell him the heartbreaks I've seen that day. He pats my face and tells me I'm an angel, but he also reminds me I have an out.

"Sweetie, this job of yours is tearing you up. It's tearing you up. You can't fix everything for everyone, Mrs. Essex. You know that; don't you? Why don't you think about finding something else? Something less hard on that soft heart of yours?"

I consider it on especially hard days. Checking groceries downtown or even delivering mail sounds easier. Transactions with clear beginnings and ends sound glorious on those days. But if I was across town bagging groceries or sorting mail, who would make that third call to the family with head lice that they need to come get all five of their kids again and be nice about it? Who would see to it that the free lunch kids have the same color lunch ticket as everyone else? Who would check on the pregnant girl in the senior class whose boyfriend just dumped her? Who would make sure the star basketball player understood that if he doesn't have the grades, he'll be benched, whether his father is on the school board or not? And who would tend to vulnerable girls like Mary Kline and Pearl Davis?

Each year, during the first days of class, I focus on the freshmen. These students are fresh meat, and I need to familiarize myself with them quickly. I can spot the smokers, the do-gooders and the ones who won't graduate, no matter how much help they receive. I can identify the girls who will get into fights in the hallways, and I have an uncanny ability to zero in on the student who will become class president with a precision that impresses everyone in the faculty lounge.

I am also on the lookout for the "tired and poor," even the ones whose families are well-off and quite capable. Those kids often suffer in silence because their parents are oblivious.

On the first day of school, my attention was quickly diverted to Mary Kline. Kline. I knew that name. I'd just bought new pantyhose and bras at Kline's Department Store.

You couldn't miss Mary. Poor girl. She was in for a rough ride. Ugh. It made me want to take her home with me and be good to her in every way possible. I'd need to keep my eye on her, though, because she was obviously in pain and needed real protection.

A few days later, another girl came to my attention. She'd just moved to town, and considering her situation, she would be placed in Bev Wand's special education class. Her files were sketchy on the details, but within minutes of meeting her I suspected mild autism and some unknown trauma from her childhood.

God Bless the Child

Pearl Davis was quite an attractive young lady, but she was slow and quiet, and I knew she was in for a rough start. She'd been brought in by an older brother, since their folks had passed a few years before.

I winced. How prepared were these two girls to make it through high school? I had serious doubts. Most of the mainstream kids were oblivious to anyone they didn't see in the mirror, and I knew that once they got a glimpse of Mary and Pearl, the two of them would be ripe targets for ridicule. Even innocent trips down the hall toward their lockers would be like walking the gauntlet. They would be at the mercy of their classmates who were inclined to torment them, and ignored by those who were indifferent. No one among their peers was courageous enough to stand up for these two. I'd been around high school students long enough to know that such a move would be far too risky. It would be largely up to me to protect them.

I invited Pearl and her brother, Frank, to sit in my office. He was uncomfortable, nervous for both of them. It didn't look like he had experienced anything positive in high school and had no clue how to set up his sister for success. I quietly wagered to myself that he didn't have a diploma. His hands were rough and spattered with paint.

I welcomed Pearl with a smile. Before I took her down the hall to her locker and class, I watched her give Frank a tight, childish hug.

"Mr. Davis, if you need anything, just give me a call."

Even though I assured him I was there to help, I didn't think Frank would ever call. Meanwhile, Pearl just stood at her locker, staring at it, unsure what to do. That combination lock was going to be a problem.

Chapter Eight

Mary Kline

Pearl had a lovely face but most of the time it appeared blank, staring into the distance. I couldn't figure her out at all until I started talking to her, and then I quickly discovered that she didn't have a deep thought in her head. Or at least that's how it seemed to me back then.

Her physical appearance, including a body that grabbed the boys' attention, was in stark contrast to mine. My calves were columns that ignored my knees and blended right into my thick thighs. Standing next to me, so bulky, Pearl was a beauty, and I was her beast. The contrast never failed to draw comments, and none of them were good.

I was a brilliant conversationalist if given the opportunity. Had I been more acceptable on the outside, I would have ignored Pearl, too, leaning up against the metal lockers with my pretty girlfriends. I wouldn't have given "the slow girl" a second glance.

Considering my unfortunate body, I would have traded places with just about anyone. I could have lived with the thousands of pimples the Fogarty twins sported on their identical faces. I could have gotten over having the limp Karen Doyle acquired after a horseback riding accident a few years back.

But there *was* a trade that made sense.

Wasn't it entirely plausible that there had been a mix-up when God created Pearl Davis and Mary Kline? I fantasized about unzipping Pearl from her body and me from mine. I'd give that dumb-dumb my blob of a shell to complete her ensemble. Her dull wits would match her new repulsive body. Then she could just kill herself. I'd dig her a gigantic hole in the ground and use a toy shovel to cover her with fresh dirt.

After slipping into something more comfortable, Pearl's body, my life would start all over again, only better. My skirts would still be tight, but this time, they would look stylish and feel fantastic. No more thick ankles for me, and I would never be shy about revealing the tops of my inviting thighs. I'd saunter my perfect and complete package down the hall and wow everyone with my wit and charm, along with my newly acquired good looks.

But no such trade was possible. Nope. I was stuck with myself. I lurched. My pace was labored, and I had little to offer anyone. Even my friendship with Pearl was arranged. Both of us definitely needed help in that department.

Chapter Nine

June Essex

"I know, Mary. I know. You're new here yourself. It's a lot to ask, but I just can't think of a better person in your class to help me make sure that Pearl Davis feels welcome."

I'd invited Mary Kline to my office to see what I could do about getting these girls together. Poulson High could be rough for misfits like the two of them, and if they had each other, at least they might both have a better time of it. Hassles and abuse would come their way, but perhaps the two could weather the storm together. I was going to have to do some convincing to get Mary on board. She was no dummy.

"You wouldn't have to do much, Mary. I promise. Pearl won't be in any of your classes. She's in the special education room, but she sure could use a friend at lunch time and maybe someone to sit with during assemblies. Would that be so bad? I know you've been raised to help other people in the community, and that your family is active in your church. Who knows what might happen with Pearl? I know she seems limited, but could you give her a chance? As a favor to me? The two of you might just turn out to be the best of friends."

Chapter Ten

Mary Kline

Pearl Davis and I became friends for one reason: neither one of us had anyone else to sit with during lunch. That had been the case since my freshman year. Pearl was a simpleton, and I was fatter than a hog.

I was a sow, a pig, a fatty, fatty two-by-four, and a lard-ass who couldn't fit through the bathroom door. But I had a pretty smile, and as the years in school passed by, I was grateful to have a friend like Pearl, who never made fun of me and always seemed happy to see me.

At least when I was eating lunch, shoving a meatloaf sandwich and brownie into my round face, I didn't have to do it alone. You see, a fat girl eating alone is pathetic. She's just asking for comments about her size, taunts about how much she's eating, jibes about what particular foods she's inhaling, cracks about the way her fat peeks out from the back, especially when her sweater rides up, and merciless teasing as she leans into a sandwich that's too big for one person, no matter how big they are.

Sometimes, another kid, even a teacher, would glance at me as if they were questioning why a girl as fat as me would need to eat at all.

For some reason, the girls in my class were compelled to display a transparent type of kindness toward me. I may have been a fat ass, but my parents owned Kline's, the nicest department store in town. The mothers of these girls did most of their shopping there. They bought tiny pairs of underpants, and socks and itty-bitty skirts from my father.

I could never fit into the clothes that my father sold in his store, so my mother sewed and sewed and sewed. She crafted my clothes with painstaking attention to detail, using high-quality fabric and notions, as if somehow those measures would make me look smaller or keep me contained. Who were we kidding? The girls kept their true feelings in check, at least for the most part. The boys, however, made up for it with their relentless comments.

The size of my gut, combined with the girth of my bottom, forced my mother to create her own patterns. She did her best to provide me jumbo–sized pleated skirts, enormous blouses that never seemed ample enough to house the upper half of me that should have been breasts. These mounds were eclipsed in size only by my stomach, upon which they rested like two enormous melons. The only thing between them was a fine sheen of sour–smelling sweat.

We never considered taking any measures to reduce my size. We had accepted my lot in life, large as it was. My bigness never came up in conversations I had with my mother. Daddy was always at the store, catering to people with normal proportions.

And no matter what she may have felt inside, Pearl never uttered a negative word. Maybe that's because she could barely speak, or maybe it's because she knew deep down that she needed me. At least somebody did.

Chapter Eleven

Mary Kline

Elizabeth was probably not the first child sired by Mr. Wonderful. He was older than us, but whispers about his "activities" were alive and well in the halls of our high school. Girls his own age already knew better and avoided his grasp. James had a habit of smothering his dates, hoping the cloying aftershave he'd slapped on his smug face would charm the pants off his long list of conquests, which included Dottie Robbins, Sue Sparks, a cheerleader from our rival, Jefferson High School, and God knows who else.

At some point in each and every encounter, James Pullman introduced these ladies to his dark, perverse side until he satisfied his urges. Screams, kicks or cries would not do. As he dropped them off at home, James had the nerve to ask for a goodnight kiss.

I suppose my size protected me from boys like James, who had no interest in pressing himself up against the likes of me. He craved raw friction, and he could have found the release he sought by rubbing up against me. Once he passed the preliminaries, the sensations would have been no different.

But James found Pearl a more attractive and forgiving target. And perfectly passive, too.

I've lived with the consequences of their trysts ever since. Most days, I don't complain. James Pullman probably saved my big, fat life. Who knows how many times he violated Pearl? While I visited my grandparents in Chicago that summer before my senior year, Pearl helped clean the South Christian Church, pastored by Reverend

Richard Pullman, the father of James, who had probably not given Pearl a second look until she was right there in front of him.

As she polished the pews, scrubbed the restrooms and cleaned the stained-glass windows, James gave her his attention. He noticed her curves and the tightness of her cotton skirt pulled across her hips as she worked. He saw it as an invitation to come closer. The fact that Pearl didn't have the wits about her to protest made the encounters convenient. Down in the cavernous church basement, in the Sunday school rooms and other empty spaces that were once the scene of Godly purpose, James found a steady, uncomplaining source of heat. He returned to that source again and again, driving himself into Pearl in the same rooms where children learned how good God could be for those who followed His Word.

When I came home at the end of the summer, Pearl had filled out some, and kept telling me James was her boyfriend.

"Pearl Davis! That's a lie. That's a great big story, Honey. Why would you tell Mary a story like that? Pearl, you know that boys don't like us. They don't like Pearl and Mary, do they? Nope. They don't. They just don't, Pearl. Did James say 'hello' to you? Is that what happened? Pearl, that doesn't mean he's your boyfriend. Trust me, Pearl. Trust Mary. I know these things. James is not your boyfriend."

But by October, I wasn't so sure.

"Pearl, Honey, turn around. Let Mary take a look at you. Are you getting fat, like your friend Mary Kline? Look at that tummy of yours, Pearl. Now, listen to me. Have you had blood? Have you had blood in your underpants, Pearl? Come on, now, you need to tell Mary about what happened. Tell me about your boyfriend, James."

By November, there was no doubt. Pearl Davis was pregnant.

Between the two of us, I was the one who learned biology, but my friend had clearly gained a leg up on me. She had more experience than I did, and it shocked me.

I didn't see it right away, and I had no idea that Pearl was capable of such a thing, but I've since learned that carnal knowledge has little to do with one's intellect.

James Pullman had finished his dirty work. It was time for the Klines to swoop in for a rescue that was just as sinister. That meant me controlling Pearl in ways no man could have conjured, even on his worst days.

Chapter Twelve

James Pullman

My sense of smell has always been keen. I've been able to sniff out the ladies with the discernment of an eager, panting puppy since I was just a pup, myself.

Grandmother Pullman's skin smelled like old lady perfume, the cheap kind I gave her for Christmas every year. Sitting on her lap, I inhaled her aroma and the stale mints she slipped me while we listened to my father drone on and on about God Almighty and something about Christian soldiers marching off to war.

Grilled onions, raw ground beef and oregano followed my other grandmother everywhere. Her ruddy, plump hands looked clean enough, but they smelled like she had fresh, spicy meat stuffed under her nails.

My mother's hair and freckled arms always smelled like they'd just been scrubbed by angels. Now that she's gone, I take comfort in holding a bar of Ivory soap to my nose. It helps me remember her cool hands touching my forehead to check for a fever.

The first girl I ever mingled with at the junior high dance had hair that must have been dusted with baby powder. If she would have allowed it, and if I hadn't been too embarrassed to do so, I would have buried my face in her curls all night.

A few years later, I discovered that the best girl smells had eluded me. Powders, perfumes, soaps and oils disguised the earthier, natural trails I detected with pants and sniffs, and later, thrusts and bumps.

Men in their modern factories cannot duplicate the inviting wafts that started with Eve in the Garden of Eden. I was entranced with what my nose experienced as I explored the inside of a girl's mouth with my tongue in what became a frenzied, licking, magnetic force, creating an urgent smell of its own.

I was driven. Dry humping created a frustrating but hopeful fragrance of its own. Even breasts had an enticing smell if I held my head between them at just the right angle. Big breasts had their own especially meaty merits, but smaller, still budding tits were a sweet treat that belonged on a dessert tray.

Locations and positions also made a difference. Sex in cars had a different aura than the same activities on a couch. Desire born in the outdoors, with fresh air blowing on exposed skin, produced a smell I could almost taste. I liked all of it. I didn't become particular, though, until my olfactory tendencies were introduced to a new scent I found preferable to all others.

Fear.

Fucking. Sucking. Humping. All of it was better, much better, drenched in alarm. Girl fear, the kind flavored with a pinch of willingness, then mixed with a pure extract of reluctance, was delicious. It was sweet enough that I found myself willing to slap and pinch and pull hair and rip pretty sweaters to get to it.

I loved the smells of my desire, infused with a fighting-for-her-life fright. Nothing encouraged me more than hearing "No" and "Stop." Screams, tears, bites and nails scraping at my face made it all the more exhilarating. As I became more skilled, I liked to delay my release until I could taste, from my lips or hers, at least a faint trace of blood.

For a long time, I could live with myself when my arousal was properly piqued. The things I did to some of those girls were no worse than what men had been doing to women for centuries. I told myself that if these girls hadn't put themselves in such compromised circumstances in the first place, they would not have been in any danger.

Young ladies who didn't want a little something didn't get into back seats or let their dates reach into their shirts, now, did they?

I resented the assumptions that my dates, their parents, my parents and the world made about me because I was the son of a pastor. They weren't willing to consider that I might have warm blood flowing deep inside me, pumping through a heart that had doubts about the God my father loved so much.

They seemed convinced that I was destined to be a good boy. I wasn't so sure.

Once I stumbled upon my vice, I came back to it again and again. I couldn't help myself, and no one could stop me. If my father or anyone in his flock had known about my dark side, they would have first pointed their fingers at the Devil, and then fallen on their knees to pray for my salvation. Meanwhile, my trysts could have continued.

Today, I appreciate those prayers, but I still don't think my nasty ways had much at all to do with some mythical beast with red skin, horns and a pitchfork. My naughty urges were all my own. They came over me as predictably as the tides. Relief was only a scratch away, and I was an itchy, itchy boy.

By the time I found Pearl, my seduction skills were well refined. Many of my conquests wanted it as much as I did, but I craved the challenge of authentic struggle. Even the ones who submitted quickly could be more fun if I got mean. A pinch or twist here or a sharp slap there usually helped set the tone for the next ten minutes, as I plunged myself into terrified virgins who weren't planning on such a rough start to their "love" lives. If they didn't cry or at least beg me to stop, I found myself forced to introduce them to new territory, guaranteed to hurt. I could promise them wounds they wouldn't show their mamas. Most of the girls were sorry they hadn't conjured up some crocodile tears for me in the first place.

Pearl Davis didn't put up a struggle. I'd just graduated from college a few weeks before and had moved home for the summer before I started seminary. One day, when my father was finishing up work in the office, I roamed the rest of the empty church building. We planned to walk home together. Dad must have forgotten that Pearl was still there. I found her in one of the Sunday school rooms, wiping a chalkboard with a damp cloth. She was startled to see me in the doorway.

"Hello, there."

She looked right at me and smiled shyly. I'd seen her around town, but never spoken to her or given her a nod. I could tell by looking into her child-like face that I wouldn't have to work too hard to set my trap.

Her tears would be a genuine reflex of pain, anxiety and fear. It would be exquisite. Impossible to pass up. Unlike many of my girls, Pearl would not extend and then rescind an invitation after we'd gotten comfortable. Hunting and "stabbing" her would be akin to catching a sweet, white rabbit trapped in a cage.

"Pearl? You know me. I know you do. I'm James."

She watched me with caution.

"Pearl. You know me. I know you."

She remained still and startled.

"Pearl, you can relax. It's me, James. I'm the Reverend's son."

My hands were open at my sides. I smiled the kind of smile I gave parents in living rooms as their daughters prepared for a night of my charms. I was a parent's dream, you see, a pastor's son with a chorus full of "Yes, Sir" and "No, Ma'am."

"Let me help you, Pearl. They're going to lock up the church soon, and you don't want to get stuck in here, do you?"

I reached for a sponge and wrung it out in the bucket of cold water. As Pearl watched me, she relaxed and smiled. Together, we washed two more boards. We were an industrious pair.

"Come on, Pearl. Don't be rude. You can at least say hello."

I teased her, feigning hurt feelings. She smiled at me again. This time, the smile was prettier and less guarded, and I was almost a bit smitten, I must admit.

"Hello."

"Oh, so you *can* talk."

Pearl laughed and covered her mouth with her hand.

I'd covered young, virgin ground before, but this was new territory. This was a piece of cotton candy, sweeter than sweet, ready to melt on the tongue. Pearl had the mind of a child, but her body was another story. It was ripe fruit, long in need of a good plucking.

"Hey, there's one more chalkboard. I'll get some clean water. We'll give it another swipe, huh?"

Pearl barely nodded and watched me walk out the door. I was skilled at this early stage of conquest, but I needed a minute to gird myself for what the next few moments would bring.

I emptied the bucket in the bathroom sink and returned to the room. I locked the door. Pearl could see that the bucket was empty. She headed for the door. I stopped her with my arms folded across my chest. I shook my head. She shook hers and backed up against the chalkboard, the one that wasn't going to get cleaned after all.

Pearl didn't cry like I expected. She whimpered a little, but it wasn't enough to arouse me. She was such a child. I couldn't bring myself to pinch her or pull her hair. She looked at me with clear eyes and just absorbed my driving need, as if she expected it, as if what was happening to her was interesting, but only mildly so.

She laughed quietly, like the nervous child she was. I panicked for a moment, covering her mouth with my hands to stifle the sound. Even that, she misunderstood.

I was completely unsatisfied. I could not finish what I'd started. I helped Pearl button her blouse and pull her skirt back down where it belonged. Instead of being angry, she shyly kissed me on the cheek and ran out the door, leaving me alone with my empty bucket.

Chapter Thirteen

June Essex

When Mary Kline and Pearl first came to Poulson High, I connected the two of them, and I was sure that I had done a good deed.

Neither girl would ever be included with any of the popular high school cliques, but at least they had each other. At the beginning of their senior year, though, I was worried, and I started to wonder how healthy their relationship was after all.

The minute I laid eyes on Pearl Davis on that first day her brother brought her in, I knew there might be a problem she would encounter that her friend Mary Kline would not. Pearl was just attractive enough to get her into trouble, and certainly naïve enough to be unable to sense the danger she was in.

By the time our fall festival arrived, there was no question that Pearl was pregnant. I was absolutely sick about it. That girl would never be able to raise a child. She could barely look after herself. The faculty determined that it was best to send her home with a certificate of completion. I made the call to her brother Frank, who agreed to meet me after school. I came prepared with a list that included two abortion clinics and three adoption agencies. Once Pearl left the school, it would no longer be appropriate for me to intervene.

Frank Davis showed up to the diner a little bit late and apologetic.

"Hello there, Mrs. Essex. Thanks for meeting with me."

I ordered the poor kid a coffee and a piece of cherry pie.

"Well, Frank, I'm just so sorry to hear that Pearl is in such a bind. She's a real sweetheart, and I'm sure you and your brother are worried."

He nodded and started eating his pie.

God Bless the Child

"Have you come up with any plan? You're not thinking of keeping the baby, are you?"

He swallowed his pie and shook his head vigorously. The pie looked so good, I decided to order myself a slice. While we ate our treat and let the waitress fill our coffee cups again and again, I learned that a plan had been cooked up that seemed unimaginable.

Edward and Louise Kline had offered to take Pearl's baby in as their own. They'd also be taking her in to live with them and Mary Kline. She and the baby would want for nothing.

The pie didn't taste good anymore.

"Frank, are you okay with this? I know Pearl and Mary Kline are thick as thieves, but Mary will be going off to college in the fall. Does Pearl realize that she'll be living there with Mr. and Mrs. Kline and a new baby, but without Mary?"

Frank shook his head.

"Oh, no, Mrs. Essex. Mary's going to stay here in town with them. She's going to live at home and help Pearl take care of her baby."

"Frank, think about this. Are you sure this is the best solution? Don't you think you should consult an attorney?"

He shook his head one last time.

"Mr. Kline said not to worry about that. He's taken care of everything. It's what's best for Pearl, don't you agree?"

Frank had a slight smile and looked away, as if he were too embarrassed to admit something. Maybe Mr. Kline was giving him money for the privilege of hosting Pearl. I didn't know, but it seemed too preposterous to ask.

The next morning, my first phone call was to Louise Kline. There had to be a mistake of some kind. Surely they were going to encourage their very bright daughter to go to college. I was the school counselor and to ask such a question was within my purview.

Louise was polite enough, but not interested in debating anything with me. I was dismissed. I needed to butt right out.

Apparently, the Klines had taken care of everything. Two weeks later, Pearl was finished at Poulson, and Mary Kline wrapped up all her credits by the new year. She'd return to walk the graduation ceremony, but there were no plans for her to attend college.

That night, as I shared this astonishing news with Bill over drinks, I wondered aloud about my initial good deed when those two girls arrived at school a few years before. They seemed to be good for each other, but I didn't feel that way any longer.

What was I thinking? Something about this doesn't feel right. Why on Earth would Mary Kline want to raise a baby under those circumstances? And why would her parents even allow such a thing?

Chapter Fourteen

Mary Kline

I didn't deserve the seat of honor. I'm ashamed to admit that while Pearl stayed in her room, crying from the painful stitches in her crotch and the agony in her hardening breasts, I held newborn Elizabeth without a second thought for her real mother.

This baby was officially mine. We Klines had made it so.

When Mother saw how adept I was, she treated me differently. She spoke to me as if I had been the one who pushed and groaned, screaming bloody murder in that delivery room. But we knew better. I would never have had the courage to do what I heard Pearl endure. I'd been arrogant enough to try and prepare her for what was to come.

"Pearl, Honey, this won't last long. Trust me, it won't. You go in there with the nurse. Mother and I will wait out here for you. The doctor will fix you right up. He will. And pretty soon, our baby will be here. Remember that, Pearl? We've got a baby coming. You and me. A baby! Okay, Mary will be right out here. Be a brave girl for Mary. Be a brave, brave girl."

Hours and hours passed. I could hear my poor swollen friend screaming like the frightened child she was. When Mother and I returned from having lunch in the cafeteria, it still wasn't over. I could hear the doctor interjecting what sounded like finishing-line instructions between Pearl's moans.

"Okay, Pearl, hang in there with me, will you?"

Pearl made a high-pitched squeak. It was a childish sound that made me uncomfortable. Mother was nervous and out of sorts, too. Pearl's cries became so loud that we could barely make out what the doctor was saying.

"I'm checking to see how far we're coming," he said. "I'm being gentle, Pearl. I know you're uncomfortable, Sweetie. Let us help you."

The turkey sandwich and chocolate pudding I wolfed down in the cafeteria weren't settling so well. Pearl's cries were heartbreaking. I wanted this part to be over.

"Where's Frank?" Pearl moaned. "Mama? I want my mama."

Pearl's screams were blood curdling enough that they probably did reach her mother all the way up in Heaven. I was sure of that, but her brother and mother weren't there to save her. And she wasn't calling for me. I didn't have the guts to come to her rescue anyway.

I closed my eyes. Mother and I listened to Pearl's final tormented pushes as the doctor continued to coach her.

"Okay. It won't be long now, Pearl. Can you breathe? Can you breathe for us?"

Panting.

"It's almost over. Stay calm. Stay calm. Push, Pearl. Push, Honey."

Moaning.

"That's it, Pearl! Give Dr. Robb one more good push and we'll have ourselves a baby."

Screaming.

"Look at that! You've got yourself a girl. A healthy little girl."

"Will you look at that hair? Good girl, Pearl. Good girl."

Once she was allowed to get out of bed, Pearl behaved more like an older sibling to Elizabeth. I'm not sure she completely understood what had happened to her in the first place to even put her in such a situation. She watched as I swaddled the baby, bathed her, fed her and clipped her little nails.

I watched Pearl fade away before my eyes, wondering if her breasts would be needed to produce milk for her little girl. Her body was responding, but none of us had signed on to play along. I was the mother of this baby. Pearl was just along for the ride.

For weeks, I let myself believe that Elizabeth was a gift to which I was entitled. But as I held her close to feed her a warm bottle, Elizabeth gazed at me, deep in baby thoughts. I imagined she could tell I was a fraud. She sucked intently, boring into me with her knowing face. This infant was not to be fooled. I gave myself away by trying to anticipate her every need, instead of letting it flow, like I thought real mothers must do. I had snatched something that wasn't mine, and no amount of loving and squeezing and smoothing was going to change that.

Pearl stared at us, imploring me to hold Elizabeth. When I allowed it, I made her sit on the sofa and bunched extra pillows around them as Pearl held out her innocent arms for her daughter. I hovered over them, as if I were the one to ensure that the baby was comfortable and safe. But I was really just trying to prevent Pearl and Elizabeth from getting too cozy. I didn't want them to recognize each other.

When I wasn't holding or tending to the baby, I was opening gifts from well-meaning friends and family. They were all a bit perplexed at the new arrangement. Some were even bold enough to clarify with Mother that I couldn't possibly have conceived the child myself.

"How is that possible, Louise?"

"Was Mary Kline pregnant all this time and we didn't know?"

"Is there a resemblance?"

Mother answered their questions with a story that sounded so convincing I often chose to believe it myself. As a family, we created our own convenient truth. An unwed young mother in my class who was slow and had no parents had gotten herself pregnant, poor little thing. Once we knew about the situation, the benevolent Kline family stepped in to help. We had the resources to take on that girl and her baby. It was the least we could do.

I was a little nervous to learn that Ruth Pullman, the pastor's wife, was going to stop by to see Elizabeth. But as I worked it through, I figured there should be no worries. Mrs. Pullman probably had no idea about her son's dark side. He was smooth and cunning and knew how to cover his tracks and hide his pawprints. She barely knew Pearl. The likelihood that she would connect the dots was slim. The only bit that troubled me was the hair. The hair! That indisputable hair. Elizabeth's hair was wild, and the color of a fresh carrot with a burst of blood. So, too, was Ruth Pullman's, and no one could hide this truth.

Pearl was napping. I had bathed Elizabeth and dressed her for company. It was like arranging a little doll. Mother had prepared cookies and tea. I sat as gracefully as I could on the edge of an armchair, cradling the baby in my arms. When the doorbell rang, Mother answered. Coats and bags were shuffled in the foyer. As Mother escorted Mrs. Pullman into the parlor, I felt giddy at the thought of another person coming to see my beautiful baby, as if I was the mother after all.

How was I doing? Was everybody getting sleep? Yes, yes, my mother assured her. It was a little chilly, so I'd bundled the baby up in a couple of blankets. All that appeared was her tiny white face.

"Oh, my," cooed Mrs. Pullman. "Let's see who we have here."

With her freckled hands, she placed a large, wrapped present on the floor in front of me. It wasn't from Kline's. She'd driven a long way to get that gift.

"Mary, Mary, Mary! Can you trust the old pastor's wife to hold that bundle while you open a gift?"

She was teasing me. She could tell how much I loved that baby.

I handed over Elizabeth with a bit of reluctance, even though I knew Mrs. Pullman had every right to hold this child. She held the baby like a professional, supporting her head and bottom, while she sat on the sofa. Those two belonged together.

Mother handed me the gift. I opened the card first, as any gracious recipient will do. I watched warily as Ruth Pullman handled my baby, my breakable doll. As she removed the blankets from Elizabeth's head and face, she sucked in her breath. The hair. That damn hair! The reveal didn't go unnoticed. Elizabeth and her grandmother shared a carrot-top bond. Theirs was the kind of hair that demanded attention.

I rustled the tissue paper as I examined Mrs. Pullman's gift, lamely attempting to distract from the obvious. My mother gushed over some girly confection in my hand that I couldn't have cared less about. We thanked and gushed and thanked some more, but Ruth was absolutely still. A woman so at ease in almost any situation became speechless, unable to conjure up any polite words. She just sat there, running her freckled hand through Elizabeth's silky orange red hair.

Mother jumped in, being her best oblivious self.

"Why, Ruth Pullman! You'd think that baby was a Pullman child! Just look at that! Two peas in a pod, you are! I think you could pass that baby off as your own!"

Ruth offered a vague smile. She ran her free hand through her own unruly tresses.

"It is remarkable, Louise. You're right. What a beautiful baby you have, Mary. You'll be a very good mother. I know you will."

She handed Elizabeth back and touched my arm. Mrs. Pullman didn't stay for cookies and tea. Mother walked her back to the foyer, helped her with her coat and thanked her for coming. When she came back to the living room, she picked up the wrapping paper and box that had been dropped on the carpet.

"Remember to send Mrs. Pullman a thank you note, Mary. That was such a nice gift."

That evening, as I bathed Elizabeth in her little tub on our kitchen table, I examined my stolen goods. This child did not look much like her mother or her father, at least not yet. Elizabeth resembled her grandmother, right down to her almost faint eyebrows and her barely visible eyelashes. The freckles would soon emerge. But that hair!

Chapter Fifteen

Ruth Pullman

When our lovely son was pulled from my body, Richard stood nearby, crying with joy. We could not believe the squirming, bundled blessing we'd just been given. God believed we deserved to have this good boy and we agreed!

With my perfect baby wrapped in my freckled arms, I was relieved that my shallow prayers had been answered. James did not look like me. His beautiful-boy skin was stark white in winter and spring, but golden in summer and into fall. He resembled his handsome father, a man who could have had any woman he wanted but preferred freckled me. I never could understand this man's preferences or my good fortune. Richard said he thought I was cute with my freckles and bright, orange red hair.

My garish hair was troubling enough, but nature had also played a nasty trick on my pasty, white skin. Our Creator saw fit to generously splatter spots all over my body. These weren't cute little freckles. To me, they were sloppy splotches. I never got comfortable with them, so I avoided mirrors and cameras, afraid I might be forced to see myself.

But that afternoon in Louise Kline's parlor, I saw my mirror image. There was no denying it. Of course, I needed to drop by with a gift. Louise and Edward Kline were longtime members of the church, and generous, Richard reminded me.

The new arrival at the Kline house was a bit of a mystery. They had adopted a baby and put their daughter, Mary, in charge of raising it. They'd also taken in the mother, Pearl Davis. It seemed a little odd. Mary was just a senior in high school. She was certainly smart enough to go to college. Maybe Louise was nervous about letting her go out into the cruel world on her own, where people would be even less kind to a girl that size than they were in our genteel little town.

Over the years, as I watched Mary Kline morph into a shapeless being who lurched behind her parents as they took their spot in the pews each Sunday, I found myself thinking decidedly *un*-Christian thoughts. I wondered what Louise Kline's grocery bill looked like and if they had reinforced their steps, dining room chairs, and even the toilet. As the pastor's wife, I kept such thoughts to myself, but others in the flock whispered similar sentiments out loud.

Watching Mary Kline was especially painful, as I know all about being uncomfortable in my own skin. My heart ached for the girl. I felt sad for Louise, too. She was forced to endure the stares and comments right along with her daughter. She was judged, too. People naturally place a good portion of the blame on the mother when a child falls short. Louise wasn't doing something right. Something was off.

During my visit to the Klines, Mary looked so pleased with herself, and she did have a motherly air about her. The bundle she handed me was soft, lighter than I remembered James as a newborn. I pulled back the receiving blanket, ready to inhale some of that delicious, new-baby scent. I was full of "ooh's" and "ah's," with all the appropriate responses for polite baby viewing rolling off the tip of my tongue.

"Oh my, what a beautiful baby!"

But I was not prepared for the child who stared back at me. The tiny thing I held in my arms was no ordinary baby. My mirror image sized me up just as her visage made a permanent mark in my memory. As we sunk into the Kline's ample couch, this baby and I recognized one another. My heart should have been thumping and pounding with joy, but it lodged sideways in my throat. While Louise squealed something about Pullman babies, I prayed a silent prayer.

"God, get me out of this house. Get me out before this girl and her mother see the tears stinging my eyes. Get me out before I throw up all over this expensive rug. Make gracious and smooth words tumble from my lips as I hand this familiar-looking baby back. Just get me to my car. That's all I ask, Lord. Get me out of this house and into my car."

I mumbled something about how great it was to be a mother and stroked the baby's hair one last time before I stumbled to the door, oblivious to Louise's patter. I made it to my car and trembled as I got the key into the ignition. I drove to the end of the block and turned a corner so that no one would see me. I parked the car and opened the door just in time to spray hot vomit onto the street.

That hair! That little girl *was* a Pullman baby.

What I'd come to suspect about my son was true, and there was nothing I could do about it. That day, I took my first bite of the bitter-tasting truth that would be impossible for my Richard to swallow: our son was *not* perfect. He was blemished, just like me, but his ugly spots were inside. He'd hurt the Davis girl in the worst way imaginable. And she'd likely not been his first. That long line of girls was hard enough for my heart to fathom as a mother, but what he had done to this poor girl, already so vulnerable and damaged, was forcing me to a lonely place I never wanted to know.

I never had the courage to share any of it with Richard. How could a man of God ever accept that his son, his own flesh and blood, could be so blasphemous with his body?

Filled with shame and dread that someone would find out, I caught myself trying to read faces and listen for the tone in people's voices to determine what they already knew about James. I no longer identified with Mary, the mother of Jesus. Instead, I felt more kinship with the mothers of one of the real criminals hanging beside him.

My son had little in common with the Savior. He deserved any type of punishment coming his way. I knew this, and distanced myself from him in ways that were aloof and unnatural. James was perceptive, and he noticed. My wicked son and I danced tensely around one another for the longest time.

Edward and Louise Kline began toting the Davis girl along with them to church on Sundays. She sat next to their giant daughter, who held the beautiful, carrot-topped baby in her arms. I should have been grateful that these fine folks had stepped into a space I would never be allowed to fill. They covered our breach, and I watched the child grow from afar. I didn't dare come closer. I could not be sure that I wouldn't snatch her for myself. I wanted to undress her, inspect every inch of her. This exquisite creature, so innocent and white and soft, had sprung into being from something so unforgivable and vile. How could my own son produce a child I could not touch, let alone love?

My James, that beautiful boy, was a beast. He could claim nothing that was good or pure in that red-headed baby. The light in her could only have come from Pearl Davis. When I wasn't looking at the child, I watched her mother move. She was so fragile and childlike, easy to be mastered in savage strokes I knew my son had delivered. I could see his cruel capacities. They ran deep, but I knew where he kept them lodged for safekeeping. I knew these things because I'd harbored him with my own body. I knew him before his birdlike bones had formed and forged themselves with baby boy bands of muscle that flexed and pushed with strong flutters against my ribs. He emerged so beautiful, but as soon as he demanded his first breath, I'd already lived with our boy longer than Richard. I knew what my good Richard could never detect. This man of mine. He believed in angels and miracles and demons, and an abundant world created in seven days, but he would never comprehend what our James had become.

Chapter Sixteen

James Pullman

My first encounter with Pearl Davis started like all the others, with a nagging, itching desire to feel that sweet kind of hum I could only know by taking someone by force.

I left the church that afternoon and walked home with my father. I was unsatisfied and restless. Richard Pullman, who was usually lost in his own lofty thoughts, even noticed. Perhaps I was coming down with something, he suggested. I should go home and go straight to bed. I took his advice. I tried to escape through sleep, hoping I'd score a wet dream in my slumber. But sleep was fitful. For the first time in years, I called upon my father's mysterious God. I told him I was sorry and that I'd be better. The old man in the clouds did not accept my apology because he knew it was not sincere. He knew I'd go back to that classroom in His house, looking for Pearl. He knew I would take another stab at her because I was a low-ranking angel, lurking on the fringes. I had a cruel streak that demanded my attention. My father's God knew I would return to the church to manipulate Pearl Davis into scratching my desperate itch.

Our first encounter had not frightened Pearl away. She seemed to be waiting for me. I had come armed with rage, determined to conquer, but Pearl possessed a gentleness that took me by surprise and felt intensely soothing. I found myself dissolved by her countenance. I could not bring myself to hurt her. Instead, I longed to put my lips on her sweet little neck and just breathe.

This time, I noticed the prominent bones in her delicate hands. Her fingers were long, and her nails had been painted a pale pink, surely, though, by someone else. A scarf pulled the hair off her neck, but a few errant strands had escaped. She rested one hand on my shoulder, and I let that quiet gesture sink in and settle. We kissed soft kisses, the sweet kind I didn't know existed.

That afternoon, Pearl did not object when I undid the tiny buttons on her white, cotton blouse. I inched my way down with precision while unbuttoning my own shirt. We stood there, breathing into each other. I cupped her face with my dangerous hands so we could be closer. We were in a trance that felt so good I could have swayed with her in silence for hours, but something stopped me. I fastened up her buttons, and she smiled at me as I buttoned up my shirt.

On the way home, I was confused, but not angry. I was ashamed of what I'd done to her the time before, worried she would remember how cruel I could be. I knew I would never hurt that girl again. I was a beast, tamed by a fragile, dim master. Was Pearl an angel sent to me by my father's God? If given the chance, he would have reminded me that Jesus Christ was an unlikely teacher and king. But at that point, I wasn't about to give Jesus much more than a passing glance.

Pearl was my savior. She broke my mean streak. I was chastened by her innocence. Each time we met I was calmed by the feel of her skin. There was nothing hurried about us. During that summer, we sought comfort in one another, but it wasn't fueled by erotic energy alone. She was pliable, and nobody was coming to her rescue.

I sought new ways for this girl to meet my needs as I struggled to maintain an illusion of gentleness. When Pearl placed the palms of her hands against mine we noticed how alike and different they were. I convinced myself that these simple gestures were sweet. God and I knew I was pretending, and we knew that Pearl was not. For her, the experience was sincere.

She extended me kindnesses I didn't deserve. One afternoon, she eased my head onto her lap and stroked my hair and temples until I slipped into an unguarded sleep. Another time, I pretended to read her fortune by tracing the lines on the insides of her hands.

I was blind to how I had damaged her future, but she never flinched, keeping her palms open, trusting me with her welfare. She misread my feathery blows for kindness, blissfully unaware that each of our gentle meetings was a heavy-handed affront to her sweet essence.

Chapter Seventeen

Mary Kline

People of average size make giant assumptions about those of us who are "extra" large. They assume that everything about us must also be massive and out of control.

These people might think that a big girl like me has orifices that are positively gaping. But really, my nostrils, my ear canals, the pores of my skin, my tear ducts, even my mouth—are all unremarkable.

Despite my unacceptable size, I've always been proud that certain aspects of my existence are quite normal. My tongue and teeth are fairly attractive, as tongues and teeth go. My sneezes have always been dainty and my penmanship tidy. My hands are beautiful and my fingernails well-manicured.

But none of this is enough. Because of my size, the world has determined that I have relinquished my rights to feel anything. They underestimate me. I *do* indulge in forbidden emotions, like love and lust, and envy and anger. I exercise my rights as a part of the animal kingdom. Female animals often take on the role of mother to abandoned infants of another species. They feed these babies, hold them, love them, clean them, and naturally feel territorial.

Once, when Elizabeth was about seven months old, I hauled off and slapped Pearl as hard as I could.

Mother and Daddy were already at the store, so it was just us three girls. I'd put water on to make hot chocolate for Pearl. The teapot whistled, so I left the girls in the parlor. When I returned to the doorway with a tray of hot chocolate, I saw the thing I dreaded most.

Pearl stood there in her long nightgown, holding Elizabeth to her cheek. She was humming soft mama songs in her baby's ear, swaying the instinctive mother-sway: back-and-forth, back-and-forth, foot-to-foot. She was a natural. Elizabeth snuggled into her mother's neck, looking more contented than ever. I froze. That sweet scene frightened me. Would I be relieved of my duties? Would Elizabeth and Pearl abandon their captain with a mother-daughter mutiny? Was I to be confronted with a natural and understandable coup?

I would not allow it. I put the tray down on the coffee table and snatched Elizabeth from Pearl. I gently laid the baby on a blanket on the floor and worked myself back to my feet, finally reaching eye level with Pearl. She smiled dimly, that smile I'd grown so sick of seeing. I hated the simple stare she gave as she watched me lavish her baby with my love.

My slap had more heft than I intended. Really. It was a full and jealous swing. Pearl was caught by surprise. Her body followed her poor cheek toward the floor. The crack and thud seemed loud enough to wake the neighbors. Had Mother been there, she would have come rushing into the room. Even Daddy would have looked up from his paper and put down his pipe. But I did nothing.

Pearl whimpered. For a hopeful, selfish moment, I wished she was dead. But I loved her. I did. I lowered myself to the floor and lifted her face toward mine.

"Oh, Honey. Oh, Honey. Mary's sorry. Mary is so sorry, Baby."

Elizabeth fussed and worked herself up into a good cry, but I could not tend to her. The rest of the day, I lavished Pearl with my love. I let her eat candy all day and put bubbles in her bath that night.

I should never have slapped Pearl. Traumatized by the birth, the pregnancy, even memories of her private moments with James, Pearl was just a confused child. Bewildered by all that had happened, she trusted me, and I guess that's why I slapped her. Pearl was counting on me to make things right, but I knew that nothing about this situation would ever be right.

By the time we celebrated Elizabeth's second birthday, Pearl was no longer my trusty lunch partner. Before Elizabeth came along, Pearl didn't speak much, but then she stopped saying anything at all. She needed reminding to comb her hair and brush her teeth, and I had to help pick out her clothes. It felt as if I had two small children on my hands. Mother could see how drained I was, collapsing into bed each night. Most of the time, I didn't even bother to slip off my shoes.

One morning, Mother told me that Daddy had devised the perfect solution. He rented an apartment just two houses away for Pearl and Elizabeth. At first, I balked. Were they nuts? Leave my Elizabeth? What?!? With Pearl?

"Mary Ann, of course, you'll stay there during the day, get those two to bed, and then come home for the night. They never wake in the night anymore. They'll be fine. You can go back in the morning, rested and ready for the day."

Mother had a point. Pearl was a heavy sleeper and Elizabeth, too. I did deserve a break. The thought of coming home each night to slip between my sheets and sleep sounded good. I loved Pearl. I loved, loved, loved my Elizabeth, too. But having a breather every night was going to feel so good. This was going to work. Both of the girls would be just fine.

Chapter Eighteen

Ruth Pullman

Being a pastor's wife had its perks. Nobody in town questioned my line of credit. Sometimes, we weren't charged at all. People assumed I was a nice person. I was, but I wasn't pure.

At first, as a young bride, I enjoyed my position as Mrs. Godly. It got me endless invitations to church functions. The nods of approval and the inclusion felt good. I had what appeared to be a revered status. My husband's sheep assumed that my knowledge of the Bible, and therefore, God, was as thorough and studied as my Richard's. What a comfort, to live with someone who could guide my spiritual growth. My husband/counselor didn't like leftovers and couldn't be counted on to pick up after himself, but he was wise and insightful, which aided me tremendously in dealing with his shortcomings.

"Ruthie, you have to pray to the Lord for specific things. He wants that. Specificity. No desire is too small or too big, Ruthie. And when He grants us what we desire, even the smallest thing, we are thankful."

Of course. Taking his advice, I prayed to myself for a minute. I prayed for privacy. I prayed for one Sunday morning to sleep in with my husband. Just one. I prayed I would stop seeing my role for the trap it was.

Those endless invitations were more than suggestions. They were summonses. I was expected to be in God's house every time the doors opened, and the lights went on. I learned that I didn't have the option to turn down an invitation to a meeting or a luncheon. If I begged off, one of the church ladies would suggest to my husband, in the most Christian way, of course, that it didn't look good for the pastor's wife to skip out. Since he had the distinction of leading them, but also being employed by them, my husband often agreed. I grew tired of potlucks. For others, they were a treat, and I had no choice but to be there wearing my best smile, but I didn't want to eat the chicken casserole, or the soggy salad, or the endless concoctions made of gelatin.

I have learned one rule as the wife of a pastor. My time, my body and my home are not my own. We live in the parsonage next to the church, which means a steady stream of traffic in and out at all times of the day. Some people don't even have the courtesy to knock. It isn't our home. It's just a place we're allowed to camp out, as long as we don't get too comfortable.

One year, I wanted to give the living room a fresh coat of paint and add some wallpaper to spruce up the kitchen. This simple, harmless request had to go before the church's pastor/parish relations committee for approval. After an hour of pointless chatter about paint color and brand, the committee decided to table the idea.

The next month, the same people listened to my request again and rehashed the finer points of painting trim. Two months later, it was determined that the church couldn't afford to paint the living room, but they would do the kitchen, and the ladies on that committee would choose the wallpaper. This meant they came barging into my home en masse, unannounced, holding samples against the wall and congratulating each other on their impeccable taste. After the wallpaper was installed, a horrible apple pattern, I was informed by the ladies that my pastoral oven and icebox were not clean enough. Those old bags looked inside my icebox!

I shared the story with Richard, who just smiled.

"That comes with the territory, Ruthie. Rise above it, Lamb. Rise above it."

Chapter Nineteen

Mary Kline

When I learned that James Pullman chose to attend seminary after college, I was disgusted, but I didn't give it more than an incredulous grunt. I was knee deep in taking care of pregnant Pearl. Then Elizabeth arrived, and her existence distracted me from caring much about James one way or the other, as long as he stayed away from Pearl.

I had myself a baby!

If the pastor's son knew what he'd done, it would have complicated what was already a challenging situation. His mother might have suspected, but she (and her husband) had too much at stake. I watched her watch us, especially Elizabeth. When James darkened the door of the church on holidays, I went out of my way to keep my Pearl far from his line of sight. They were hypocrites, those Pullmans, all three of them.

We Klines got on with our business. Daddy worked at the store. Mother, Pearl and I stayed home. Elizabeth grew from a baby to a toddler. We moved her and Pearl a few doors down so I could get my fill of them during the day and come home to rest at night.

Elizabeth turned three, then four, then five. We went to church together on Sundays, making room for Pearl and the red-headed carrot top of a little girl we'd saved.

Mr. Wonderful had completed seminary. Good for him. Good for the Pullmans. He was serving a congregation, his first, far away from us. Good for us that he was far away.

An announcement was made right after the doxology but before joys and concerns, that James Pullman would be coming back to town to serve alongside his father. This was not a joy for me. This was, however, without a doubt, a big concern, something that needed prayer and perhaps plotting. I was ill.

The old hens clucked. Having this nice, young son of the pastor back in the fold made for such a full circle story in the local newspaper and church bulletins. Reverend Richard must have been so proud to have his boy return to follow his righteous path, and right under his sanctimonious wing.

But Ruth Pullman was another story. On the surface, she nodded and smiled. She had no choice. She stored gracious responses and affirmations in her cheek to keep pleasantries and chit chat sounding natural. But the maternal pride that should have been so easily within her reach was harder to catch. From my pew perch, at chicken dinners, rummage sales, and practices for our Christmas pageants, I suspected that this pastor's wife, the one who tried her darndest not to stare at Elizabeth, was also concerned, and she had every reason to be.

I'm not sure why I showed up at the open house for Ruth's prodigal son, but I did. Something in me wanted to see and taste the fatted calf. I helped myself to some lemon bars and a brownie, as I waited in line for the meet and greet. The chatter that filled the church basement was friendly, even boisterous. This was cause for celebration, a homecoming no committed parishioner should miss.

I heard the guest of honor teasing the old bags with the tone and tenor one might expect.

"Of course, I remember you, Rose!"

His hands looked smooth and soft, only capable of good works. As I moved ahead in the line, waiting my turn to welcome him, I wondered if James Pullman had spent any time on his knees, apologizing to Jesus for his misdeeds. I imagined, at the very least, that Jesus had lent him an ear, nodding with understanding. After all, temptations of the flesh are strong, and boys will be boys. Jesus always did hang out with a rough crowd. He liked prostitutes, tax collectors, and hot-headed fishermen, so he probably welcomed James with open arms.

I figured James had been forgiven. But I wondered if his confession was worthy of Jesus. Did Jesus know that James' trysts were never mutual? Did he know, like I did, that James force-fed his little lovers, shoving his hot gruel into their mouths whether they were hungry or not? Did Jesus know about Elizabeth and Pearl? Did the Lord remember *me*? Did He expect us to file down the center aisle on Sundays and drink His blood from a cup served by the hands of the pastor's son? James Pullman had probably washed his paws thousands of times since he'd pawed Pearl like a dog, but they would never be clean enough for me.

Perhaps Jesus could see beyond black and white and knew the gray truth. Jesus lent us both an ear. On one side, he heard James' apologies, excuses and lies. On the other, I stood ready to whisper, just between us, my own unpunished deeds.

Jesus didn't need our confessions. He knew we were sinners. James committed his with thrusting hips and invasive lips and hands capable of bad deeds, but I was no better. Like a greedy child, I accepted a gift that was not mine. I took Elizabeth for my own like she was a toy on a shelf in our department store, a possession I felt entitled to own.

Long before I came face to face with our new associate pastor that afternoon, Jesus knew I was a thief both blessed and burdened by the goods I had stolen. He understood that my brand of aggression was that of a woman unloved. He'd seen my kind before. We are many. We can be spotted with ease. Some of us are ugly, others ugly and foolish, while others are ugly and foolish and needy. I was all those things, and fat.

These truths fueled me as much as any beef I had with James. I picked a fight for reasons even I could not comprehend. When it came to Pearl, I was indignant about what she'd endured, but thankful she had because I was the first one to benefit. Without James Pullman's sins, I would have never had Elizabeth. Now, despite having Pearl and Elizabeth to fill my days, I was still empty and wanting, a young woman, only 24 to his 27, and when we came face-to-face that afternoon I wanted to be seen and heard, thanked and feared.

He would have no trouble recognizing me. I'd initially thought about bringing Pearl along, even Elizabeth, to officially welcome James to the fold, but this first encounter needed to be mine. I didn't want to show him all my cards just yet.

As the welcome queue shortened, I finally faced the young reverend. For almost a week, I had rehearsed what I would say to him, laboring over my brilliant and bitter speech. I'd never uttered a word to James. He'd never said anything to me, either. Our paths had not conveniently crossed in school. But we'd been in the same church for years. Our parents talked to one another as if we were great friends who chummed around together, sharing secrets and ice cream sodas, but each of us knew we shared nothing like that.

As Reverend James Pullman extended his hand, an entirely new thought surfaced. Was it a message from above? It was entirely plausible that James didn't have a clue that I knew about him. Why would he? I was fumbling for words I'd committed to memory. I had assumed that the young reverend knew about my friendship with Pearl. But how? Pearl and I were of no concern to someone like James. There was so much he did not know. Seeds had been spilled during his trysts with Pearl. The repulsive beast standing before him knew all about it. And now, I was bathing and feeding his child.

I offered the associate pastor my hand.

"Mary Kline! How are you? My, it's good to see you! You haven't changed a bit! What have you been up to?"

His smooth, familiar tone suggested that we had been the best of friends, but we'd never spoken in all the years we'd been in church together. He hoped with his eyes and smile that just this once I would dismiss the inconvenient truth.

I fell for it. I'd never spoken to anyone as handsome and charming as James Pullman. His smile was intoxicating, and his aftershave was anything but cheap. I could see how easily poor Pearl and the others became ensnared in his lovely trap. His hands were warm. It would have been easy to melt right into him and let him walk me to Jesus.

Ruth Pullman felt a nervous kind of pride as she watched me shake hands with her son. The way she held her mouth, chewing the inside of it in thought, reminded me of Elizabeth. She did the same thing with her mouth whenever she was in some kind of trouble. The recognition jolted me out of my reverie.

"James! You haven't changed either! I'm still here, keeping busy, living with Mother and Daddy. And Pearl. Pearl Davis. You remember Pearl, don't you, Reverend? I was planning to bring her with me this afternoon, but she was tuckered out."

The color drained from his handsome face as James peered into mine. As he searched his files, I could tell by the way he patted my hand that the good Reverend was trying to determine just how close Pearl and I had become. How much had sweet Pearl shared? What did the great big girl know?

Jesus, forgive me. I could have crushed James Pullman, flattened him like a pancake, but despite my girth, psychological warfare was my game. I'd spoiled his little homecoming.

I waddled my way back toward the dessert table with the Devil on my shoulder. I watched Reverend Wonderful squirm a little under my critical gaze. This was going to be fun. Feeling lighter than a feather, I plucked a lemon bar from the buffet and ate it slowly, like a lady.

Chapter Twenty

Richard Pullman

My Ruthie should have been happier about our news. I needed her to nod and smile more. I needed her to beam. But she was dodgy and skittish about the whole business. She'd been distant around James for longer than I liked. When I brought home the front-page article in the newspaper, her lackluster response irritated me.

"Look at that, Mrs. Pullman! Will you look at that?"

I slapped a stack of papers on the kitchen table, right in front of her.

"Five copies, Reverend? Five?"

Pride was sinful. I knew that, but the Lord would understand this time. We'd made front page news, and to celebrate like proud parents was within our rights, just this once.

"Awe, Ruthie, just enjoy this, will you? We're on the front page! Above the fold, Mrs. Pullman. *Above* the fold!"

She took the top paper from the stack, scanned the article and handed it back to me with a nod and that infuriating prim smile that could steal joy from a baby.

"That's real nice, Reverend."

"Real nice? Ruthie, what's gotten into you? Our son just finished seminary, made the front page of the newspaper because he's coming back home to serve in our church with me, and that's all you've got to say? Real nice? Where is that proud mama who loves her boy?"

She took off her glasses, squinting to eyeball the smudged lenses and wiped them with the edge of her sweater.

"Richard, it's real, and it's nice. I'm glad you're so happy about it. I am. I just think Jamie would be better off working first with some other congregations. He needs to spread his wings, not be so coddled and fussed over like he has been here. It seems too soon to come home. He needs to cut his teeth someplace where they don't know him."

"What do you mean by that, Ruth? Just what do you mean by that? He can learn a lot from me, Mrs. Pullman, quite a lot. Would it kill you to congratulate him? To congratulate me?"

More silence. Satisfied with the job she'd just done with her glasses, Ruthie slipped them back on her freckled face, offered me the same nonplussed smile and walked across the kitchen to warm up her coffee. I followed her with a paper in my hand.

"Damnation! What is the problem, Ruthie? What is the problem?"

I slapped the paper and poked at the photo of us standing in front of the church. I'm beaming. Jamie's beaming, and Ruthie looks tight and grim as ever.

"Look at that, Mama. Would it have hurt you to crack that smile open a little for the photographer? Show your teeth, Ruthie?"

She shrugged, and poured cream and sugar in her coffee, stirring carefully while chewing the inside of her cheek. My red-headed wife was a stubborn one. My own mother warned me about red heads, but I wouldn't listen. With her cute freckles and sweet way about her, Ruthie had the makings of a good pastor's wife, exactly what I needed coming out of seminary. She met the mark quite well for the longest time, always taking care of the home front and Jamie while I tended the flock. Oh, sure she got her feathers ruffled by the church ladies from time to time, but nothing that couldn't be solved with a pep talk and pointing to scripture.

Soon after James left, this empty nest of ours didn't look good on her at all. It made me wonder if maybe we should have tried to have one more child, like Ruthie wanted. But I didn't budge. We had our hands full with James and the church. We fought and fought. Every time I baptized a baby after that, I could see Ruthie out of the corner of my eye, sitting in the front pew with James, tight lipped, her hand on his thigh to keep him still, refusing to meet my gaze.

Oh, Lord, my wife sure could hold a grudge. When she lost a battle or harbored a worry, she nursed it long past its due. When she went tight and quiet like that, it made me wonder if we were as evenly yoked as I'd once thought. But the grudge at hand would pass, and we carried on till the next one. James and I grew used to his mother's occasional sulks, and shrugged them off as hormonal in nature, just the price two men paid when living with a woman.

But this particular mood was different. There was no snapping out of it, no sunshine after the gloom. Ruthie changed on me not long after James left for seminary. His visits home were infrequent, and who could blame him? His mother offered only a chilly, perfunctory kiss on the cheek when he opened the parsonage front door and a quick nod as we said our goodbyes before I drove him to the station to catch the train back after another tense visit.

"What's got into that mother of yours, young man?"

"Not sure, Dad. I'm just not sure."

"Were you disrespectful? Does she know something about you I don't? James, have you gotten yourself into some trouble she might know about? We talked about this. Living in a small town like Poulson doesn't give a young man much wiggle room for error."

He nodded.

"I know that, Dad, I know. You don't need to remind me."

"James, I'll say it one more time, so look at me while I say it."

"I'm looking."

"When you're in the ministry, Son, or someone in your family is doing the Lord's work, there's no room for blunders. You got me?"

"I know. I know."

"So, I'm asking you one more time. Is there something you need to tell me?"

He shook his head.

"I can't think of anything, Dad. Really, I can't think of a thing."

I didn't believe him. Our son was a good-looking boy. Always had been, but he could be shifty from time-to-time. I'd gotten him out of a scrape or two that his mother didn't know about. Better to keep some things between men. No sense getting Ruthie all riled up when boys will be boys, even ours.

Once James came home for good, we made him a little church office next to mine. He moved back into his boyhood room at the parsonage, just like old times. Lord knows things were tense. Ruthie stayed for the church service, but usually ducked out right after, claiming she needed to get home to make us lunch. We'd come home to a roast chicken and dressing, or tuna salad sandwiches, but the table was set for two, not three. She'd retreat up to our bedroom for a nap instead of eating with us. I started hearing grumbles about her not participating in the women's Bible study, and she only signed up for one shift of the fall bazaar. She begged off helping with Bible School, too. That was a bridge too far.

"Now, Ruthie, you know that's part of the deal when we lead a church. We're a two-for-one deal, Mrs. Pullman, and you're not keeping your part of the bargain, Lady."

She sighed and looked straight at me.

"Richard, it's high time we let some of the younger women in the church take these things on. I'm fresh out of new ideas, and I've done plenty. I'll make some cookies and help with setting things up. That's it. Now stop hassling me."

I sighed and backed off on Bible school. But when it came time to officially welcome James to the church with a reception, I needed Ruthie's full cooperation.

"Mrs. Pullman, you need to bring your A-game for the welcome reception. Do you understand? I need smiles and nods, and confirmation that you're proud of our son. I deserve it, and so does he, so pull it together. This is a big day for James and a big day for us, and I don't need to be worried about you scowling and acting all dodgy on me. I mean it, Ruth."

She did a little better for the reception. She wore the yellow dress that looks so pretty on her, and had her hair pinned up. She stood next to me and Jamie and smiled, greeting everyone in line, nodding along just like we needed her to do. After the line died down, she retreated to the kitchen, helping put cookies on trays and filling up pitchers of lemonade, like she was just another lady in church, not the mother of the guest of honor.

Jamie smiled and charmed his way through the afternoon. He could press flesh, that one. You can't teach that. His grades from Seminary weren't that bad, either. Not as good as mine, but admirable enough. There was still plenty this young man of mine could learn about serving the Lord. He hadn't done a funeral yet. Weddings would come more naturally once he got married himself. We'd need to find him a wife to keep him out of trouble.

He'd get better at baptisms once he had a child of his own, too. That would cheer Ruthie right up. That's what she needed. We needed to get that boy married, and once we had ourselves a grandchild, she'd soften right up.

Chapter Twenty-One

Mary Kline

The power I'd allowed myself was making me heady and bolder than I'd ever imagined.

Every Sunday, I watched the young reverend with a smile that made him uncomfortable. Being fat and mean are not necessarily related. I'm fat all the time. I'm naturally good, almost saintly, when I want to be. I'm also capable of being extremely mean if I feel it's justified.

I'm not sure what I wanted from James Pullman. An apology to Pearl would have been pointless. I certainly didn't want him to have any access or responsibility for Elizabeth. I wanted him to unzip his pastor's robe to reveal the wolf suit underneath. If this wolf had come back to town as an insurance man, a banker, or a farmer, even the owner of a department store, I could have forgiven his past. But I found his career choice offensive and not worthy of the God who loved all of us, even me.

I appointed myself James' temporary judge, and relished the role because his crimes were worse than my own. I couldn't control my eating, and I'd taken a baby as my own for all the wrong reasons, but I wasn't a rapist planting my seed into an innocent girl. The notion that someone was more repulsive than Mary Kline was convenient.

I started slipping the young reverend well-crafted notes, beginning with my first taunt.

Reverend James,
I have a theological question for you. Being fresh out of seminary, I'm sure you'll have the answer.

Is it advisable to fornicate in the House of God?
A concerned Christian

Two weeks went by. No reaction. I didn't appreciate that. A second note was necessary.

Reverend James,
Where does God Almighty stand on the treatment of pretty, young slow girls?
A confused Christian
P.S. Do you think the Big Guy forgives us for everything?

That got his attention. All I wanted was his acknowledgment.

He caught me leaving church the next Sunday. I felt his warm hand on my shoulder.

"Mary Kline. I need to talk to you. Do you have a moment?"

Others stood nearby, assuming that the new young pastor was reaching out to the resident fat lady. Perhaps he was going to ask me to serve on a committee or teach Sunday school.

I followed him through the sanctuary back to his office. It was a thrilling walk. I was about to be alone with this very bad but very good-looking man. A real creature of God. I prayed he would close the door, which he did, with a look of genuine concern.

"Mary, what's bothering you? You know that you can come to me at any time. We'll talk and pray together. Just say the word, and I'll be happy to help you work through whatever might be on your mind."

Damn, he was good. I could see how he could seduce anyone with a heartbeat. For a moment, I pretended I wasn't fat, and that James wasn't a slimy snake. He was the blue–eyed angel he appeared to be, and I was a pure and shapely woman. We were about to profess our love for each other, and then he'd whisk me away to the parsonage, where we'd start making babies right away.

"Mary?"

I snapped back to reality.

"Nothing's the matter, Reverend. Really."

"Mary, I don't believe you. And I must tell you, something's bothering me."

"What?"

"I think you know, so let's get this out in the open right now. I'm going to be here for a long time, and I think the two of us need to come to an understanding."

"What kind of understanding would that be, James? Or should I call you Reverend? You have to earn that title, Buster."

"You should know I won't be harassed, Mary. Is that understood?"

I had to ponder that. I thought I understood where the poor fellow was coming from. It's hard to look that good and feel so confident about being an ambassador for the Lord when someone's got you pegged.

"I think so, Reverend."

"Good."

He smiled as he opened the door for me.

"Then we understand each other?"

"I'm not sure I would go that far."

I waddled out, already thinking of my next missive. I was getting to James, and there was nothing he could do about it.

I waited a week to send my third note. I wanted him relaxed.

I used my neatest handwriting to pen my next love note.

Reverend James,
Just wondering if you think God protects all of us all the time.

Where is God when a young pearl of a girl gets a little too much of a boy?
An understanding Christian

This time, my young pastor let me have it. I guess it didn't help that I showed up for a Sunday chicken dinner and smirked at him from the dessert table while he schmoozed the crowd. If I had not been there, they would have eaten out of his hands, but my presence made him self-conscious, and he must have felt foolish making nice-nice while I saw right through him. Honestly, I was just there to slice the pie.

The next morning, James knocked on my door and forced his way into the foyer. My parents were already at the store, and I was about to head over to see Pearl and Elizabeth.

"Why, James! What a nice surprise!"

He was having none of it.

"Listen, you fat bitch."

Wow. No more mister nice guy. His holy veneer had worn thin. For the first time, I saw a flash of the fiend who lurked underneath his smooth exterior.

"I won't have this, Mary Kline! You have no idea what you've accused me of doing. You can shut your fat mouth and back off. If you don't, I'll make sure you're one sorry pig."

I should have trembled, but I didn't. I knew there was nothing James could do to me. The Klines had been longtime members and supporters of the church. Our endowment had made it possible for the church to hire the associate pastor and our family money bought the soap that James Pullman used every morning to wash his filthy body.

I admonished him like a schoolboy.

God Bless the Child

"Now, James. Do you think that's the kind of language a pastor should be using with a member of his flock? Jesus might have to rap your knuckles."

My bravado was making me say and do things that were stupid and based on a false sense of security. I followed him out to the porch and watched him walk to his car.

"I'm warning you, Mary. Back off!"

As he opened the door, he pointed at me one last time.

"I'm serious. This is over."

The young reverend was almost cute when he was angry. I couldn't wait for him to punish me more. This was the most fun I'd had in a very long time.

Chapter Twenty-Two

James Pullman

It's one thing to disappoint God, but quite another to know you've punctured the heart of your own mother. I was an arrogant novice, bursting with knowledge of the spirit and all the Biblical trivia I'd digested during seminary. Jesus loved me! God loved me! All of my sins—past, present and future—had been forgiven, bartered for me by the agonizing hours my Savior spent twisting and gasping for breath on a cross.

Purified after four years of college, seminary, and a short stint with a small congregation, I returned home ordained, ready to occupy the seat next to my earthly father, Reverend Richard Pullman, a man I hardly knew, but felt compelled to honor.

He never said it, but I believed he was proud. I didn't need his words. I'd never had them, so their absence didn't create a void. My father was the source of wise counsel wherever he went. He was available at any time of the day or night, to anyone and everyone but me.

Even my mother enjoyed more of his attention. She had her role as the attentive assistant to a master magician whose stage was the pulpit. That's where he pulled rabbits out of hats and convinced his captivated crowds that water could be made into wine, the lame could walk, and the blind could see.

Once the show was over, spent from his performance and needing to prepare for the next, my father became distant and distracted, which made me lean into my mother. The two of us were thick, and she kept her lad in line, correcting my faults and praising me when it was merited. For a long time, I was a good boy, and she had no reason to think that I might stray beyond what she could tame under her watchful eye. I'd gotten into a few foolish scrapes early in high school that were brought to my father's attention. He swooped in swiftly, cleaned up my mess, and together we agreed that there was no sense bringing my mother into any of it.

I expected her to be pleased that I chose to attend seminary after college and that I would take my rightful place in our home church. That narrative should have been glorious for my mother, but she had changed. When I came home for a visit after my first year in seminary, my father greeted me with more genuine warmth than my mother. During that week, she said little and barely made eye contact. The woman who always asked about my classes and friends had gone mute. She didn't ask if I needed anything and didn't even slip me pocket money as we said our goodbyes. Her coolness left me uneasy.

On the train ride back, nagging thoughts about what might have hardened her once palpable devotion kept me from taking care of the required reading I had neglected. Perhaps the pastor's wife had caught wind that the pastor's son was no angel. That was entirely plausible. The fact that my long list of misdeeds, which began in high school and stretched through college, had not come to her attention yet was hard to believe. My rough dalliances were frequent and furious, but punctuated with pauses of short-lived remorse, justification and shades of shame. More troubling than the acts themselves was anxiety I had about being found out. It seemed miraculous, if not mathematically impossible, that one of the girls I'd plundered had not reported something to someone. In my arrogance, I took those still waters as confirmation that my behavior was acceptable, a sign from God that I was within my rights to keep going.

My mother's rebuke, silent and unmistakable, persisted. It wasn't a passing mood or misunderstanding. She had made a savage statement with her quiet resolve. Across the dinner table, during countless church services and over holidays when I came home from seminary, she kept her gaze diverted, even as she passed the salt and poured my coffee. She performed these tasks with a discreet hostility. Perhaps she was distancing herself, like mothers must do, once their sons and daughters emerge into the world of adults. Yes, that's surely what was happening.

I possessed just enough conceit to compare myself to Jesus, who also reached a point in His own ministry when He, too, put physical and emotional space between Himself and his mother. I cherry picked what I needed from the Gospel of Luke. I claimed the ever-expanding space between my mother and me as my own preference.

If Ruth Pullman chose to claim me again as her son with motherly smiles and the pride all sons deserve, I would rebuke her in the same way the Savior did his own mama.

"My mother and brothers are those who hear God's word and put it into practice."

That's what the good Savior said to his mother when she tried to play her maternal hand, and that's what I would do, too. It hurt me, but I would have to look at my mother as just another parishioner. I would shake her hand after church each Sunday. I would offer her the same cup and chunk of bread that others received during communion. I would even counsel her, like any good pastor should, but Mrs. Pullman would have to make an appointment like anybody else. There. *She* wasn't the one who created the space between us. That quiet, empty chasm that separated this mother and son was *my* creation and *my* choice, a line *I* had drawn in the sand.

My good, gentle mother had been such a sweet force for so long that her violent reaction to my turning the emotional tables on her startled me. It cut me to the quick. I'd never expected my freckled, sweet-smelling mother to have a dagger tucked between her breasts, but there it was, and she pulled it out and held it to my throat when I let myself get too big for my holier-than-thou britches.

Once she detected the mounting tension between me and Mary Kline after I returned to church, she pounced.

"James, your mother would like to speak with you."

It was the longest sentence the woman had uttered in my direction in at least five years. I was so good-looking, I was almost pretty, but despite my schooling, I still had shit for brains. I responded with a tone I thought witty and superior, appropriate to the state of our relationship.

"To what do I owe this pleasure, Mrs. Pullman?"

My mother saw right through me and refused to accept my sass. The look she gave me told me that I might get a good, hard crack on the butt, the kind she used to give me when I was a kid and misbehaved in church.

There I was, a grown man, wincing at the thought of her giving me a sharp pop. She closed the door to my church office and locked it. Was she going to whip me? The phone rang.

"Don't answer that, James."

I didn't dare. I stood behind my desk, stunned and paralyzed, waiting for a reprimand that had obviously been building up for years. Perhaps I deserved what was coming.

"You will listen to me, James. You will give me as much time as I like because I'm your mother. Is that clear? Reverend?"

I swallowed. It had been an awful week already. I'd received another note from that pain in my ass, Mary Kline, and I wasn't up to another drain on my patience.

"Alright, alright, Mother. Now, calm down."

Her return glare told me to remove my associate pastor hat and sit my self-righteous ass down. My mother wasn't messing around. She was here to conduct some serious business and I'd better look her in the eye.

"What's going on with the Kline girl, James?"

"The Kline girl? You mean Mary Kline?"

I was stalling, hoping to put off a conversation long overdue, one that would finally put me in my place. I knew it, and so did she.

"Son, what's she got on you? I need to know. Now."

The Kline girl *did* have something on me. I'd spent time unwisely with her friend, Pearl Davis, right there in my own father's church. My mother didn't need the details. One time with Pearl was unforgivable enough and would mean heartbreak for any mother.

I didn't have the courage or the words to reveal the brutality of our first encounter, or the subversive softness of all the other afternoons I spent with Pearl. She would not need to know about any of the other girls or how Pearl disrupted my mean streak. What my mother knew about Pearl was enough to break her.

What I *didn't* know was how much my mother *did* know.

For the next hour, with a quivering voice, she told me all the things she knew about me, James Pullman, son of a reverend, a young man who had let his crotch become his compass for a few years. The cocky bastard she described sounded like an old friend I knew well. My mother had heard about my backseat reputation, but at the time, she had refused to believe any of it. How does a man admit to his mother that he'd dipped his young wick by force into just about any girl available? How would Jesus recommend I confirm this with my mother, that I'd taken Pearl, the "slow" girl, on a number of occasions in the church where my own father was pastor? Even Jesus would have to take that straight to God and get back to me.

While my memo sat in the Savior's inbox, my mother dumped something quite humbling into my lap. What she shared next explained her lack of enthusiasm for me since I started seminary, and her reluctance to welcome me upon my return to South Christian Church. My good mother knew more than I did.

"Mary Kline has an arsenal of ammunition, doesn't she, James?"

She was staring at me coolly, waiting for me to say more.

"I'm sorry. I'm so sorry, Mom."

What else could I say? I'd made some horrible, brutal mistakes. I had quite a resumé, not what you'd expect from a man of God, the son of Reverend Richard Pullman.

"Does Dad know?"

She shook her head and spat at me.

"No, James. Your father isn't *capable* of suspecting something like this. He's just not capable. I could hold that red-headed, freckled child right under his nose and he wouldn't be able to comprehend it."

Child? A redheaded, freckled child?

My mother watched me as images of my afternoons with Pearl flooded my memory. She'd smelled so good and had smoothed my rough edges. She'd shown me how to get the hum I craved without brute force and fangs. Soft on the surface, but undeniably dangerous, my times with Pearl were beyond the pale and unforgivable.

She didn't cry through any of it, and her sweet acceptance of all the wrong that took place made room for me to classify my crimes with Pearl as different than all the rest. *She* was different than everyone else, and I had taken cruel advantage of that.

With my own tearful mother standing before me, I learned that those stolen moments had consequences. I was a father. I had been for some time.

Chapter Twenty-Three

Elizabeth

I never asked Mary Kline about the long stretch of nights when she left me and Pearl to fend for ourselves. It wasn't until I was a grown-up that I understood how wrong and dangerous it was.

When the front door to our apartment clicked shut each night, it was just the two of us, my dim-witted mother and me. Pearl didn't like being left at night. Sometimes, Mary had to do quite a bit of convincing before she could get out the door.

"Pearl, Honey. You don't need Mary Kline during the night. No, you don't. You'll be sleeping, Honey. And I have to go back to my house to sleep, too. That's all. First thing in the morning, I'll be back, right here, making you and Elizabeth pancakes. You don't need Mary here at night. You and Elizabeth will just be sleeping, Honey. Be a big girl for Mary."

Pearl was the "adult" in the house at night, but she never popped her head in to check on me, or to tuck the covers up around me a little tighter. I never ran to her bed, either when I had a disturbing dream, or some branches clicked against my window. Mary Kline was always there in the morning when I walked into the kitchen, making breakfast and reading the paper.

"Good morning, Baby!"

Most mornings, Pearl, Mary and I feasted on chocolate chip pancakes, French toast with syrup and powdered sugar, eggs with crispy bacon, or sometimes donuts from the bakery.

Now that I'm a parent, I'm astounded that I was left alone with Pearl night after night, with no one else to take charge. With a child in

God Bless the Child

the house, things can happen any time, but especially at night. A little one might need a drink, a midnight bath in tepid water to stave off a fever, or someone to clean up pools of vomit. A child can become vulnerable at night from bad dreams, scary sounds, a sick tummy, loneliness, or monsters in a closet or under the bed.

As a little girl fending for herself, I learned the source of each sound in the house: the radiator hissing, drip drops from the kitchen sink, and the muffled grunts and shuffles from Pearl's room down the hall.

I'm not sure how long it went on, but Pearl had company most nights. I was just a small child, but I could tell from the sounds that her visitor wasn't invited.

Pearl's guest came for visits with the regularity of the cuckoo clock in our living room. It was always after ten cuckoos, but never after two. After two cuckoos, I could fall asleep, instead of listening with interest at the loud thuds and moaning coming from down the hall.

Pearl's visitor moved down the hallway with purposeful steps. It couldn't have been Mary Kline. Her footsteps were heavy, and every step was accompanied by toiling breath. Moving her girth from Point A to Point B required calculated effort and a significant exchange of air that was noisy and labored. Besides, Mary loved me so much she never would have passed my door without a motherly gesture—a pat on my head, a rub on my back or some fussing with my blankets and pillows.

On the nights the visitor came, I could hear Pearl whimpering, and as I grew older, I gathered that something unpleasant was taking place, but I never ventured down the hall to find out or offer any comfort if it was needed.

I had no idea . . .

One night, the sounds were less muffled. A man was talking with a gruff voice that sounded scary, but somewhat familiar.

"You're not going to say a word, are you, you dumb, little slut? You've had this before, haven't you? Yeah, you've had plenty of this. I can see that. You don't say much, do you? I like that about you. You're just what I like. This is a nice little arrangement, don't you think? I like your new place, Pearl. But let's make sure we keep this between you and me."

I knew that voice!

The next night, I was powerless (again) to prevent the same thing from happening. The visits seemed to go on and on. Pearl and I had birthday cakes in our little kitchen. Mary moved her sewing machine into the living room, and I stood on a chair by the front window as she hemmed the skirt on a new jumper I wore for my first day of preschool. Life was normal, at least during the day.

During the night, however, Pearl's whispering visitor sounded just threatening enough that I never said a word. I didn't want my mother to get in trouble.

One night, the pace and tone of the exchange took an alarming turn. The same low voice Pearl and I had come to know so well had new and threatening things to say.

"Pearl, I'm getting tired of you. I think we're ready for something fresh. Don't worry. I'll come back to you, whether you like it or not. I think I'll take a stroll down the hall. What do you think about that, Pearl? You've got yourself a little neighbor, don't you? There's a little girl here, isn't there? I wonder if she's as simple as her mama. Tell you, what. I think it's high time we find out tonight, don't you? My little bitch? I like that idea."

I heard a surprising, guttural grunt from deep in Pearl's throat, followed by a loud thud against her wall. The visitor howled and cursed, and Pearl matched him with screams that reached a panicked pitch. I'd never dared to venture out into the hallway on these nights, but this time, I did. I saw shadows from the living room window that illuminated the dark hallway, but as I moved toward Pearl, who was frozen but hysterical, I came face-to-face with our visitor. Holding his bloodied face, he tried to turn away from me as he staggered out the front door, leaving it wide open. Pearl was still wailing, crying out for Mary Kline.

I snuck down the front steps onto the sidewalk in my footie pajamas. I'd never been outside at night like that. The cold of the night air rustled through my hair, which was still damp from my bath. I raced as fast as I could to the Kline's house, where Mary slept. I was proud that I could reach the doorbell.

Mrs. Kline answered the door in her housecoat and slippers. She looked down at me, surprised, and yanked me inside, shutting the door behind us. Mary stood at the top of the stairs, looking sleepy and dazed.

"Mary Ann! Get yourself down here! How did Elizabeth get out? Didn't you lock the door? Elizabeth, what are you doing here in the middle of the night? Where is Pearl?"

Mrs. Kline had my upper arm in her grasp, but she eased up a little and stroked my head while we waited for Mary to make her way down the stairs. As soon as she reached the bottom, she lunged for me, forcing her mother to make room.

"Elizabeth! Baby! What? What is it? My God, why are you here?"

She held my shoulders tight.

"What's wrong? Where's Pearl, Honey? Where's Pearl?"

By that time, I was crying and couldn't answer. Mary, still in her nightgown, didn't bother to put on slippers. She flung the front door open and dragged me down the sidewalk, waddling as fast as she could.

Pearl was in her room, crying and shuddering.

"Mary Kline! Mary Kline!"

"Oh, my darling Pearl. Oh, my honey. Oh, my girl. All right. All right. Mary's here. Mary Kline is here. Oh, my honey. All right. All right. Mary's got you."

Later, as I sat on Mary's lap, wrapped up in her enormous sweater, I told her about Pearl's visitor, about all the visits, and what he said. She seemed shocked and ashamed of herself for leaving us alone like she'd been doing for so long. She seemed to know exactly who the intruder was, too. She was so sure of herself that it made me confident she was right. There was no need to say who it was. Mary Kline was taking care of us. She dressed us and fed us and tucked us in at night. Pearl and I could count on her to protect us.

The next day, Mary had us moved back in with her and her parents at their house, where we'd be safe.

Chapter Twenty-Four

Mary Kline

James Pullman didn't get back at me directly. He got me where he knew it would hurt. He came back for Pearl, but not because he wanted her. He came back because she had no fight in her and hurting her would hurt me.

My worst fears had come true. When Elizabeth showed up at our door that night to tell me someone had been in the apartment hurting Pearl, I wasn't sure which I felt more: shame or stupidity. What kind of a mother leaves her children alone like I did? Mothers who weren't really mothers at all, that's who. I deserved to be punished, just not by that fucker.

James deserved to hang one cross away from Jesus, and I had earned my own spot on an extra-large cross on His other side. Reverend Pullman and I were pitiful criminals, and even He couldn't promise either of us salvation. He was too disgusted with us, so He let us hang there, gasping for breath and glaring at each other.

The next day, I tried to casually pry information out of Elizabeth. I wanted her to tell me everything she'd heard, seen, smelled and suspected. But my informant was just a child, and I didn't want her to realize how irresponsible I'd been.

Pearl, the only other witness, would never be able to explain what had transpired. How many times had this happened? I wanted to know about each and every thud and bump. I needed dates and times, and I'm ashamed to admit I would have even let my little Elizabeth see the whole thing if it meant someone else would know the truth about our blessed shepherd boy.

I was now James Pullman's judge and torture master, and the self-appointed duties were getting to me. I'd gotten sloppy. I envied Pearl. I despised James, but I lusted for him from afar for his exteriors. Why hadn't he come after me? This was between us. I would have enjoyed even a slap. What did Pearl have that I didn't?

I was a worthy opponent. James and I were meant for each other. We were both nasty and liked to be on top. We shared a common bond. Both of us used Pearl to gratify ourselves. We deserved each other.

The night attacks drained Pearl of any dignity she had left. As she lay weeping in my arms, I hugged and comforted her, knowing I'd practically escorted a monster right to her door. I was thankful that my friend depended on me. Most of all, I was thankful she didn't know what a piece of shit I was. Still, I wasn't going down without making sure I splashed and smeared some of myself on James.

After settling the girls back at the house, it was time to darken James' door. I put on my best tent and painted my long fingernails blood red, so I'd look the part of a woman scorned. This wasn't going to be a courtesy call. James and I had played around long enough. I came to his door ready for a fight, but quickly learned my war paint, my fantasies of a bloodbath with James, were all for naught.

I didn't even say hello. I pushed myself into his foyer, pleased that I'd caught Mr. Wonderful by surprise.

"You are a fucker!"

Even as I said it, I noticed how nice he looked in his jeans and sweater. He had a puzzled expression, but I wasn't fooled.

"Mary, what do you want? What is it that you want from me?"

Other than his scalp, I wasn't sure.

"An apology, Mary? Is that what you think you need from me?"

His voice had the calm of an exasperated counselor.

"Mary, what do you want? You are right, okay? You're right. I took advantage of Pearl. I did. There. Does that make you happy? It was a long time ago. It was very, very wrong. I was a stupid kid. Is that what you need, Mary Kline?"

Wow. I'd always imagined his confession to be more pleasurable. However, it didn't feel as good as I'd hoped. Where were the streamers, the confetti, the cake, the blood?

"James, I don't give a damn anymore about what you did when you were a horny little bastard. I'm talking about your latest crimes, you miserable fucker."

His blank stare looked authentic, but it couldn't be possible.

"What the hell are you talking about, Mary?"

"Oh, no, James. Don't start with me. You know exactly what I'm talking about!"

"Please, Mary, enlighten me. I don't want to play games with you anymore. I don't want to look at you or speak to you or be in the same room with you, Mary, but God expects more of me, so here we are! What is it that you need from me? What will end this? Right here, right now. What will end this?"

"You couldn't keep away from her, could you?"

"Keep away from who, Mary?"

He had about one ounce of patience left to spare me.

"Reverend, give it up. You disgust me! We have a witness! What did you think when you ran into that little redhead in the hall last night? Huh? If you didn't notice her in church, I bet you got a good look at her in the hall last night on your way to Pearl. You might want to take a closer look. Guess what, Daddy? She's yours, you arrogant fuck!"

There it was. I'd just shown James Pullman the point of the knife I planned to plunge it into his holy, black heart. My switchblade was no sharper than a butter knife. Damn. I was breathing heavy, angry breaths. James was calm and waved his flag of surrender.

"Mary, I haven't seen Pearl in years. You haven't brought her to church since I came back. I don't know what you're talking about. What happened last night? I don't have any idea. I don't. But you should know that I am aware of Elizabeth. I've known for a few weeks now. My mother also knows. I don't know what to say to you. I know that Pearl and Elizabeth are blessed to have you and your parents. Mary, what you've done is wonderful. I'm sure Pearl and Elizabeth are in the best possible hands. I wish I could change what happened, but I can't."

We stood there, James and I, eyeing each other. I have to admit he was convincing.

"I have to go on with my life, Mary. I'm not the person I was back then. I've done terrible things, and I must atone for them, and I'm doing that. I'm just thankful that Pearl and Elizabeth have what they need. Do they have that, Mary? Do you want me to be involved in caring for Elizabeth? I will. I'll take responsibility for her. I'll contribute money. I'll spend time with her. Whatever you ask, I'll do it."

I didn't believe him for a minute, but I wanted to. This pretty beast had exacted his revenge for my taunts and now he was playing his "I'm–a–reformed–bad–boy" card. He knew I had no more cards to play. I had to fold. I could never go to the police or hold him to account for attacking Pearl without also exposing how irresponsible Mother and Daddy and I had been. We'd left a child in our charge alone, night after night, with Pearl Davis, a young woman who didn't know her own address or phone number.

"No, James. Do *not* even think about sliding into place with that child, now, or ever. I'm not going to let you have that kind of satisfaction. Don't ever, ever come near her or Pearl again. Just leave us alone, you fuck. We don't need your help."

"Alright, Mary. If that's what you want, that's what I'll do. Let's leave things where they are, Mary. Let's just leave things alone."

I didn't want to call a truce, but I had no choice. All I could do was go back to Pearl and Elizabeth and start protecting them, like I should have been doing all along.

Chapter Twenty-Five

Elizabeth

As a kid, if I said the word, "poop" three times in a row I couldn't help smiling.

Poop plopping in the toilet, bird poop splattered on the windshield of Mary Kline's car, dog poop in the yard, elephant poop on the African plains—all of it was funny.

Poop. Poop. Poop.

Mary Kline didn't appreciate my humor, but Pearl chuckled along with me. I was probably the only kid whose mother appreciated good bathroom humor. Sometimes, while Mary cooked supper, I'd find Pearl in the living room, hunched over a magazine, and I'd start with my poo–poo jokes. She cracked up every time. All I had to do was mouth the word and she couldn't suppress a smile.

"Hey, Pearl, pull my finger. Go ahead. You know you want to. I wonder what Mary's fixing for supper, Pearl. What do you think? Are we having a poo–poo platter? Pearl, you know that's funny. I bet Mary's whipping up a batch of her extra fudgy brownies, extra, dark, you know, like shit brownies, brownies with corn in them. Shit on a shingle! Come on, Pearl. Pull my finger. You know you want to. Okay, let me pull yours."

Mary would holler from the kitchen.

"Elizabeth! E–liz–a–beth! That's enough! You are a piece of work. I'll never understand why you think bathroom humor is so funny. I mean, a bowel movement is a natural, human function. Everyone has them, and there's nothing funny about that. Good Lord!"

"Did you hear that, Pearl? Everybody has bowels that move. Have your bowels moved? Where did they go? Mary Kline is trying to say that everybody takes a shit, a dump, a crap in the crapper. Even Mary yanks down her drawers and cops a squat. Did you ever think about that? Even Mary drops the kids off at the pool, at least once a day, and sometimes twice."

Mary would always object.

"Enough! That's not funny, young lady and I don't want to hear it anymore! Do you hear me, Elizabeth? Pearl! Don't encourage her!"

Pearl and I were both testing our limits with one of the body's most hysterical functions. It was fun at the time, but later on I realized that all my birth mother and I were doing was bonding over a big, steaming pile of shit.

As I grew older and understood the mechanics of sex, my humor took a more sophisticated turn. The whole business was ridiculous to even imagine, so I spent hours alone on my bed, trying to picture my teacher, Mrs. Jarvis, doing it with her husband. My humor with Pearl was confined to the toilet variety, so these sex funnies were mine, and mine, alone.

Once I had experimented enough with sex to recognize what some of the fuss was about, it didn't seem all that silly. I was happy for Mr. and Mrs. Jarvis, but I hoped she took off those black–rimmed glasses before they did it. My mind grew nasty, as I searched for material I could use in my one–woman comedy routine. Mary Kline and Pearl became the butts of my internal amusement. These two mothers of mine looked ridiculous in just about everything they did. And imagining either of them as their erotic selves made me laugh so hard, I cried.

Mary Kline must have had breasts, but I couldn't see anything appealing about them. After I noticed in a *National Geographic* magazine how women fed their children with milk from their breasts, I was more grossed out than ever. Not even a baby starving in the jungle would be enticed by Mary's mounds. She probably would have smothered a child with her ample bosom, force feeding the kid until the poor thing puked. Mary's size made her an unlikely candidate for much beyond hand-holding. In fact, I felt sure that Mary Kline had no sexual identity. It was just too cumbersome and funny and sad to be possible.

Pearl was another story. The notion of her sharing an intimate moment with a man was less amusing, especially after I knew that she was the female who birthed me, which meant she had to have had sex or I wouldn't exist.

Pearl, my mother, this child–like adult who needed help getting dressed and sometimes drooled, had made actual contact with a man! How on Earth had Pearl been able to attract that kind of attention? How could anyone kiss her? Imagining Pearl doing the deed was impossible, but then again, I had heard her on the wrong end of the act many times as a young girl in the middle of the night.

Even worse and more disgusting, was realizing that the man who found my dim–witted mother attractive enough to get naked with her had to be my own father. This man had unimaginably low standards, and my mother somehow met them. If the two of them were such a perfect match at the time, what did that make me?

I didn't find that funny at all.

Chapter Twenty-Six

Mary Kline

I knew we'd reached a point in Elizabeth's life when some of what I had to offer became irrelevant and even inappropriate. I could prepare delicious meals, make holidays memorable, scrub stains out of clothes, bring elaborate cookies and cupcakes for parties at school, drive here and haul her there. I could cut out intricate patterns and create showstopper clothes for this girl. In matters both practical and frivolous, I appeared capable.

But a cumbersome truth inched its way between us. It separated my little charge and I into distinct camps. As Elizabeth's body took shape, this girl, who wasn't mine in the first place, was destined to scale a wall I'd only gazed upon from afar. For so long, Elizabeth had filled my need for contact, never in a sexual way, but through the charms of her passing innocence. As a small child, she offered me hugs with the brush of her hair against my fat cheeks. But as Elizabeth grew, she hoarded those sensations for herself, depriving me of my simple pleasures. She was saving her touch for something more promising with someone who could appropriately reciprocate.

I knew that sex was a worthwhile endeavor worth pursuing. I was so hungry for touch of any kind that I often settled for the only thing readily available: my hand. Anchoring myself in skin-on-skin dreams I'd only seen in movies, I sent myself to Heaven. Eventually, even my own hand betrayed me. It didn't have eyes, but it could feel my fat and it became as disgusted with me as any imaginary lover.

Among our sad triumvirate, Pearl, with her backlog of ramming sessions with James Pullman, qualified as the resident expert in the sexual arts. Even some basic mechanical information might have proven useful to Elizabeth, but by then, Pearl had disintegrated. Even before I brought the girls back to live with us, she stopped talking.

As Elizabeth evolved into a young woman, her flesh-and-blood mother was taking giant steps backward, regressing to the lower levels of Maslow's hierarchy of needs. Pearl seemed satisfied with the bare necessities: food and drink, and warm, dry clothes. When she pored through magazines, it was to look at the pictures, like children do when they pretend to read.

It was as if Elizabeth wanted genuine approval, asking "Mother, may I?" Pearl was useless and so was I. We stood on the sideline to watch this girl of ours scissor-step and bunny hop her way across boundaries we'd never braved ourselves.

Pearl and I were easy to leave behind.

Chapter Twenty-Seven

Mary Kline

Mother and Daddy had gone to look at a property 40 miles south of town, a storefront Daddy hoped to open as a second department store. On the way back, they hit an icy patch and the car flipped into a ditch.

The weeks that followed were filled with relatives on both sides of the family flocking in to pay their respects. Elizabeth was happy to miss school that entire first week, but after a few days of having a 14-year-old home around the clock, I was ready for her to go back.

She sulked in the corner at the funeral home, barely mumbling her version of a greeting to those who filed through to express their condolences. Pearl was restless as well. Both were a distraction as I tried my best to field the attention, write thank-you notes, and for the first time ever, make decisions about the store.

I inherited Kline's and all the management headaches that came with it. Payroll, accounts payable, accounts receivable, inventory, advertising, quarterly reports to the board of directors. You name it; all the business Daddy had attended to for years was now mine to manage. I had not yet shed tears over the loss of Mother and Daddy, but the paperwork presented by lawyers and Daddy's longtime assistant manager, Roger Fleming, brought me to tears.

When the lawyer contacted me about the will, I learned that Daddy had signed a contract the afternoon of the accident to lease the new space for a trial period of one year, with an option to buy. Perhaps that was the type of contract they should have arranged for my family: a trial period with an option to make things more permanent later might have been better for all of us.

Roger, bless him, stayed on and took over much of the decision making. I needed him to rescue me like he did. I was not capable of minding the store, especially while managing surly Elizabeth and poor Pearl. Roger came by the house a few times a week with papers to sign and updates about decisions he'd made. He was kind and gentle with me in a fatherly way.

One afternoon, less than a month after the accident, as he packed up his briefcase and slipped on his overcoat, he stopped and looked at me with concern in his eyes.

"Mary, I'm worried about you. You look exhausted. Are you getting enough rest?"

I shrugged. I wasn't sleeping much at all. Elizabeth was running wild, sneaking out of the house, and I was sure she'd been smoking. I found cigarettes in her room and the school called three times that week about one disciplinary issue or another. Pearl was Pearl, sitting in the corner, watching the theatrics unfold between me and Elizabeth.

"You know, Mary, I might be overstepping here, but I have some advice if you're interested. You might think about getting Pearl into a home. You've got your hands full as it is. That would simplify things for you, and she won't know the difference, will she? She might be better off, Mary. No one would blame you. Your whole family has done quite enough for that girl. Think about it. You've got the money to cover it."

I shook my head.

"Oh, Roger, I would never consider it, not ever. No way. Pearl and me, we've been through it."

He shrugged.

"I know it will be hard but promise me you'll think about it."

I promised.

That night, once I was sure Elizabeth was in her room to stay and the dinner dishes had been scraped and rinsed in the sink, I helped Pearl into her nightgown.

"We're skipping a bath tonight, Pearl. Mary's beat. We'll get you scrubbed up tomorrow, Miss Pearl."

Pearl nodded and let me guide her into bed. I slipped into my own nightgown but didn't bother to wash my face or brush my teeth before I tossed and turned myself into a fitful sleep.

The next day, I started going through Mother's things. That night, I slept deeply for the first time since the accident. Roger's suggestion about Pearl had taken root. Maybe he was right.

It took me a few months to pull the trigger, but I finally arranged to move Pearl across town. The facility was clean, and Pearl could have a room of her own. I made a big fuss about that, making her a pink bedspread with matching pillows and curtains. I hung her clothes in the closet and put away her underwear and socks in a chest of drawers.

Elizabeth had said goodbye to Pearl at the house, offering a quick, forced hug that irritated me with its brevity. Pearl deserved better from her daughter. She teared up on our way over in the car, and I soothed my friend as best I could.

"Now Pearl, don't you cry. I'll bring Elizabeth over to see you all the time. All the time. And Mary will visit, too, Honey. I'll bring you magazines and candy. Mary Kline will do that. You'll see."

I ate lunch with Pearl in the cafeteria. The meals wouldn't be as good as what she had at home, but I promised myself I'd bring her something yummy on my next visit. I walked with Pearl back to her new room.

"It's time for old Mary to get home now. I need to start supper."

I was trying to sound casual, as if this were an ordinary exchange and not the day I was leaving my sweet friend with strangers. Pearl started to make a fuss, and that wouldn't do. I gave her a giant Mary Kline hug and felt her frail body shudder against mine. My simple friend was not to be fooled. She knew exactly what was happening, and so did I.

"Bye, Honey. Mary will see you real soon, Pearl."

I walked to my car, shaking and feeling weak. I sat there in front of Pearl's new home, looking up at her window. Sure enough, she was standing there, looking for me. She waved, and I waved back, blowing her a kiss.

I cried all the way home. I shed tears that I hadn't been able to shed for Mother and Daddy. I was headed home alone, where Elizabeth and I would continue our scrapping and posturing. Maybe I was getting what I deserved.

Chapter Twenty-Eight

Elizabeth

I flipped on the light in my room. My hair reeked of smoke, and my jeans and shirt smelled like spilled gin and lime. Thankfully, Mary Kline was asleep on the sofa.

My shirt was inside out and backwards. An hour earlier, that shirt, my jeans, bra and underpants had been wadded into a heap and kicked to the floor of John Clapp's pick-up truck. The two of us had been panting inside the confines of his front seat, stripped to our socks. It was much too cold to take our party for two out to the bed of his truck.

But we didn't let cramped quarters or the chill stop us. We kissed for what seemed like hours until he asked me to take off my shirt. He helped me peel it off my back and over my head so he could see and feel my stomach and breasts.

We didn't go all the way that night, but my hips and lips felt bruised. We devoured each other, marking our territory. Our necks were covered with dark love bruises. John Clapp showed his affection for me and my body by matching me hickey for hickey, tongue for tongue, and thrust for thrust.

It was scary, but delicious. My reward was lying in his arms as we drifted into a satisfied sleep. To me, the falling asleep part was more intimate than anything that had just taken place. Letting my mind drift into autopilot while someone held me was more sacred than any of the bases I'd blown past with an assortment of boys.

We awoke in the dark, threw on our clothes, and emerged disheveled from the truck. As my latest lover drove down the street, I noticed that the hair on the back of his head was matted into a nest. He was dreaming of the next chance we'd have to grab each other in his dirty vehicle, fogging up the windows with our senseless bucking.

By the time I'd discovered the rubber string that runs from the tips of my breasts to the place where my legs parted ways, Mary Kline and I had been living together for a long time. Her parents had passed away. Lucky Pearl lived in a nursing home across town. Mary and I had been left to spar and posture our way around each other in her messy old house until I figured out that I could come and go as I pleased.

Compared to Mary, I was a seasoned lover. After the first time I allowed Gregory Pinnell (or maybe it was Leo Ames) to slide his cold hands down the back of my jeans, I was the experienced one, a veteran tongue wrestler who knew her way around a backseat.

Mary stayed home and kept the house from blowing away while I ventured out into the world, hips first, daring every man-child to slap me, tickle me, or touch me any way they would. I grew to appreciate the musky smells of arousal. Sometimes, I'd wait a day or two after an encounter to bathe so the funky smell of hungry, lusty boys could keep me company.

Chapter Twenty-Nine

Elizabeth

I found the clean design and lack of color in the abortion clinic soothing. At home, we kept things we needed and things we did not. In the examination room, the blank walls made it clear that we were in a place where anything extra was quickly discarded.

Mary stood in the corner of the room with a determined stare. The two of us were not speaking. The barbed words we'd exchanged the day before had really stung. I'd hit Mary in her most tender spots, and like any bewildered animal in pain, she responded in kind.

I had kept my pregnancy to myself, hoping it would go away on its own, sure I would fool my poor excuse of a mother. Compared to me, Mary was a novice of love, but she wasn't stupid. She passed biology. My condition was the natural progression of a reckless pursuit of all activities carnal and dangerous, and even a big fat virgin could have figured out my predicament.

The leverage I held over Mary had run dry. In spite of being wildly popular with boys of all ages and backgrounds, at 17, I'd never been on an actual date. Not one of those young panting dogs had ever bought me a soda or taken me to see a show. Boys weren't interested in pinning a corsage onto my dress, when they knew I'd probably let them remove that very same dress.

I was the girl they picked up after they took their dates home from the school dance. I'd kicked more than one empty corsage box off the back seat of a car while wriggling out of my jeans, intentionally worn two sizes too small. With their porcelain dates tucked safely back at home after a dreamy night of swaying in one another's arms, my boys were ready for something less demanding but far more satisfying.

Mary Kline had spent hours at the sewing machine, creating what she thought were beautiful dresses for me to wear to the dances, the homecoming, and the Sweetheart Ball. I didn't care. To be hateful, I refused to even try on the finished products. Mary would sigh and hang her latest creation in my closet.

As a little girl, I was always ready to give Mary and Pearl a fashion show, but those days were gone. I didn't bother about Mary's feelings. I found her attentions smothering and irritating. At first, her renewed interest in my cycles amused me, but her continuous probing quickly grew annoying. I responded with my most potent weapon: silence. Lonely Mary despised my silent treatments, and she usually responded by shuffling away to do something else for me.

Mary Kline did everything on my behalf. She cleaned my room and stocked the refrigerator with homemade meals, but I never gave her the pleasure or the courtesy of sitting down to share a meal with her. She often ended up throwing containers of rotting food away. I was surly, aloof and rude. I read her ability to withstand my abuse as tacit acknowledgement that she deserved such treatment.

One morning, after she'd slapped two steaming pancakes onto a plate in front of me, I felt her pudgy hand on my shoulder. I pretended it didn't matter, but this time, Mary didn't walk away to lick her wounds. She grabbed my arm with surprising force. I tried to jerk away and in doing so, my fork clattered to the floor.

"Elizabeth!"

Her voice was harsh. There was nothing singsong about it.

"You will listen to me!"

Mary Kline bellowed. I tried to move, but her grip was decisive.

"You have a child inside you, Elizabeth. If you miss your period, it means you are pregnant. I *knew* this would happen. You are a stupid girl! This will ruin your life."

I refused to meet her gaze, so she cupped my chin like she had when I was a little girl, forcing me to look into her fleshy face.

"We're going to a clinic tomorrow to take care of this. You're such a pretty girl, but you don't care about anyone but yourself. I won't raise another child, Elizabeth. I won't."

My lips formed a wicked smile, one I'd been saving for a long time.

"Mary, you are talking to me as if you are my mother, but that's not who you are! Who are you, Mary? Who are you?"

She slowly crouched, fearing the blow she knew was coming.

"To be a mother, Mary, you have to get fucked, and we both know that no one would stick it in you. Don't we? That's right. You're too goddamned fat!"

This was the first time I had described her like that, but the words didn't feel as satisfying as I had imagined they might. For years, I wanted to be the one to tell Mary how huge she was, and I'd finally done it. But the moment didn't feel as yummy as I'd guessed.

Mary Kline did to me what she should have done long before, at the onset of my rebellion. She slapped me. Not too hard, but with just the right firmness of a mother who has had enough. That slap across my face transformed Mary into the mother I needed and restored the balance of power between us.

I dashed up the stairs to my room. Mary heaved herself up the stairs behind me and struggled to drag a chair down the hallway to my closed bedroom door. Finally, I heard her wheezing as she tried to catch her breath. I wasn't going anywhere the rest of the day.

The next morning, we dressed and ate breakfast, without speaking. We rode in silence to the abortion clinic in a town 30 miles away.

Because of my age, Mary accompanied me into the procedure room, where I endured the cold and careful scraping of what felt like a metal razor blade. The doctor who performed the procedure was calm and quiet, as he scraped the territory where I'd casually invited so many guests. Mary Kline clenched my hand in hers, giving me love squeezes I'd resisted for so long.

When it was over, the doctor left the room, but his stern nurse remained to clean up. My freckled thighs were still draped with a white sheet when she approached, carrying a stainless-steel container, shaped like a kidney. She held it out for Mary Kline and me to see. What we saw assaulted our senses and made Mary retch. My screaming was interrupted by the nurse, who was determined to make her point.

"Young lady, you need to see the life you've chosen to end. Here. Look at it closely. This isn't a science project. This is a tiny person. Inconvenient, isn't it? You've come here today, filled out a few papers and thrown this human being away. Take a good, long look."

Once my blurry eyes focused on the contents of the bowl, I couldn't divert my attention. I was repulsed yet riveted by the creation my sensuous body had harbored. This was a fusion that had happened most likely in the back of someone's car, late at night, without love or even a cursory introduction. The unknown father of this baby didn't know me and was just one of many warm bodies I'd hugged with my legs. Still, his magic parts and my magic parts had mingled together one night, and a miniature heart had begun to beat.

Mary Kline and I sobbed all the way home. For the first time in years, the woman who raised me the best way she knew how held me in her bed throughout the night.

The next morning, I awoke to a tray of hot pancakes. We watched Mary's favorite movie, *Some Like It Hot*, and howled together at Jack Lemon and Marilyn Monroe cavorting together in the sleeper car.

Mary Kline and I talked about Pearl and how I came into this world. I learned that I was just a byproduct of interactions that should never have happened. I didn't know yet who my father was, but as I sat there, crotch throbbing, my thoughts drifted to my poor mother, Pearl. She was just a vessel and Mary Kline, her only friend, had taken her in with me aboard.

I'd been allowed to thrive and enter the world because someone saw a use for me. That someone was Mary Kline. For that act alone, didn't I owe her my gratitude? Did Pearl ever thank her for saving us? Did Pearl know, deep down in her empty head and simple heart, that I belonged to her? Did it ever occur to Mary that she owed us something, too?

Chapter Thirty

Elizabeth

After we aborted my first baby, Mary Kline and I became thick again, mostly by necessity. The abortion had startled us both, and we agreed that I'd take back my own body. No more trespassing.

The summer before I left for college, I taught myself how to douche. I cleansed myself again and again, determined to disinfect my past. The new Elizabeth was clean. The next time I found myself horizontal with a man, I'd do it for a better set of reasons, and it would take place in a bed, with clean, crisp sheets.

By the time I met David after college, I'd practically achieved a faux–virgin state. During our first months dating, David was more pet than boyfriend, a good dog who didn't mind the collar and leash I put on him. Eventually, his doggy features seemed human. He evolved from my pet with a girl's best-friend potential into something much more. He hadn't come to me expecting anything and that intrigued me. He seemed disinterested in the delights I might offer. For months, our skin only touched as our fingers fumbled in the popcorn box at the movies. Always a gentleman, he let me have the pieces I prized.

Even after I'd known David for a year, I'd grown so accustomed to having my body to myself that I was stingy with physical affection. After a reasonable amount of time, we had a love affair through kissing. My lips liked his lips, and the feeling was mutual. Our kisses blended, one into another, for hours. It was the first time I'd placed kissing into its own little container, boxed with boundaries.

My body tried to join in, but I wouldn't allow it. David's body also came knocking, but I let him wait. I became a bit of a tease, and he was one frustrated boy. I didn't play my fuck card until I was sure he was at the breaking point, when I felt convinced he might just love me.

David loved me beyond what I deserved. I could stretch him like a piece of rubber. He seemed willing to play along, so I pushed the envelope. One time, I refused to speak to him for several days. He was wounded, calling the house again and again. I let the phone ring and watched from my bedroom window as he knocked on our front door for an hour before giving up and moping back to his car.

I was ashamed of myself, knowing full well that I was squandering his affections just like I had rebuffed Mary Kline. The cruelties I meted out were my version of a protective ten-foot pole, a reliable tool for fending off anyone from smothering me.

When I emerged a few days later and saw him in the hall at work, he asked me out for lunch to talk things over. I shrugged, but grabbed my purse and sweater, following him out of our building. David was angry, and we didn't have lunch that afternoon. We went straight to his apartment. I lifted the lid off the kissing box, and we both called in sick for the remainder of the day. He'd finally given me what I wanted, a boundary, the fair fight I craved. I let him worship me in all the ways he'd been dreaming about until the next storm came through.

Chapter Thirty-One

David

I tried explaining Elizabeth's upbringing to my parents. After I was dating her for more than two years, it must have crossed their minds that she could be *the one*, which finally propelled them to probe a little more, beginning with my mother.

"David, will Elizabeth's mother be joining us for dinner when we're all in town?"

"No."

"So, should I make reservations for just the four of us?"

"No, Mom. Elizabeth will bring Mary Kline with her."

"That large woman?"

"Yes. That one. Mary. She raised Elizabeth. I told you that before."

"David, I don't think I heard that. Where is Elizabeth's mother?" My father interrupted.

"Julia, David told us. You did, David. I remember."

"Well, it's still unclear to me," said Mom.

I sighed.

The whole thing had started to seem normal to me, too, so translating the dysfunction to my uncomplicated parents was a tiring task.

"Elizabeth's real mother is slow. Her name is Pearl. Mary Kline is an old friend of Pearl's, and she took care of Elizabeth since she was born. She took care of Pearl, too."

"Where is Elizabeth's father?" Dad said.

"I'm not sure about that. I don't think Elizabeth even knows."

My parents needed more information.

"Where were Pearl's parents?" said Mom. "Why did Mary take over like that? Aren't they about the same age? What about Mary Kline's parents? Where were they?"

"Mom, I don't know the whole story. I wasn't there."

Elizabeth and I weren't even engaged yet, and already I was weary. I didn't have any good answers.

"Well, I guess it turned out okay, Mom. It's a little strange, but it's over. Elizabeth is fine. She's smart. She's funny. She loves Mary Kline like a mother, and Mary is the one who will join us for dinner."

"But what about her *mother*?"

Mom could not let this go.

"What do you want to know, Mom?"

I could barely maintain my patience. Why did any of this matter? They knew I loved Elizabeth. They had started to love her, too. What was the point of this questioning?

"I think Pearl is in a home of some kind. She went away when Elizabeth was in high school."

My mother quietly processed this new information.

"I guess it doesn't matter, David. I just wanted some clarification."

As I came to know Elizabeth longer and became privy to more and more information about what made her tick, I guess that's all my wife wanted, too: clarification.

Who was her family? Who was her mother? Who was in charge?

Chapter Thirty-Two

Johnson Kuhlman

Just because I like fabric and sewing, it doesn't make me gay. My mother told me I came by my interest genetically, that it runs in the family. My grandfather was a tailor, as was his father before him. They were both disappointed that my mother didn't take to sewing like they had, but she assured me that they were smiling from heaven at my seemingly girlish inclinations.

My sweet mother pointed out a truth that anyone cultured and educated would naturally know, that some of the world's finest fashion designers and tailors had been and still are men. Sewing is only "women's work" to minds that are closed for business.

My father was horrified by my early preoccupation with how clothing was made. By six or seven, I would spend hours inspecting the inside of his sports jackets or turn his trousers inside out so I could see how the pockets were made.

Santa left thimbles, thread, and pincushions in my stocking every Christmas. One year, I got a professional quality tape measure and my own pair of scissors.

"Now, maybe I'll be able to find my good scissors when I need them!" my mother teased, as my father grumbled.

I could spot sloppy stitching from across a room. By the time I was nine, I could instantly distinguish skilled hand stitching from that of a machine. I could replace zippers and buttons better than my mother, and my parents had their biggest fight when my father caught my mother and me working together on a new set of crisp café curtains for the kitchen.

I was 13 when my father finally walked out on us. On my 14th birthday, I received a brand–new sewing machine, the same one I'd been coveting for my last two birthdays. Because it cost my mother a fortune, she couldn't afford any needles, thread, and materials. For those, I'd need to get a job and make my own money.

I figured I'd just snag an after-school job at the fabric store downtown. I was old enough, but the storeowner, Mrs. Phelps, said she'd have to think about it and reluctantly let me fill out an application.

"Are you sure you want to work here, Mr. Kuhlman? Have you applied at the grocery store or the hardware store? They always need big, strong boys to carry out groceries and stock shelves. Why don't you try there, Honey?"

I came back the next week. The help wanted sign was still in the window. Mrs. Phelps had no takers, and the Halloween season was weeks away. Black fabric for little witch costumes and pink for fairy princess gowns would be flying out of the store. Mrs. Phelps still held out. She hadn't made up her mind.

I came back the next week, and the next. Exasperated, Mrs. Phelps hired me, but with this warning:

"Son, I think your friends and classmates are going to give you a hard time. You'll take some ribbing for this. Are you sure this is what you want?"

I think she was genuinely concerned about my social wellbeing. That's when I told her about the sewing machine my mother went broke to buy me and showed her the quilt top I'd pieced together with scraps from home.

Mrs. Phelps cleared her throat and looked at me over her glasses. Suddenly, we understood one another. I'd finally broken through to become Caroline Phelps' protégé. I started working at Phelps Fabrics that

Saturday. It was October 11, 1974, and except for Sundays, I've worked there ever since.

I stocked thread, zippers, buttons, needles, and pins. Bias tape and ric rac came in every color on the spectrum. Cards were wrapped in lace, one more intricate than the last. I quickly learned that Phelps Fabrics carried the largest selection of ribbons in three counties.

The most exciting part of the job was helping Mrs. Phelps unload new shipments of fabric, bolt after bolt of varying grades and colors of cotton, coarse and complicated plaids, blinding checks, and stripes that went for miles. The raised bumps on the dotted Swiss felt good on the palms of my hands. Calicoes, prints, denims, fine-gauge corduroys all became my personal candy store.

The best part of my job occurred as we neared the end of each bolt because the remnants were mine for the taking. I hauled bags of fabric home every night, much to my mother's dismay and chagrin.

"Johnson Kuhlman! We don't have room for another scrap!"

She only half meant it.

"Don't bring home another piece until you've done something with what you've already nabbed!"

I used my earnings to buy additional fabric and patterns, which I stacked in neat piles around my room. My cousin, Janet, told me she didn't find my passion for all things fabric disturbing or girly at all.

"Johnson, if you think about it, these patterns are just like the blueprints other boys use in shop class. The only difference is your building materials are soft and theirs are hard."

I've always loved Janet. I could have kissed her right on the lips. The dress I made for her to wear to the Poulson High School Valentine's Ball looked fabulous. It was the first time I'd ever made something from material that had been specially ordered.

God Bless the Child

I was nervous. Auntie Jean had paid $2.39 a yard for the russet satin. I labored over it with the same zest other boys had for the souped-up old cars inside their fathers' garages.

Janet came by the house the night of the dance so my mother could see her in the dress. I eyed it with subtle pride. Her dork of a date, Aaron Stells, had managed to get the right color corsage, and my cousin looked like a cupid for the school dance.

I didn't want Aaron to catch on that I was the one who had sewn his date's dress. I let him think my mother was the master seamstress. I wasn't ashamed of my talent, but it was just better this way. Less hassle. Mrs. Phelps had a point.

My mother and I watched Janet and Aaron head off together into the night.

"Johnson, you should be taking someone to the Valentine's Ball. You're handsome enough. Any girl would be thrilled to go with you."

I smiled at this beautiful woman who also happened to be my mother. I could tell by the way she measured her words that she was probing for signs of my homosexuality. My father had planted warning seeds before he left, and she kept a close watch.

I heard him one night, hissing at her under his breath.

"That kid is a faggot, Marilyn. A faggot. And I'll be damned if I'm going to sit around and watch you fluff his skirts!"

Mother didn't have anything to worry about. I liked girls. One day, I'd find just the right one. That girl would understand that I was an odd, fabric–loving bird, and she'd love me anyway. I knew it might take time to find this woman, but she would surely be worth the wait.

Chapter Thirty-Three

Mary Kline

Johnson Kuhlman has always been kind to me. I remember frequent trips to Phelps Fabrics with Mother as a child. Johnson was just a teenager back then, older than I was, a toad, waddling to the store, following my mother.

While Mrs. Phelps measured and cut yards and yards of fabric at the counter and Mother looked for sturdy zippers, I ran the palms of my hands over rows of lace, letting the light touch of its edges tickle my palms. Mrs. Phelps furrowed her brow in my direction, but she never said anything to Mother. After all, we were her best customers. Johnson didn't mind that I touched all of the ribbons and the laces.

My mother didn't enjoy sewing, not like I do. Not like Johnson does. Mother sewed because it was a necessity. She wanted me to wear nice things, and nothing from Daddy's department store fit quite right.

I watched her from afar as she worked. She didn't hum to herself or talk to me while she sewed. She wore the same face creating my Easter dresses as she did while scrubbing a dirty pan in the sink. Her determined grimace was uninviting enough that I never worked up the nerve to ask her to show me the ropes.

I learned how to sew from Mrs. Lend, my home economics teacher. She liked me. A bit plump herself, she didn't seem bothered by my size. I was a natural. Mrs. Lend's praises felt like caresses. It was such a relief to come into her classroom after a torturous hour of crabby old Mr. Rivers trying to pound geometry theorems into my thick head. I took Home Ec every semester of high school and graduated knowing how to cook and sew like a champion.

"Miss Kline, you're going to make some lucky man a wonderful wife," Mrs. Lend crowed one day after tasting my French onion soup.

The girls in the class snickered and elbowed one another, shooting each other amused glances. Fat Mary Kline? Someone's wife? Ha! She'd have to get a date first.

Years later, I told Johnson that story and he got tearful on me, right there on my living room couch.

"Johnson, are you okay?"

"I'm sorry, Mary, but that just makes me so sad to hear that story."

I watched him wipe his eyes with a hanky from his pocket.

"Why are people so cruel? Oh, I wish I'd been there. I wish I had. I would have given those twits a smack!"

My Johnson. He's so good to me. I suspect that with his lilting voice and sensitive nature that my love has endured his fair share of taunts and unkind assumptions. I no longer care what anyone thinks of us. We know what we've got. We *both* know.

Chapter Thirty-Four

Johnson Kuhlman

Louise Kline spent much of her time and energy sewing clothes, even though Kline's Department Store had everything anybody with money might want to buy.

By the time I was 19 and had been working at Phelps for four years, I learned that most of our regular customers made their clothing as a cost–saving measure. A thrifty homemaker could make three nice dresses for the price of one from Kline's. There would still be fabric left over to make some doll clothes, a small pillow, or a pincushion.

Louise Kline bought expensive fabric and lots of it. Almost every two weeks, our shipment included three or four large pieces of material for her, as well as high–end buttons and sturdy zippers purchased from what Mrs. Phelps called the "quality catalog."

I often delivered to the Klines. Mrs. Phelps was miffed that what she had in stock wasn't good enough for the picky Louise Kline. Usually, when a customer came in to buy fabric and notions, they also purchased a pattern. Louise Kline never bought patterns. On a slow day, as we shared a quick tuna salad sandwich in the back room, I asked Mrs. Phelps about it. She finished chewing and wiped the corners of her mouth with a cloth napkin made from remnants.

"Louise used to buy patterns, but she hasn't for some time now. I wondered if she decided our patterns weren't good enough, but after she brought her girl in, I figured it out."

My boss was about to say something unkind. I could tell by her hushed tones and the way she shook her head. What she was about to say was a dirty job, but somebody had to do it.

"The child is *e–nor–mous*, Johnson. Absolutely enormous."

She stretched her arms out like she was telling me a whopper of a fish tale about the one that got away.

"That poor woman makes the girl's clothes because they can't buy them big enough. Now, she can't even find patterns that fit the child's proportions. It's awful. It's just awful."

At the time, I'd always seen Mrs. Kline come in the store alone. I didn't know she even had a daughter. Just how big could a child be? It seemed awfully unkind to be talking about a little girl that way.

"Louise hasn't brought that little piggy in here with her for a while, and I can't say that I blame her. It's a disgrace!"

Mrs. Phelps sneered.

"That plump little porker keeps Phelps Fabrics in business!"

She wadded up the sandwich wrap and looked at her watch.

"Wash your hands before you come out, Johnson. We're going to inventory the bridal section between customers. Wedding season's coming up, and everywhere you look, it will soon be bridesmaids, bridesmaids, bridesmaids!"

I was intrigued by Mrs. Phelps' description of this oversized girl, so it seemed like forever before another parcel needed to be delivered to the Kline home. Finally, the day came, but the package was too big for me to deliver on my bicycle. Mrs. Phelps rolled her eyes as she handed me the bulky, brown package and her car keys.

"Must be expanding over there, again," she said with an evil wink. "Perhaps you'll get lucky, Johnson, and see the little whale today."

As I pulled up to 363 Blossom Street in Mrs. Phelps' Cadillac, I felt the same curiosity that must have driven nobles and scholars to seek a visit with John Merrick, the Elephant Man, hoping for a sighting of the freak. I pictured myself sleuthing around the yard, peeking in windows for a glimpse of the big Kline child. I figured she couldn't be that hard to find.

For a brief and cruel few seconds, I let myself imagine that the Klines had been forced to install a swimming pool in their backyard, and that their whale of a daughter would be found floating in circles and coming up for air when she needed it.

Little Mary Kline wasn't as large as I'd been led to believe. She couldn't have been older than five or six, sitting there alone on the front step. I recognized the fabric of her jumper, which was too tight. She looked uncomfortable, but she wasn't a beast at all. If I squinted my eyes just slightly, she was just the other side of chubby. There was something haunting about her face. I don't think she was pouting, but her puffy cheeks made it look like she was. She had snapping blue eyes and just enough pudge around her neck to draw attention from her pretty face.

"Hello."

She looked up at me and quickly glanced down again.

"I've got something for your mother. Is she home?"

The fat little girl nodded, stood and disappeared into the dark hallway that led into the house. A few moments later, Mrs. Kline emerged. She thanked me for my trouble and gathered the parcel into her arms.

When I returned to the store, Mrs. Phelps didn't waste any time questioning me.

"Well? Did you see her? Did you see the girl?"

I nodded but chose to say no more. I wouldn't give her the satisfaction of a comment or any lurid details. The Kline child was on the heavy side, but she was not an animal or circus freak. I chided myself for letting my imagination get the best of me before I'd even seen her.

Shame on me. Shame on Mrs. Phelps.

Chapter Thirty-Five

Louise Kline

Watching Mary dress up Elizabeth was painful, especially when I wanted to dive in with my giant girl and help her overdo it. I let myself slip a few times when I came home from our store with boxes of beautiful outfits and dresses.

My generous gestures were not as well received as I'd hoped. Mary was territorial about our baby doll from the moment we brought her home. She rebuffed my grandmotherly advances, turning her back to me cruelly as if I didn't deserve to be included.

I could have helped with diapers, warmed up a bottle in a pinch, or kept Pearl occupied, but Mary never invited me to enjoy the sweet deliciousness of having a little girl in our house. She devoured that treat whole and licked the plate clean.

I wanted to let our daughter know that I had also been robbed. I'd been deprived, too. My own little doll, the one I dressed up and fussed over, did not stay lovable for long. She knew too much and could blurt out truths that would ruin us. We stuffed her and didn't stop her when she stuffed herself. As she grew steadily thicker, her expansion drew comments from family.

"Louise, Darling," said Cousin Sally, "what is that child eating? For goodness sake, you've got to take care of this. If you let it go on too long, she'll never lose it. Never."

She was right. So was the pediatrician, who clucked his tongue at every checkup and sent us home with diets of grapefruit juice and cottage cheese. My own mother shook her head each time we visited.

"You simply must put that child on a strict diet, Louise. Strict. If she keeps that pace, she'll never leave."

Edward just shrugged when I told him there wasn't any clothing appropriate for a little girl her size at Kline's.

"Don't you have some specialty lines for children like Mary? There must be some other options, Edward. Our child isn't the only fat kid in the world."

My husband and I looked at each other and silently acknowledged that our girl was the fattest one we'd ever seen. We knew that she could not be contained and that she was our heavy burden to bear. When Edward bought me a sewing machine, I took on the task of keeping Mary covered. From then on, whenever the three of us entered or left a room, we held our heads high and let people say what they wanted.

As Mary grew older and became aware of the taunts and jokes made at her expense, I could not protect her from each barb. After an especially cruel day at school, after she'd cleaned her plate and asked for a second dessert, I heard her crying quietly in her bed, which we'd moved next to mine. I wanted to go to her. I wanted to pick her up and give her the comfort she should have received from her mother, but each time I tried I regretted the gesture and resented her for trying to gobble me up with her roundness.

I'd disentangle myself from her hungry clutches and retreat to my empty bed, loaded with shame for the distance I put between us, angry with her for choosing such a visible and vile cocoon for herself, and wistful and weepy for how sweetly it had all started before we allowed it to go so horribly wrong.

Chapter Thirty-Six

Johnson Kuhlman

Back–to–school season always put Mrs. Phelps into what my mother called a dither. Industrious and thrifty mothers within a 30–mile radius of town descended upon Phelps Fabric at the beginning of every August, ready to purchase material, and lots of it.

Hundreds of little girls needed a "first–day–of–school" dress or jumper, and Caroline Phelps carried just about any material their prickly and demanding seamstresses could dream up. By late July, many mothers were distraught to discover they wouldn't get one more season out of their daughters' old plaid skirts or that there was no more hem to let out on their dresses. Budding young teens needed more give on their blouses.

If you wanted to witness a good catfight, Phelps Fabric was the place to be in late summer. Mothers can be as vicious at that time of year as they are when Easter dresses and prom gowns are at stake. Purchasing fabric was serious business, and women make the cattiest bunch when they're in shopping heat.

On a hot summer afternoon, when the first day of school was still a few weeks away, Louise Kline came flying in, breathless and on a mission. As she made her way to the counter, her daughter darkened the door. Mary Kline was panting and sweat rolled down her neck and the sides of her jowls. She wore a shapeless sundress made of green fabric with large yellow and brown sunflowers. I remembered cutting that material out the previous spring.

"Mrs. Kline. Miss Kline. How are you ladies today?"

Mrs. Phelps was working hard for a sale, but I wasn't quite sure why. The Klines spent more money in our store than any of our other customers. I'd measured and cut and folded more orders that day than I thought possible. We'd also run out of all of our white thread by noon. Mrs. Phelps was barking at me in front of the customers to save face for her lack of planning.

Louise Kline rolled her eyes and nodded to her daughter.

"Well, it looks like we're in need of some more material, Caroline," she said.

"Mary," Mrs. Phelps said. "How was your summer? You were in Chicago with your grandparents, right?"

The boss was putting on the charm, and it was about as genuine as a slap in the face. Mary detected it and didn't respond. Louise spoke for her.

"I think we had a good time, didn't we, Mary Ann?"

Mary grunted and shuffled toward the cottons.

"Let's see," said Louise. "We'll need blouses and skirts and a few dresses. Caroline, what kind of plaids do you have, or will I need to order some?"

Mrs. Phelps looked straight at me, trying to hide her irritation, like I was her ally. She must have forgotten how nasty she'd been about the thread shortage less than an hour before.

"Well, Louise, we have a lot of new plaids, so I'm sure you'll be able to find something you like. We just need to make sure we have *enough*, don't we?"

As a young man whose passions lie in the bosom of a world dominated by women, I tended to champion the underdog. I appointed myself goodwill ambassador for Phelps Fabrics, and Lord knows, I was needed. Caroline Phelps had the best selection of material in town, but she could be a viper. If she decided she didn't like a person because of one flaw or another, her decision was final.

I tried to make eye contact with Mary as I measured yard after yard of the polished, white cotton her mother purchased to make the girl's underpants. I said to her with my eyes that I didn't mind her big butt. I tried to tell her with a twitch of my lips that it was okay, that *she* was okay. I imagined her friendless and trying to be the nice young man my mother raised me to be, I made small talk with Mary while her mother stocked up on thread and needles.

The fat girl shot me down with what I eventually came to know as her trademark bite.

"What's your name, again?"

"I'm Johnson. Johnson Kuhlman."

I wanted to make sure she understood that I came in peace.

"Well, look, Johnson, I'm here to get some material and then we're leaving. I don't need a friend, or someone to give me pitiful looks. We're here because I'm as big as a house and my mother's trying to make me some clothes that fit. I don't need a friend, and if I did, it sure wouldn't be some guy who pussyfoots around with yarn and lace in a fabric shop. That's pathetic, so just take care of your own little freak show, and I'll take care of mine."

Until then, Mary Kline had begun to look pretty to me, in a big mama sort of way. Perhaps she was a beast after all, and my pity had been misplaced.

"Just trying to be nice," I said.

"Whatever."

She sulked like the big teenager she was while Mrs. Phelps added up the bill.

"Mary Ann," said her mother, "help me with this stuff. Caroline, let me know when the fabric for the nightgowns comes in."

"Will do," Mrs. Phelps said. "Will do. You girls come back."

Later that day, Mrs. Phelps treated me to lunch, so I picked up a steaming bag of hamburgers and two strawberry shakes at Slapp's Diner. As I waited at the counter, I saw Louise and Mary in a booth. The waitress brought Mary a big piece of apple pie à la mode. I turned to look the other way. It just didn't feel right watching her. Eating dessert looked like it might be an intimate act for this girl, something that should be done with as much privacy as possible.

Chapter Thirty-Seven

Mary Kline

My mother was efficient with her moves—ordering fabric, ordering food, ordering me to move this way and that as I hurried along with her to the next function, the next appearance, always squeezing into the next painful place we needed to be.

"Hurry up, Mary Ann. We haven't got all day, and I'm sure you can move a little faster if you want to. That's the key, Mary. When you want to do something, when you put your mind to it, your body will come along for the ride."

That was easy for Mother to say. She was slim and trim. She could move with a swift, clipped precision and never wasted a moment to linger. There was no window shopping for her. That was for dreamers, gazing at perfect, lifeless forms covered with costly clothing without being disappointed as their fine reflections stared back at them.

Mother rarely looked at her full self in the mirror. We shared that trait. She was satisfied with periodic peeks in a tortoise shell compact from the cosmetics counter at Daddy's store. She inspected her face one mirrored circle at a time, patting a shiny nose into submission, pushing a stray strand of hair into place, and tending to ruby red streaks that bled beyond the confines of her lips. Satisfied, she'd snap that sphere of herself shut until the next show time.

Mother was consumed with the quality of all that bubbled to the surface. Coverage concerned her. We needed strong fabrics with nimble give that understood their assignment, to cooperate, to meld seamlessly with sturdy notions that shifted on command to contain my flesh into shapes that ran concave or convex.

I was a blob of circles, hills, curves and valleys, with no angles to offer her. The intersections of straight lines my mother craved were only within her grasp when she wrapped packages in foil paper, folded into crisp, creased triangles, squares, and rectangles, pressed to impress the recipient of each gift she brought home from the store.

Mother was so good at wrapping gifts that Daddy put her in charge of training the girls at the gift wrap counter, where standards were high. Gifts from Kline's came nestled in white tissue, confined in tidy white boxes wrapped tighter than the white sheets of a boot camp cot, and all of them had a signature red bow embossed with the letter K.

On the surface, all gifts were created equal. No trinket from Kline's was too small to receive the full treatment. Keychains, mittens, even scarves from the last chance rack were packaged and presented with the same trappings as cashmere sweaters, leather gloves and the most expensive dress in the store. A gift from our store could yield delight or disappointment, but the contents of each package didn't matter. The most important thing was how each gift looked on its way out the door.

There wasn't a box big enough to package me, but Mama worked with what she had. As she held the tape measure to my waist or across my shoulders, sucking in her breath with each expansion, I longed for her to touch me like I was her girl, not a mound to be measured.

Once, when I was home from school for a few days with a cough and sore throat, I felt her cool hand on my forehead as she checked for a fever. It was gentle and soft, and when she moved it to rest on my hot cheek, I reached up to hold it there a moment longer. I kept my eyes closed, so we could both pretend I was asleep, that she had not let herself linger and that I had not so greedily soaked in her fleeting display of affection. I wondered if her eyes were also closed, so she could feel her way in the dark to my fever and pretend I was a girl who was easier to hide, package, and love.

God Bless the Child

Her hand left my cheek, and as the door to my room clicked shut, I fell into a fevered sleep, craving something more substantive than chicken soup and crackers and remnants of a motherly touch cautiously doled out when no one was looking.

My hot-cheeked dreams swept me into long lost places that beckoned me to a soft landing. I was smaller, less burdened with flesh. My face nestled into my mother's velvet neck, where my warm, wet breath was welcome. I reached for her hair and worked a piece in soothing circles between my fingers. She encouraged my baby advances with kisses planted on top of my head as we swayed together in a sweet dream that made me wonder if it wasn't a dream at all, but a memory I deserved to enjoy.

That fever broke, as did the reverie. I was no longer in my mother's embrace, but alone in my bed, sweating, hungry, and wondering what I could find that might fill me to the brim.

Chapter Thirty-Eight

Johnson Kuhlman

Caroline Phelps retired and offered me first option to buy her out. I wanted it, for sure. The store was home, and I'd been there long enough to know how happy it made me.

I had just moved into the little apartment at the back of the store, which became my home sweet home. Sometimes at night, I'd walk through the shop, fingering the bolts of fabric. As crotchety as she had become over the years, Mrs. Phelps had been my company for a long time and now she was gone, off to live with her sister in Texas.

Her customers became my family. I knew which mothers would look for which fabrics. I understood the families that purchased fabric on credit and paid a little bit back at a time. I could predict which mothers I would see for formal gowns.

I marked time with many of these families. Mrs. Lively had five daughters, and she had come to Phelps Fabrics five separate times to buy material for bridesmaid's dresses, but she made only one bridal gown. All five girls wore the same one down the aisle. That's how she could justify the amount of money she spent on that one single gown.

Families grow and change. Little girls once delighted with frilly frocks now preferred jeans and store-bought tee shirts. In some cases, their mothers kept sewing. Mary Kline was one of these mothers. Elizabeth grew from a cute little pixie of a girl who loved coming into the store with Mary to pick out patterns and material into a teenaged bitch. I shouldn't have felt that way, but sometimes I just wanted to strangle that girl. At 15, she knew better. She treated her mother so poorly. I hated to imagine how things were at home when nobody was watching.

Mary usually showed the girl an assortment of fabrics.

"Elizabeth, which one of these do you like best?"

The brat wouldn't even respond. One time, she told her mother to shut up. I almost leapt over the counter to shake her. I wanted to spank that kid if only Mary Kline would have let me. But she just bought the material and shuffled out of the store while her ungrateful daughter waited in the car.

I could barely contain my fury.

"Don't let her talk to you that way, Mary. That's unacceptable! Does she understand the time you put into the things you make for her? Do you want me to tell her?"

I was livid, but it didn't matter.

"Oh, Johnson, that won't help. It won't help at all."

"I'm sorry, but it makes me mad! I don't like to see you treated that way, Mary Kline!"

"I know, Johnson. Thank you. We'll be all right. She's just an angry girl. It'll pass."

Mary waited a long time for it to pass. I worried about her, alone in that big old house, her parents gone, Pearl, too. She was left there with that miserable girl. Nothing good would come of it. Not one good thing.

My heart softened even more for Mary. Her skin was beautiful, and she had a pretty smile. She was a skilled seamstress in her own right. Her passion was evident, and we grew to respect one another for our talents. As we matured, it seemed like she appreciated me, too. I found myself hoping that she would come in soon to buy patterns and fabric. I loved how she patted and smoothed the fabric with her agile hands and carefully manicured nails.

Chapter Thirty-Nine

Mary Kline

My hands were the only part of me that did not elicit shame. Unlike the rest of my body, my hands could be counted on to move nimbly from task to task. They were a bit fleshy, but they were not so distorted by bloat that they invited an extra look or cruel comment.

When I looked at my hands, I imagined average, maybe even delicate bones beneath the surface of muscle, tendons and a thin layer of fat and skin. They went about their work not knowing how good they had it. If the bones in my hands ever had the chance to trade war stories with other parts of my body, they would be thankful they had it so good. My forearms didn't have much to complain about, but my poor spine had a sad tale to tell. It was no small task serving as the load bearing axis responsible for supporting all my flesh. My pitiful knees had plenty to say, too, as did my overworked tibias and fibulas. And those tiny, burdened bones in my feet screamed with pain each time I stood for too long or moved forward. They were trapped, forced to work like slaves in the galley of a ship.

I wondered what my frame might do if given a get-out-of-jail-free card that released it for a night on the town, unfettered and free to dance down the sidewalk. It would stop to show off in a hopscotch challenge with a group of happy children or jump rope all the way to ten without needing to catch its breath. It would sashay to the park, looking for boys to see how small it really was, how worthy of a second glance, even if it was just an ordinary bag of bones.

I did what I could with my hands. As I grew older, I made my best feature look and feel even more delicate and feminine by filing my nails and carefully painting them all the fun colors that felt off limits in the clothing I wore. Hot pinks, firetruck reds, creeping corals, lilacs, plums, mauve, taupe, even a daring neon orange were there to remind me I was a woman. I added sparkling rings and enjoyed watching the prisms catch the light as I prepared meals for me, Pearl, and Elizabeth.

It made peeling potatoes less dreary. Chopping onions was more pleasant. I liked the way the soapy suds sparkled on my hands under the kitchen light. Standing at the sink, the twinkling made me feel like a princess. With my hands, I could assert my womanhood, dominate fabrics, take command of the steering wheel, sign my name to checks and documents, wield my good scissors, master my measuring tape, put pins in their place and piece together fabric confections that looked good enough to eat. For the longest time, my dimpled dream weavers gave me quiet pleasure, a private consolation prize for my eyes only.

I went to Phelps Fabrics every few days, especially when Elizabeth was younger. I always needed something—buttons, ribbons in every color of the rainbow, cottons, fleece, tulle, thread, bias tape, needles and pins. They had zippers and piping, ric rac in every color, fresh bobbins, eyelet and yards and yards of the loveliest lace.

By the time I was making my own purchases, Mrs. Phelps and her scowls were long gone. The far more pleasant Johnson Kuhlman was in charge, and he always greeted me warmly, even though I'd been beastly to him when I was a teenager.

We batted friendly banter across the counter as he carefully measured and cut whatever fabric or notion I wanted to buy. When making something yummy for Elizabeth or Pearl, I thumbed through the pattern books for just the right thing. They were normal in their proportions, so there was no need to craft my own patterns like Mother had to for me. But I could do that in a pinch. Johnson always asked what I was making and seemed delighted when I made matching dresses or nightgowns for my girls.

One day, after he wrapped up green velvet, matching ribbon, green thread, and a packet of tiny green sequins I planned to sew on the skirt of Elizabeth's dress for the Christmas pageant, he placed his hand on top of mine and kept it there for a moment.

"Mary, this is going to be a beautiful dress against that little girl's mop of red hair. Perfect choice, just perfect. I hope you'll take pictures and bring them in. I'd love to see the finished product."

Breathless, I nodded, and felt my face flush. I needed to get home. Mother was there with Elizabeth and Pearl, and I'd promised I wouldn't be gone too long.

The compliment from Johnson felt like a caress, which caught me off guard. He'd always seemed just this side of feminine, but as I saw the contrast of his hand against mine, it was positively manly. His entire hand covered mine completely. It was warm and solid. I noticed for the first time that the backs of his hands were covered with dark hair that must have been even thicker on his forearms, which were buttoned up underneath the long sleeves of his shirt.

I drove home thinking first-time thoughts about a person I'd known nearly all my life. Those hands had touched almost every piece of fabric that had ever touched my body. But just moments ago, he hadn't let the fabric get in the way. His skin touched mine, and not by accident. His manly hands had found the most feminine body part I had to offer and touched them so softly and kindly that it took my breath away.

That night, after we'd eaten dinner, and I'd tucked Pearl and Elizabeth in for the night, I told Mother and Daddy goodnight and made my way up the stairs to my room. I looked in the mirror, turned on the lamp, and leaned in closely. My skin wasn't that bad. It was soft and unblemished. I slipped on my nightgown and got into bed, thinking about

Johnson's hands and his smiling eyes and the genuine message that tumbled from his lips, just for me.

The next day, I decided I might just need an extra spool of green thread. I painted my nails a deep shade of plum, two coats, and slipped on an aquamarine ring Mother had given me for my birthday. I combed my hair and slipped on some lipstick before I headed out the door, feeling a bubbly sensation at the back of my throat and in my belly. I waited at the counter as Johnson tended to customers in front of me. Finally, it was my turn, and his eyes were on me.

"Well, Miss Kline, long time, no see. What can I do for you today?"

As I inquired about the thread, he smiled and nodded. I watched him walk toward the counter behind him and reach for a spool.

"I thought you might need this, so I pulled it for you after you left yesterday. I was going to give you a call when things calmed down."

"Oh, great, Johnson. Great. Thank you."

I watched him ring it up with those hands. His sleeves were rolled up, and my suspicions about his arms were correct. They were manly alright. I could see tufts of that same hair peek out from his shirt toward the top, too. Johnson was a man who had thought about me when I wasn't in front of him, spending money.

I paid for my thread and prayed that he'd find a way to let his hand touch mine as he slid my purchase across the counter. There was no good way to make that happen, but I thought I could see in his eyes that he was also hoping for something. His smile would have to do.

"Thanks, Mary. Get busy with that dress!"

I think he was flirting with me. I flirted right back.

"Don't you worry about me, Johnson. That red-headed child of mine is going to be the best dressed little girl at that pageant. I'll have photos to prove it."

I sewed that dress with more joy than I'd experienced in a long time. It was the holiday season. The tree was up, as were the stockings. There were packages wrapped expertly by Mother under the tree. We baked and decorated cookies, and Elizabeth still believed in Santa. She even still believed in me back then.

Once she and Pearl were tucked into bed, I sat by the light of the tree and sewed tiny green sequins onto Elizabeth's Christmas dress. The tree twinkled, and so did my elegant, womanly hands.

Chapter Forty

Johnson Kuhlman

Mary Kline and Elizabeth entered my store one Saturday morning. It was still Phelps, but by then I'd been the sole proprietor for years. I'd never bothered to change the name. We still had the largest selection of fabric, and I'd expanded to offer sewing machines and repairs, tailoring services, and a whole section of knitting supplies, including miles and miles of every color of yarn imaginable.

Mary was out of breath, but not exasperated. The girl was no longer a child. Mary's little doll had grown up and seemed to have softened. The teenage scowls and rolled eyes were gone, and I was glad to see Elizabeth, now a grown woman, with a surprisingly pleasant look on her face.

"Mary Kline!"

I squealed like a girl. I'd seen Elizabeth's engagement announcement in the paper, and I figured I'd be seeing my old friend soon. A bridal gown! How lovely! I was so happy and excited, not about the wedding or impending marriage, but the dress. I could tell by her smile that Mary was thrilled to be at my counter and even more thrilled to need wedding dress patterns and fabric.

"Johnson, I bet you know why we're here, don't you? Elizabeth, you remember Johnson, don't you?"

Elizabeth and I exchanged pleasantries. I pulled up two stools to a side counter and brought out four bridal pattern books.

"What time do you close, Johnson? We may be here a while!"

I was pleased to see that the bride could smile and play along with her mother's triumphant moment.

"For you ladies, and forgive me Elizabeth, for you, Mary Kline—I'd stay open all night. If you're good, I might let you take a few books home with you."

"Oh, Johnson, that's very sweet of you," said Mary. "We might just take you up on that offer, but we'll try to be good anyway."

Mary Kline winked at me. I'm sure of it. She winked! I floated to the back room to make some coffee while Mary and Elizabeth pored over pages of beautiful, happy brides, wearing handmade gowns that looked like fluffy, gorgeous clouds.

When I returned to the front of the store, I tried not to hover.

"Elizabeth, what do you think?" said Mary. "Do you remember Jill's wedding dress? You'd look like an angel in something like that."

Elizabeth mumbled a response, turning her way toward the back of another book.

"Mary, Jill Freeson is a blue-eyed blonde with a stick for a body. I'd look like a warthog in drag with that kind of collar and sleeves. Don't forget, my arms aren't exactly pretty. We'll want to cover them, for sure."

Mary didn't disagree with her daughter.

"Well, Jill's dress was pretty, but perhaps you're right. I've always liked your little freckled arms, but we'll do whatever you want, Honey."

"Mary, this isn't about what I think," said Elizabeth. "This is about what looks good, and what doesn't. Arms that are pasty white and covered with hundreds of red freckles are best not displayed. That's not an opinion. That's just a fact."

"I think you're awfully hard on yourself. You're a beautiful girl, and David must like your arms just the way they are."

"David is blinded by love, and I don't think he sees the spots. Really. I don't think he sees them."

God Bless the Child

I understood what the girl was talking about. I did! With my eyes, I could see Mary Kline's size. I mean, it—*she* was right there, in full view, wheezing in front of me, but once the visual shock lost its impact, my eyes refused to deliver the fat message to my heart.

This David person couldn't see freckles and I couldn't see flab. I saw a talented, nurturing woman with skin that was dewy and fresh. I hoped her plump hands would touch mine as I spread material out on the counter for her inspection.

"Elizabeth, we'll do what you want. You choose the dress, and Mary Kline will make it."

I watched the two women relay a silent message. It was a lovely, tender second that made me feel hopeful and glad for my friend.

"What about tea length, Elizabeth?" said Mary. "That seems to be back in style."

"That might be nice, but I'd like something with a bit of a train."

Several minutes passed as the two flipped through the large pattern book pages.

"Oh, Honey, this is you. This is you, Elizabeth."

Mary was sure. Elizabeth craned her neck to see what her mother had found, and the two smiled at each other. Eureka! They'd found something that I'd learned could equate to the Holy Grail for mothers and daughters on a quest for the most important dress in their lives: a wedding gown they could agree on! This was a major feat—a specific accomplishment—one I'd only seen on rare occasions in my shop.

I'd seen many mothers and daughters leave the shop in tears. There was a lot at stake: reputations, money, time, and independence. The wedding dress symbolized so much for both mother and daughter.

I'd come to learn that it was the final frontier for many, the last battleground where mamas and their babies could shed blood over turf they'd been tugging at their entire lives. I was pleasantly surprised with what I'd seen thus far between Mary and Elizabeth Kline. I'd seen the two draw their swords in the past, especially when it came to details.

Mary Kline liked ribbons and lace. She'd buy lace with no plan for its use. I thought it was odd, but who was I, a mere clerk, to argue? I recalled that Mary's mother, Louise, never bought lace, fancy buttons, or anything frilly when Mary was a child. Elizabeth's arrival was Mary's chance to make the dresses she never wore at that age. For a long time, Elizabeth allowed it. Mary added lace wherever she could, on cuffs, hems and collars. When she brought the child in to model her latest creation, even I thought she'd overdone it on the extras.

Elizabeth's tastes changed as she grew. As a preteen, she refused to even look at the lace. She and Mary would leave the store with everything they needed for a dress but the lace. Mary would let Elizabeth believe she'd won the battle, only to return later alone to buy what she originally wanted.

"How's that going to go over?" I'd ask, knowing full well the battle my friend was about to wage.

"We'll see," Mary said. "Maybe I'll make one dress plain and the other one how I like it."

I shook my head and watched Mary leave the store with yards and yards of her intricate, expensive ammunition.

Those battles were over now. Elizabeth had matured and moved away. Perhaps some time and distance had mellowed the pair. How delightful this was going to be! I started bringing bolts of white satin and a heavier linen for them to consider.

"We won't want satin, Johnson," said Elizabeth.

She waved off the two bolts I held in my arms.

"Too shiny."

"Well, Honey, this is a wedding dress," said Mary. "I mean it's okay for it to shimmer, just a little."

"Shimmer? This isn't a Hollywood party, Mary. It's a service, a church service. I want something classy."

"Classy, yes, but what do you have in mind? Surely, you'll allow something with a little bit of wow. This is a bridal gown, Baby. What about some brocade? I bet Johnson could help us find a nice white brocade, couldn't you, Johnson?"

Elizabeth started chewing the inside of her mouth. She was holding back, I could tell, and so was Mary, but not for long.

"What if we consider changing the shade, Elizabeth? Perhaps white wouldn't be as flattering, but I bet a nice ivory in satin or brocade would look nice. Johnson, can you bring us some ivory to put up against her little old arm?"

I headed to the bridal section in search of ivory satin and brocade.

"Ivory, white, whatever. Mary, satin is shiny. So is brocade. If the dress is shiny, the pictures will look horrible. And you know I'll be sweating, so I'll have a shiny face and a shiny dress. I'm telling you it's got to be subtler than that. If we're going to go for something shiny and tacky, then why are we even in a fabric store? Let's order my wedding dress from a Sears catalog. That will save you time, and you'll get what you want—some fluffy-ass thing that's not me at all!"

Mary took her time to respond and cleared her throat.

"Johnson, I was mistaken. I think we're here for a pilgrim dress, not a wedding dress. Bring me your ugliest, cheapest cotton."

"Alright, Mary, enough. Enough," said Elizabeth. "That's cute."

The bride-to-be looked like she was searching for an ally. I'd seen enough of these bloodbaths to know that my opinion was only going to get a dirty look, probably from both sides. A neutral, possibly gay fabric storeowner was my safest position in a case like this.

"Johnson, this is going to be a garden wedding," said Elizabeth. "The dress needs to be elegant, but not overdone. The flowers will be wildflowers, not the formal, stiff kind of cookie-cutter arrangements you see at most weddings. I want this to be special, not some forced-looking nightmare. I don't want a great big Easter dress!"

She turned to her mother.

"Mary, we've done the Easter dress thing, the confirmation dress, and the formal dances for high school. I'm not a little girl anymore you can dress up however you want. This is my wedding dress. Mine. For once, can you try to see where I'm coming from? I want to feel good in this dress. Please, for once, can you make something the way *I* want it? I don't want shiny, or fluffy, or lacy or any of that crap. I've never wanted any of that! Mary, can this day, this dress, be about *me* and what *I* want? Please?"

Daughter was hurting mother. I could see that. Mary Kline's eyes welled with tears, but she didn't allow them to roll down onto her cheeks. I ached for her. I wanted to come to her rescue.

Don't cry, Mary! Don't cry!

"Ladies, we have all kinds of options, and I think you'll be surprised to see there's got to be something that will work. Let me order some samples and I'll call you when they're in. I think I know just what you're looking for, Elizabeth, and there's even some lace out there that's really subtle and tasteful, Mary."

Mary paid for the pattern and the two left. A few weeks later, they came back, and after some artfully controlled negotiation, Mary Kline spent $800 to order two bolts of raw silk in a hue called oyster. She even ordered matching silk thread and four boxes of the tiniest seed pearls I'd ever sold. She was resigned, but on a mission to make the dress of Elizabeth's dreams. Elizabeth agreed to entertain the idea of a barely visible, expensive, imported lace on the hem of the skirt.

Making the simple, elegant gown with its smooth and graceful lines would require restraint and supreme sacrifice for someone like Mary

Kline, but she seemed prepared to rise up and suffer in silence. Just like many mothers, she waved her surrender flag for a battle she'd anticipated her entire mothering life.

Chapter Forty-One

Elizabeth

When Mary Kline dared to mount a flight of stairs, which was rare, the entire staircase groaned to support her, making it impossible for her to sneak around. But sure enough, I heard those stairs groan again one day when Mary huffed and puffed her way to the first landing, where she paused to catch her breath.

"Mary?"

I sounded so impatient. I hated myself for being such an ungrateful, critical bitch to the woman who raised me. Still, I pressed on with my exasperated tones.

"Mary, you don't need to come all the way up. I said I'll be down in a minute."

"Elizabeth, I just want to get up there to . . ."

"To what? You want to get up here because I'm not getting downstairs fast enough to suit you. I'll be down in a minute."

"No, that's not it. I thought we'd better go over the invitation lists again, and I thought I had some addresses up here in the dresser. Some of our Kline cousins will expect an invite."

I had to laugh. I had no Kline cousins. Mary didn't either. We'd never seen these people who lived six states and ten bloodlines away. But Mary felt compelled to inform them of the meaningful events in our lives. If they read her letters and Christmas cards, they knew when I arrived in the Kline household, that Mary had adopted me, that her parents had died, and that I'd graduated from high school and college.

I wondered if they knew Mary weighed nearly 350 pounds, and that my real mother was practically mute in a nursing home across town.

God Bless the Child

I tried to imagine what they might think if they saw Mary Kline's downstairs bathroom and the rings of rust in her toilet. I wondered if they had any idea that Mary held on to every piece of paper that ever came into her hands, and that all of it was filed haphazardly in several locations in the house: atop the grand piano and on the floor beneath, on Mr. and Mrs. Kline's old bed, inside an unused tub in the upstairs bathroom, and lately, filling up two laundry baskets she kept next to the couch. Anything on paper from the last two years could probably be found right at her feet if a person were willing to dig for it.

Each time I came home from college, I felt myself tighten up the closer I got to the front door. My head usually began to ache within ten miles of town. Instead of graciously eating what Mary Kline had prepared as a welcome meal, I took a few bites and begged off dessert so I could lie down. I heard Mary cleaning up, but I never got up to help.

By morning, I'd be awake, but not rested. My teeth clenched so tightly throughout the night that I could feel a ridge forming at my temples. My irritation with Mary Kline had a pulse of its own that outthumped those in my head and heart.

Eventually, I consulted a dentist, who recommended a rubber guard to control my stress, especially at night. My subsequent visits were punctuated by an uneasy tension, and I ground my teeth more than ever, but the mouthpiece kept my jaws from locking up for good.

I couldn't stand myself for how I treated this woman who adored me. Why did her presence annoy me so badly? Why couldn't I eat her food and thank her for it? Why didn't I ever acknowledge her for the hours she spent stooped over the sewing machine so I would have beautiful things to wear? Why did it bother me that she was so huge? Why should I feel so embarrassed by her? Mary wasn't my mother, but I felt tethered to her like a daughter. I owed this gigantic person everything, but I could give her nothing.

I hoped to figure out a way to distance myself from our odd little family. But for this visit, I had to overlook my locking jaws and stick around because my wedding gown was hanging in the bedroom. Mary had begun putting it together and I couldn't wait to see her progress.

She was pleased with herself, and I managed to act grown–up enough to indulge in a tender exchange, the kind we both always dreamed of but hardly ever managed.

"Mary!"

I was stunned and ashamed and touched by the confection that hung from a hook in the ceiling. We'd decided that the sheen of white silk would not flatter my white skin, which was dappled with red freckles. We both felt deep down that the purity of white would not match the other parts of my makeup, either. We chose a color called oyster, in a raw silk. Mary Kline spent a fortune having the fabric imported, as well as some lace. I only allowed a bit of lace on the hem, preferring nothing fluffy or busy.

For once, Mary honored my taste. The only other adornments were seed pearls barely visible to the naked eye, which Mary attached to the waist and on the sleeves and hem of the dress, by the hundreds.

She fashioned a simple circlet for my head with silken scraps held together with leftover lace. From the back flowed a gauze-looking veil. Mary Kline had done something right. I hugged her bulbous body next to mine, thanking her again and again for the gown. She smiled, acting like it was nothing, but knowing it was really something.

We had dinner together that night, just the two of us. I ate a plate of her beef tenderloin and parboiled potatoes and even asked for seconds. I think it was the best day and night of Mary Kline's life.

Chapter Forty-Two

Johnson Kuhlman

It was a perfect spring day. I held in my hands an invitation to the Kline wedding, which instantly told me I was part of an elite group. For one thing, the wedding wasn't in town. It was two hours away, in a chapel next to a fancy country club.

Over the ensuing weeks, I figured out that virtually no one from town had been invited, and I cheered for Mary Kline. Her social station in town was unique. Most people her size would have been banned to the outskirts of civilization, deemed freaks of nature, and barely tolerated. While Mary was familiar with that kind of treatment, she was allowed to mingle where other outcasts wouldn't dare.

The reason was simple. Kline's Department Store, and the money people spent there. No matter your station in life, if you needed underwear, an emergency pair of stockings, or a quick birthday or anniversary gift, Kline's was your destination. The store carried nice things. It was right downtown, and the clerks insisted on gift-wrapping every purchase in white tissue paper and a sturdy box. When you left the store, you felt like you had purchased something special. Even a new box of hankies felt good, coming from Kline's.

After Edward and Louise Kline died, the store was run by a longtime employee, but the profits went to Mary Kline. People soon figured out that Mary's checks always cleared. They wanted none of her, but they loved her money.

Mary got her hair done every week at Missy's and paid to have her fingernails painted to perfection. She purchased a new car every year, with cash.

I was glad to see that poor Mary understood it all, that none of the bitches in town cared about her or Elizabeth's wedding. I was happy she'd taken this opportunity to shun them, and I felt honored to have one of her coveted invitations.

I let all my customers know that the store would be closed on that special Saturday. The night before, I laid out my suit and tie, pressed my shirt and polished my shoes. I'd just climbed into bed when the phone startled me.

"Hello?"

I answered pensively. It was after ten o'clock. At this hour, I figured it must be bad news.

"Johnson? Is that you?"

"Yes, yes, this is Johnson."

I was unsure of the voice on the other line.

"Johnson, it's Mary. Mary Kline."

Mary Kline! Mary Kline was calling me! At night? At home? I'd never been part of a fabric emergency, but I was aroused just thinking about racing to Mary's rescue in my pajamas with a pincushion in one hand and my good scissors snugly placed in my holster.

Mary Kline had never called me at home. What had gone wrong? Had she scorched the material on Elizabeth's dress with her old iron? Had she accidentally stepped on the bustle and ripped a giant hole in the back?

"Johnson, I need you. I want you to come look at something."

She needed me. Mary Kline *needed* me.

"What is it, Mary? Are you hurt or something?"

"No, no, nothing like that. Can you come? Right now?"

I'd never felt so needed in my life and my God, it felt good.

"Yes, Mary. I'll be right there."

"Johnson? Can you do me a favor?"

Could I do her a favor? Didn't this woman know I would do her hundreds of favors? All she had to do was ask.

Just ask me, Mary Kline.

"Anything. You name it, Mary."

"Can you bring me some fresh needles and a bolt of that ivory lace? The Alencon? Remember the one I almost picked up last time I was in the store?"

I knew the bolt. Mary Kline was about to commit what amounted to a felony, a heinous, premeditated, mother-of-the-bride crime, and it was my job to stop her. I was on my way to struggle over good taste with the most beautiful woman I'd ever known. And in my pajamas, no less. It was going to be up to me to pull her back from the tacky edge. I headed toward my car in sneakers and a bathrobe. The Kline wedding, or at least the dress, needed saving.

The front porch light was on. Mary came to the door, looking frazzled. She wore a pink housecoat that she couldn't quite button and her enormous breasts heaved beneath a flowered, flannel nightgown that set me on fire. Oh, Jesus! Why hadn't I thrown some pants on before I left? My pajama bottoms were doing a poor job of hiding my feelings for Mary.

"Johnson!"

Did she notice?

"Come in, come in. Thank God you're here!"

Oh my God, I certainly was!

Mary Kline's face shone in the light. When I saw the chocolate frosting on her chin and her milk moustache, I ached for her like a schoolboy, a 40–something year old schoolkid with nothing between me and my dream girl but a raging hard–on and too many wasted, loveless years that I'd let slip through my fingers.

"Come with me!"

She frantically licked the chocolate from her fingers. Sweet Jesus! I followed her into her bedroom. Her bedroom! Was this possible? A slob! This beautiful thing was a slob! Oh, sweet, sweet Jesus!

In the corner of the room stood her sewing machine, littered with scraps and empty spools, scissors and pincushions. I saw the tattered tape measure around her adorable neck and almost lost control of myself. I wanted to ease this sweet big mama over to her messy bed and fuck her beautiful, talented brains out.

"Johnson, look at this!"

She was crying.

She'd smeared chocolate frosting, the dark kind, on the dress. A big, dark brown stain was streaked across the bottom. Thank God it was on the hem.

I snapped into action.

"Honey, wash your hands with soap and water."

One didn't handle expensive raw silk and eat a cupcake at the same time. It was sacrilegious. My darling girl knew better, but she just couldn't help herself.

When she returned with clean hands, the two of us looked at the beautiful wedding gown she'd created. The triumph that hung from a hook on the ceiling of this woman's bedroom sealed the deal for me. I wanted to spend the rest of my life with the splendid soul who'd created this work of art before me.

The raw silk hung just like I'd thought it would! Any hands that could stitch the thousands of nearly microscopic seed pearls with such precision had the potential to be a skilled, albeit patient, lover—just what I needed! Those pudgy hands were dream weavers, and I wanted to hold and kiss them.

I felt like her husband, and I was perfectly ready to engage her in a matrimonial spat right there in the bedroom. We could kiss and make up later. Right now, this big, buxom honey of mine had been a bad, bad girl, and it was my duty to reprimand her. I relished the task before me.

"Mary Kline! How much did you spend on this material? You shouldn't hold a cupcake, a chocolate one, no less, within a ten–mile radius of this dress! What were you thinking?"

My sweet, sorry baby wasn't thinking. She'd been feeling, just feeling, and because they go hand in hand, she'd been eating.

"I don't know. Oh, Johnson. Help me! Elizabeth will never forgive me. Never!"

The love of my life was weeping in my arms. I'd never been so close to her. A counter had always stood between us, but here she was, needing me enough to call in the middle of the night with this embarrassing crisis.

"Alright. Alright. Let Johnson think a minute."

My heart was breaking for this bad, hungry girl, but it was hard to think. My brain had migrated to my pants.

"Bring me some cold water and cotton balls."

We'd try to coax the chocolate from the fibers without smearing it into a bigger mess.

Bad news: the cotton ball trick didn't work.

More bad news: the smear looked worse after we worked on it.

Good news: My brilliant seamstress soul mate had thought ahead enough to build in some extra fabric at the fold in the waist.

More good news: we could take out the stitching at the waist and let the extra fabric flow to the floor, cutting off the section where the offending cupcake had landed.

The best news of all: it was going to take me and this specimen of a super woman *all night*! I had a promising night before me of sewing side–by–side with the sweetest, sexiest woman alive!

It was six in the morning when we finally stood in the corner of the room, staring at our love child. I'll never forget it. Once we convinced ourselves we could fix the problem, we both relaxed, laughing and talking as we worked. I even teased her a bit about the cupcake and her initial plan to cover the spot with more lace. She felt comfortable enough with me to laugh.

"Well, I guess I'll see you at the wedding," I said.

We stood together on her front porch. The light was still on.

"Yes, Johnson. I'll see you this afternoon. How can I thank you?"

"I'll have to think about that one."

I winked and spent the rest of the afternoon thinking about all the ways my beautiful Mary Kline could thank me.

Chapter Forty-Three

Mary Kline

The night Johnson rescued me after I'd dropped a cupcake on Elizabeth's wedding dress counts as my first date. I'm not sure, but I think it was probably his, too.

I like to fall asleep thinking about that beautiful night when he arrived on my porch, ready to save me.

I liked Johnson, but I'd long suspected he was gay. My desperate call to him was not a romantic overture. I was in crisis mode, and he was the only one I could call. Long ago, when Elizabeth was a little girl, if I ran into a sewing snag, if I'd sewn myself into a corner, I called on old Mrs. Lend, my home economics teacher, to help me out. But unfortunately, she'd passed away a few years before I was stupid enough to stand over my daughter's white wedding dress and eat a chocolate cupcake.

I must have been a sight that night in my ratty old nightgown and a housecoat. Johnson says he thought I looked cute, and that it made him love me even more.

"Just how long did you have the hots for me before that night?"

He laughed and gave me a quick peck on the cheek.

"I've cared deeply about you, my sweet, for a very long time, but I never thought I stood a chance until that night. I still can't believe how lucky I am."

"Me, too," I said.

Johnson scolded me for being so careless with Elizabeth's dress. He knew how much I'd spent on the imported fabric.

If it had been any other dress, any other night, I would not have panicked. But this was Elizabeth's wedding dress. If she'd known about my cupcake mishap, her anger would have reached new and horrible heights. I could already hear how she would punctuate her attack.

"Mary, what the *hell* were you doing adding *more* to this dress?" Haven't we established that this dress was fine? Just fine? That it didn't need one more thing. Not one more sparkle, one more inch of lace, or one more fucking pearl!"

She'd go on and on. She'd probably accuse me of intentionally dropping the chocolate frosting on the dress. Through her critical lens, my cupcake bomb was nothing but sabotage, a way to add more of my tacky lace to her dress, even though I knew she didn't want any.

"This is rich, Mary Kline, even for you!"

Fortunately, the nasty conversation between my daughter and I only existed in my imagination. That night, Johnson, my darling Johnson, saved the dress, the wedding and me.

After I calmed down and Johnson contemplated our next move, he got on his knees and billowed the entire train up like a tent, poking his head, and then his entire body under the dress to survey the damage. From underneath yards and yards of oyster-colored raw silk, I heard him click his tongue and mutter softly to himself. After what seemed like an hour, he emerged with a determined look on his face and his hands on his hips.

"Here's what we're going to do, Mary."

Using tiny scissors and a seam ripper, we removed the skirt and train from the bodice of Elizabeth's gown, stitch by stitch. There was enough reserve fabric at the top of the skirt to let it down far enough so that we could cut off the chocolate stain. I guess I *had* learned something about sewing from Mother. She always, *always* left plenty of extra fabric tucked up into seams so that she could let them out as needed, as my large frame expanded.

Once that was done, Johnson and I had quite a task. We were two highly-skilled surgeons performing a life-saving procedure on a dress that had just had a near-death experience. I was charged with removing the lace and seed pearls from the original hem and sewing the whole works back onto the new, unstained skirt and train. Johnson worked to reattach the skirt to the bodice, by hand, of course.

Once we were sure that our plan would work, we breathed normally again. I started removing and reattaching thousands of seed pearls. Johnson worked deftly, pulling his needle in and out, in and out. We agreed that we'd never work with raw silk again.

"I'm going to refuse to even sell raw silk to anyone who comes into the shop," he said.

"Yeah, I know what you mean. I'll never buy the stuff again. If it had been up to me, I wouldn't have picked this fabric in the first place, not for a wedding gown."

"Well, Mary, it was what your customer wanted."

He held pins between his teeth.

"And it suits Elizabeth's coloring."

"Yes. But how are we supposed to *adorn* the dress? Raw silk has all those damned little nubs in it. It's not exactly easy to sew seed pearls on and get them evenly distributed on raw silk. It's tricky, Johnson."

"Don't fight the fabric, Mary. Work the needle in as close to the nub as you can and then thread the bead on."

"Johnson Kuhlman, are you telling *me* how to sew on doodads?"

Johnson grinned.

"Mary Kline, I wouldn't dream of instructing you on this finer point of sewing. You are, after all, the Doodad Queen."

I winked.

"What's that supposed to mean?"

"It means that I've been selling fabric and doodads to you for more than 20 years, and I've noticed that you like to decorate."

"Ouch."

"No barbs intended. Just an observation and nothing more."

"Damn!"

I'd not only pricked my thumb with the needle; I'd been tripped up by one of those nubs.

"See, Johnson? This is what I'm talking about. See how the pearl lays funny on the nub?"

He considered my dilemma and then said the manliest thing I'd ever heard him say.

"You've got two choices. Either let the pearl do what it naturally does when sewn on raw silk or don't put a pearl on that spot."

I appreciated his practical approach, but I wanted to smack him.

"Johnson, you and Elizabeth seem to have forgotten that this is a wedding dress."

"But if the bride wants something simple, that's what you must give her. Mary, you know that for Elizabeth, less is more."

Johnson was right. Elizabeth just wanted something simple from me. That's all she ever wanted. But I kept insisting that she needed more—more sequins, more seed pearls, more lace, more extravagant gestures of my love for her.

Johnson and I sat in silence, working feverishly to put life back into Elizabeth's gown. I suspected that he might have felt like he'd said too much. He tried to lighten the mood.

"Mary, can I ask you a question?"

"Yes."

"Were you honestly going to try and fix this mess by covering up the stain with lace?"

He looked right at me with a smirk.

"Well, I was desperate, Johnson. You don't know Elizabeth. She can be so hateful sometimes. I was in a panic."

"Mary Kline, I *do* know Elizabeth and I've seen her in action enough times to know that you put up with way too much. If you ask me, that girl needed a couple of good swats right on the butt. She could probably still use one."

I laughed. He was right. I should have disciplined her more. But it was too late now.

"Mary, I'm sure glad you left some leeway up at the waist."

He pushed up his glasses.

"If you hadn't, we'd have ourselves a mess."

I nodded and kept working.

"Hey, Mary."

"Yes, Johnson?"

"Will you do me a favor?"

I looked up at my friend, who was looking straight at me.

"Promise me that you'll never *ever* eat a cupcake with *chocolate* frosting while working on a white wedding gown!"

I smiled.

"The gown isn't white, Johnson. It's *oyster*. And I promise."

"I don't believe you."

"No, really. I promise."

"Hold up your right hand please and repeat after me."

I laughed.

"Repeat after me, Mary Kline. I, Mary Ann Kline . . ."

"Hey, how do you know my middle name?"

"I don't know. I just do. Now get that hand up."

"I, Mary Ann Kline . . .

"Do solemnly swear . . ."

"Do solemnly swear . . ."

"That I will never, ever, *ever* . . ."

"Johnson, you're silly."

"Repeat after me!"

"I will never, ever, *ever* . . ."

"Eat a cupcake with chocolate frosting while working with expensive, imported, almost-impossible-to-find raw silk . . ."

We laughed and sewed and teased one another through the night and into the morning. It was romantic. I'd never felt so safe and loved.

It was the best night of my life.

Chapter Forty-Four

Johnson Kuhlman

The wedding went off beautifully and Elizabeth's dress looked perfectly elegant. Not one guest, nor the bride and groom, had a clue of how Mary and I had feverishly resuscitated the dress the night before by removing all evidence of the flying chocolate cupcake.

Our ministrations and intimacies from that night became a defining moment for our friendship. Mary had let me inside her world, and when she discovered I wasn't repulsed, I became a frequent, welcome guest.

She was an accomplished seamstress, of course, but I was delighted to discover Mary's skills in the kitchen to be equally refined. Everything she created was a succulent masterpiece. Her meats glistened and steamed at the appropriate moment. Her soufflés never flopped. Her gravies were lump-free, and her vegetables crisp, accented with just the right amount of butter and spice. Even Mary's bologna sandwiches looked nicer on the plate than they should. With her touch, the most ordinary sandwich was elevated beyond its humble beginnings.

"Mary, you're trying to fatten me up, aren't you?"

She'd just put a piece of warm apple crumble in front of me, sprinkled with cinnamon, along with a cup of hot coffee.

"Admit it. It's part of your evil plan, isn't it?"

She smiled at me coyly.

"Maybe, Johnson. How's the crumble?"

"It's perfect, Honey. Just perfect."

We didn't ride off into the setting sun as quickly as I'd hoped. We settled into a comfortable routine, sharing one of her meals every Saturday night, without fail. I came with something pretty in my hands, always—sometimes a bouquet of flowers, other times a few new thimbles or a book of the latest patterns from the store.

We shared our separate creations. I'd show her my latest quilt top and she'd respond by bringing out a dress she'd been working on.

Mary's hands tempted me. Sometimes, I'd try to hold them, and she'd usually allow it. For what seemed like years, we allowed ourselves to slip into a comfortable rhythm, just like an old married couple, or maybe it was more like a confirmed bachelor brother and his fat, spinster sister. This brother's feelings for his sister often strayed into inappropriate corners, but I held back. Something about Mary seemed fragile. She was lovely to me in every way, and I felt so honored to be her friend, that I rarely dared to act on my true feelings. I didn't want to scare her. Almost every Saturday night, after resisting a hundred opportunities to kiss her, I'd leave, ashamed of myself for my cowardice.

I was becoming an accomplished flirt, but nothing more. With our words and our eyes, we gently batted the possibility of love back and forth between us. All the while, our bond stitched itself together with threads no thicker than spider webs. Had I understood how difficult it was for this old girl to thread together even the flimsiest kind of trust, I would have wept over each forward step she made.

On my way home after another lovely evening, I wondered if Mary could comprehend just how much I wanted her. I wondered if she wanted me as badly.

For a long time, I dangerously assumed that Mary's lack of confidence was a consequence of her weight. I didn't know that her size had little to do with food and that it was a defense mechanism she'd never been able to turn off once it started. A body like hers could usually be counted upon to repulse and drive men away, but I, Johnson Kuhlman, was no ordinary man. I wanted her. I wanted this great, big woman in a way that felt quite sexual, but I wanted the introductions and the conclusions as well. I lusted to hold her, to wrap my hairy arms as far around her as they would go. I yearned to see her body, and I wanted her to see mine. I dreamed of making a big and beautiful quilt with this woman and wrapping us together in it for a long, afternoon nap.

Most of all, I wanted to experience the ultimate act of bonding: I wanted to share my good scissors with her.

After each meal we shared in the quiet of her kitchen, I insisted on doing the dishes while she sat at the table, and we talked. In her presence, I felt like a man as I rolled up my sleeves for the task ahead. When I was finished, Mary Kline thanked me and I told her with my eyes and by the way I neatly folded the drying towel, how much I loved her.

"You're welcome, Mary. You are *so* welcome."

Chapter Forty-Five

David

I might be the only person who can see beyond the darkness that is my wife, Elizabeth.

Somewhere in the shadows is a woman who smiles and tells the dirtiest jokes I've ever heard. Somehow, when she told them to me, they didn't sound vulgar. When a beautiful girl says words like *fuck* and *ass*, men are either incredibly aroused or repulsed. I was in the arousal camp because I was sure this baby doll didn't really get the jokes she told. She was a pretty little parrot, spouting provocative words without knowing their meaning. Once I figured out that she knew *exactly* what she was talking about, I was provoked and hopeful.

We dated for a year before she even let me pick up the bat much less reach any bases. By then, I was furious with her for barely letting me touch her breasts. As driven by my needs as I was, I'm surprised I stayed around as long as I did. But there I was and here I am, still taking her fits and teases like delicious beatings. I loved them. I hated them. I knew they'd go away, and I knew they'd return. They always did and still do. I'm no child. I'm a big boy and could have walked away if I'd wanted. That's the thing. I never wanted to take that walk.

Elizabeth was loose enough to eat popcorn that literally floated in butter, wash it down with a foul-smelling cream soda and call that supper. She wouldn't talk to me for days, but I never found myself cruel enough to give her some of her own bitter medicine. Most of the time, she was funny and deep, and all too aware of her frailties.

When we played around, or I teased her and the mood was right, I called her a pain in the ass and she roared with laughter, pleased that she was such a challenge. On another day, the same words could reduce her to tears. She knew I was kidding, but she also understood that what made the joke funny was the truth it represented. She knew she *was* a pain in the keester. Her moods ebbed and flowed, but the highs were so pleasant that I was willing to stick around through the lows.

After three more years of mood swings and some of the most inventive sex I'd ever imagined, we were married in a lavish ceremony paid for by Mary Kline. She liked me and grew to love me. My parents thought Elizabeth was wonderful, and most of the time she was.

When I pulled back her veil to plant a kiss I knew what was underneath: somebody wonderful and funny, who loved me the best I'd ever been loved, a beautiful baby doll with a dark side and a foul mouth. I loved it. I loved *her*. I wanted to ride off into the sunset, eating and drinking her up.

That's what we did in the beginning. On Sundays, we went to church, but didn't concentrate on God or the message. We came home, stripped off our dressy clothes and fell back into an unmade bed to recapture all that had happened the night before. We'd drift into a satisfied sleep and wake up hungry. My wife could cook. After our Sunday rolls in the hay, she would prepare something wonderful for us to eat at our tiny kitchen table while we read the newspaper cover to cover. We'd devour her omelets and quiches along with the headlines, then let the afternoons slip away with no chores or obligations, just comfort sex and comforting food. I loved falling asleep on those glorious Sunday nights with our legs entwined and her warm breath on my neck.

It wasn't always blissful. Sometimes, I'd find Elizabeth soaking in the tub, in the dark, with a tear-streaked face, unable to pinpoint why she was crying. Long, hard, messy sobs wracked the same person who only hours earlier had thrown her head back in raucous laughter at one of our impromptu parties.

It was such a treat when Elizabeth had the giggles, deep, genuine, and throaty. I missed them most when she was sad or angry. I usually remained calm when her anger reached its predictable peaks. This enraged her all the more. She operated on high or low. If I wanted to stir things up, I could do the unthinkable. I could point out the bright side. She hated that.

Over the years, after some nasty encounters we can never take back, I came to understand why the bright side was so irritating to my wife. It was simple. She wasn't often capable of seeing the light. It did not come naturally to her, and when anyone opened her curtains to let in the sunlight, it was too glaring, intruding on whatever dark funk she happened to be brewing.

Elizabeth and I agree that if we could remove one blemish from our early married life, it would be the exchange that occurred over a table we bought for the kitchen. She'd pushed me plenty of times before, but the table argument took my patience to the brink. I snapped. Anger alone does not adequately capture what drove me to bellow at her like I did. Elizabeth wanted the table. I thought the price was inflated and wanted to keep looking. She was set on paying and hauling the table home right away.

I'd experienced Elizabeth's mood swings, which can reveal the best and worst of a person. But the table incident frightened me. Her eyes, usually deep green, morphed into tearful, black pits. I'd never seen her face stretched in such a hateful snarl. In that moment, all she cared about was having that table.

She threw a juice glass into the sink and seemed satisfied that it broke into shards. She aimed her nasty words at me like never before and boy was she a good shot.

The table incident, as we refer to it now, was certainly the most hateful version of herself that Elizabeth revealed to me.

God Bless the Child

But my beautiful wife said she was sorry, and I did, too. We bucked and blended our way back to neutrality. That always seemed to work, at least temporarily. The fact that we still own the table speaks volumes. I've often wondered if the memory of that whole night might disappear permanently if I took that thing out to the yard and set it on fire.

The table is still here, and every time we share morning coffee or a Saturday afternoon lunch, make grocery lists or pay bills on its smooth surface, we honor the savage hallowed ground we've made of it.

Chapter Forty-Six

Elizabeth

The enormity of the dirty little secret I shared with Mary Kline did not haunt me until we learned that my body became host to another life. David and I welcomed this exciting news, like one would expect a happily married couple to do. This new child was wanted and fit neatly into our plans, and we looked forward to her thriving undisturbed.

Her tiny heartbeat was strong enough for her to dance inside me. My little ballerina mastered arabesques and random leaps across my womb. She was the tiniest performer, and my visions of perfect pink tutus buoyed me through uncomfortable parts of the pregnancy.

While we awaited her arrival, I caught myself reaching for Mary Kline. I wanted her to help me prove that I could start something *and* finish it. She needed to see me do my mothering correctly. I wanted to school her first, then grant her something that would settle our matters once and for all.

Long before this new baby emerged wet and slippery from my body, I knew her name would be Mary. It was my peace offering.

Our baby did not appreciate the eviction. David was cheering us on, but he looked pale. Poorest of babies, my darker side mused. Which of my first two offspring had received the better deal? At least Mary Kline and I had set my first little waif free, crudely aborted but allowed to become one, organically, with the Earth beneath my feet.

This red dancer I held to my chest screamed and shrieked her newborn bray. She seemed to know already that so much would be expected of her. She eyed me warily, waiting to see what I would do next.

That first night in the hospital, I had a dream that frightened me so much I never dared share it with anyone. My first child, the one Mary Kline and I had tossed in the garbage, had pinned a note to the north wall of my womb.

"Watch out, brothers and sisters! This mother will eat her young."

I awoke startled, wondering what they did with the little alien who had been removed from me years before. Was it wrapped in an old newspaper and tossed in the dumpster behind the clinic? Did the nurse wait until the clinic door closed behind us before she tossed it, like a little fish, into the toilet?

At the time, I didn't care so much. I would have been the first one to flush that spooky little thing down the sewer, where it could do the backstroke and fight its way through the shit all the way to the ocean.

Little Mary might have also been better off being released into the sewer before it was too late. As I picked at the whitish scales on her new, pink skin, I figured the poor thing deserved a mother who at least looked the part. I pulled on my mask, so she wouldn't see the old crone who lurked underneath.

I had to admit, I was not the stuff of which real mothers are made. Trapped in the role, I feared I probably would find a way to sniff out its rotting, decaying parts, rendering me as uncomfortable as a mother as I'd always been as a daughter.

Neither role suited me. Whose footsteps should I follow? Mary Kline's? Pearl's? Louise Kline's? And what path could I forge for this bundled girl that was mine? Would I leave a paved path or merely drop breadcrumbs that had every chance of being gobbled up by hungry birds before she looked up to discover I was long gone?

Chapter Forty-Seven

David

Birth is a bloody business.

I had no interest being with Elizabeth in the delivery room when our Little Mary was born. I would have been content to keep up the long-standing tradition of cowardly, weak-stomached fathers waiting for the big news in the waiting room. But that was no longer in vogue. All the cool dads stayed in the trenches, and Elizabeth was determined that I, too, would be a cool dad. She pressured me and laughed when I brought up the subject.

"You're gonna be right there with me, Buster. If I can take it, so can you!"

She threw her head back and guffawed at her ridiculous husband, the weenie man.

My wife, and most women, will say it's the mother in the birthing scenario who deserves pity and admiration. This is true. Elizabeth did all the heaving and panting and bleeding and sweating.

The doctor asked her if she wanted a mirror placed at the end of the delivery table so she could see our baby's head crown. I assured my wife that she did not want to see what I could see. As excited as I was to meet our first child, I was also sickened by the sight of my wife's sweating body, toiling to work out its destiny.

Little Mary's arrival was a relief. I was more than happy to hold that red, squalling child so Dr. Hannigan could tend to Elizabeth. After what I just witnessed, I was sure I could never think of her in the same terms. The whole process was horrifying.

Elizabeth and I were no pioneers.

God Bless the Child

    I had to give it to the good doctor. Any man who can witness and manage the perils and contortions that take place during birth has grit. Secretly, I wondered what such visceral and constant trauma had done to the poor doctor's psyche and erectile function. After what I'd just seen, I was certain my own had been forever compromised. Selfishly, I wondered how long I would have to wait to find out.

Chapter Forty-Eight

Elizabeth

Little Mary brought us joy. We'd already fallen in love with her from the way she kicked with such vigor inside me. What a character she would be! What a most beautiful baby. Her nursery awaited a prince or princess. We crowned her before she was even born.

Every night, I drifted off to sleep, replaying the events of her birth and homecoming. It was warm and soft, and so was she. I loved the smell of her tiny neck with its downy folds and creases.

I didn't mind that my nipples were bruised and blistered beyond recognition those first weeks. My new little friend came for frequent visits, always wanting to know what she could eat. The pain started to feel good, even satisfying, once I heard the baby gulping back big glubs of milk. What a good mother I was! The tiny droplets of milk that gathered on her pink lips satisfied me as much as her.

I was giving her my best, and as much as she wanted. I came to her in the darkness, giving bluish-white nectar that flowed in an endless supply. She took and I gave, keeping pace with her frantic sucks.

I sat in the rocking chair in her room, my chest bared to my waist, there for her taking. My Little Mary gummed me so hard that it hurt, but I never winced. Each cut felt better than the last—the more blood the better. If my milk were laced with blood, it would fortify this child.

I *wanted* my daughter to hurt me.

Mama could take it. I craved her feedings as much as she did. I filled her and she emptied me. Each time she relieved me of my burden, I filled to bursting again.

Little Mary's infancy was a delightful blur. I loved every minute of being home with her, loving her, falling asleep with her in the afternoons, the two of us snuggled in my bed, waking up with a faint sweat between us. The sticky smell of her I'd come to love clung to me. Her breath was sweet, and I liked the smells she brought into our home: fresh Play-Doh, a box of fat crayons, and a new box of animal crackers. I even found the faint smell of her slightly wet diapers satisfying.

Her new words delighted us. I wanted to blow bubbles by the hour and read book after book. We knew she was a brilliant creation. Each new trick was a treat, a miraculous feat. For a while, Little Mary's beginnings felt like *my* beginnings. I loved her and I loved David again. I had healed for good. Temporarily at least, we were healed by our child.

By then, the kitchen table incident was a distant memory. We ate dinners and breakfasts at that table. One night, after our babe was asleep, we even made love on it, whispering breathy phrases that turned us on but may have frightened others.

David and I loved each other. We did, we did, we did.

It had been too long. It had, it had, it had.

David missed me and would take whatever parts of me I could give.

He asked, and I answered.

He pushed, and I pulled.

We were desperate, and I clung to him like I might be drowning. David worked hard to save me, to pull me back to the ship.

As our baby slept, we made up for lost time. My breasts had blessedly been restored from two milk possets to the plump treasures David never tired of exploring. He was grateful to be invited back into territory that had once been exclusively his. Little Mary served as a balm for old wounds and a shield for future fires. We enjoyed the lull, while it lasted.

Over time, the bliss brought out the restless side in me. I began to bubble and snap and pop and hiss. Frustration caught me by surprise and clogged my throat. I could never stay on top of the laundry or the dishes, and an unmade bed made me feel sad and unworthy. I'd sob and gulp and steel myself to conquer the disorder that surrounded me. During these sieges, the people around me weren't always safe.

A grilled cheese sandwich broke me. My toddler's favorite, something I'd made hundreds of before, needed far more attention than even the most deserving sandwich should have. After multiple tries to get both sides of the bread grilled to perfection and then sliced into four even squares that made clean breaks with no cheese spilling out, it became clear to me that I'd never make a grilled cheese the way Mary Kline made them. Her sandwiches were golden and even. I tried and tried until I ran out of bread and cheese. After about an hour watching Mama toss her lunch into the garbage can, my Little Mary lost interest and toddled into the other room, content to paw through her books with her little hands.

That evening, David noticed the grilled failures in the garbage and questioned me about the waste. He asked what I ended up feeding our little girl. I was horrified when it dawned on me that she had gone without any lunch at all! She didn't have the words to say she was hungry, and Mama was off in the kitchen, wrestling with white bread, American cheese and some demanding, invisible critics who were more important than feeding my child.

My brain outpaced my hands and feet, which were no match for a ticking clock that teased and tempted me to take on more. The sorted begged to be resorted, the stacked restacked, and the unsmooth, smoothed over. Decisions were never final. There was always checking and rechecking, and labeling and aligning. My world expanded and contracted without mercy, leaving little room for anything or anyone but my long lists of tasks at hand.

What was happening to me? I'd never known perfection, but my newfound quest for it could not be quenched.

Chapter Forty-Nine

Little Mary

Across the street from our house sat a big old Victorian that had been renovated into a boisterous preschool.

I liked standing with my nose pressed against the glass in our living room, watching the children in the fenced-in yard as they played tag and twisted round and round on the swings. Sometimes, they'd laugh and smile. Other times, these same children would cry, either clinging to their exasperated parents or howling because of a scraped knee.

I must have been only about four years old by then, but I'd already figured out that it was best for me to stay smack in the middle of happy and sad. Swinging too high made Mama nervous. Being motionless made her edgy. Dragging my feet in the dirt in a serious back-and-forth motion was safe. If I stayed firmly fixed to serious, Mama could flit from project to project, mood to mood, and still find me when she needed me.

She'd come to me for a fix of lipstick kisses, and then flit off again. Her lip prints all over my face were proof to outsiders that I was an adored child. Moments later, the same woman who planted those lip marks would have me pinned to the floor so she could wipe off the evidence of her affection with a spit-covered finger.

Love was dirty.

Mama made sure that I never saw her and Daddy in an embrace. When he tried to hug her from behind, she'd recoil and shrug him off. He was a nuisance, and so was I. We were both a bother, and often in the way of her plans.

God Bless the Child

Mama's loving was never granted upon request. Instead, anyone around her waited to receive her morsels of affection on *her* terms. She wasn't unlike a cat, coming around only when it suited her. And she was no dog! You'd never see my mother begging and wagging her tail or panting for us like a puppy.

One morning I stood with my nose pressed firmly against the cold glass, watching the children coming and going into the school, dragging their big people behind them.

A dull thump and screech of wheels launched a small child's body into an arc through the air, ending with a thud against the pavement. The woman in the offending car stood in the middle of the street, shrieking. Another woman barreled down the sidewalk, falling onto the heap of bloody skin and broken bones. Her screams mingled with the howls from the driver who had unwittingly hit the little girl. More cars stopped. People jumped out and slammed doors, standing still and moving toward the scene. Children's faces were being turned away so their eyes could be shielded by grown-up hands.

The sounds were loud and disturbing enough to beckon Mama to the window. She snapped the curtains shut, scolding me for my interest in such an appalling scene, but she watched the chaos herself. I tried to join her, but she shooed me away.

I wished I was the hurt little girl on the pavement, with my mother weeping over me, so sorry I was gone. She would scoop up my limp body from the street and rock me right there in her arms, oblivious to the crowds that had gathered to gawk. Mama would rock me and rock me, stopping only to plant a kiss on my smashed in skull.

Chapter Fifty

Elizabeth

One year for Christmas, Little Mary received a gift from family friends—a brand new, Fisher–Price barn. As a child, I had an earlier version of this classic toy. But the gift our daughter opened was new and improved. The words on its box said so. The mother and child on that box looked delighted with their new barn! They were frozen there, caught happy as they placed mother cow and baby cow together in their stall for the night. The rounded, squat little farmer didn't seem to mind that his behind was in the shape of a circle that had only one place to sit: the green tractor. He spent his days pulling a plastic mound of pumpkins and molded yellow square of plastic that was trying awfully hard to look like a bale of hay. Farming is a happy life, especially when it comes wrapped up perfectly in a box.

That happy mother on the box obviously hadn't had the toy out of the box for long when the photo was taken. I wanted to track her down and see how she felt about the new and improved barn. I wondered if she shared my disappointment when she discovered all the flaws of this new and improved version of the barn. When I was a little girl, every time I opened the front door to my barn, a tiny cow hidden deep in the mechanism of the hinges bellowed out a satisfying *moo*! Little Mary's new and improved barn offered no such feature. There was no moo. Nothing. Not a sound. Not even a quack or an oink.

I would have also loved to see that mother's face when she discovered that the new and improved barn didn't have a silo like the old model. This was a significant flaw that no self-respecting toymaker, farmer, or mother could abide.

A barn with no silo meant chaos. Just where did those ever–improving toymakers think we were supposed to store those adorable animals? The tractor? The trailer? The pigs? The cows? The horses? The farmer? The pumpkins? The hay? Where were we supposed to store pieces of white fencing? The inside of the barn was not a viable option. The pieces fall out the windows, and you needed a degree in engineering to cram the whole works in just right so you can close the fucker.

When I saw an older style for sale at a garage sale, just like the kind I'd had as a child, complete with a silo and a gate that mooed, I snatched it up and nearly had a car accident getting home. While Little Mary was in bed, I packed that brand new, "improved" barn and all the frigging animals back into their box and taped that piece of shit shut. I put the older barn on display in the living room and Little Mary never asked about the other.

Some of the things from my past worked. The barn was one, and going back to that was easy enough. But there was just as much about growing up with Mary Kline and Pearl that wasn't good at all. Sorting out what I needed and still wanted consumed me in ways I could not explain to anyone who had not been there. The only people who had been in the thick of it with me were these two mothers of mine. One was skilled at suffocating me, and the other, the one whose blood ran through my veins, bore witness but would never be able to commiserate with me or remind me to be kind.

Chapter Fifty-One

David

Keeping up with Elizabeth's preferences drained me. I'd come home from the office tired, but ready to have dinner with my wife and play with our little girl a little before it was time to tuck her into bed.

On nights when it was clear that Elizabeth was riding one of her obsessive waves, there was little room for niceties. Each obsession demanded to be satisfied with its corresponding compulsion. Anyone who stood between the two did so at their peril, including our child.

Our Little Mary mastered the retreat early on. When her mama was on one of her days-long quests for order, she made herself scarce, even as a toddler. This child seemed to know instinctively that there were times when it was best to let her busy mother remain busy. Some children would respond to this lack of availability with frantic clinging, but not our girl. She was good at quietly pawing through her storybooks, doing puzzles, or watching the comings and goings outside from the front window in the living room while her mother whizzed and whirred about the house, scrubbing, aligning, and reorganizing all the invisible disorder that troubled her.

Most of the time, Little Mary and I leaned into one another (and Elizabeth's increasingly ridiculous demands) like troopers. But we'd invariably get sloppy with the building blocks or the books or those fucking Barbies, which meant it was easier to get out of our taskmaster's way. I was miserable and could only surmise that our little girl was, too.

To keep the peace and manage the madness, I'd excuse the child from whatever task du jour was on Elizabeth's absurd to-do list each night and on the weekends. When it was finally time to sink into bed on nights when Elizabeth was on one of her jags, I wasn't even tempted by her naked body next to mine. If I caught her being short or impatient with Little Mary, I'd intervene, first with a raised eyebrow, and then by shaking my head. On cue, Elizabeth would challenge me.

"What is the problem, David? I'm just asking our child to take care of her things. I don't think it's too much to ask that she keep things sorted. She's expected to do that in school."

Little Mary inevitably looked confused as she hustled to please her mother, and I'd feel anger build quickly from my guts to my chest and up my neck before I'd snap.

"Oh, for fuck's sake, Elizabeth! Do you hear yourself? Do you?"

I'd snatch up Little Mary and whisk her out the door to get as far from the orderly chaos as feasible. Most of the time, Elizabeth would not even acknowledge our exit. I knew my wife. She was secretly pleased to have us out of her way. There was sorting to do.

Little Mary and I would stop by to see my folks, or hit the park, the zoo, the mall, or the movies. Any place was better than our house. When it was time to go home for bed, we'd tiptoe inside. I'd deposit our sleepy child into her bed and find her exhausted mother tangled in her own sheets. She would be worthless to us for the next few days, paying off the heavy debt of energy she'd accumulated as she spent beyond her means during her latest organizing spree.

The cycle became so normalized, woven into our home life, that we lived between cautious spurts. Had our Little Mary not been there to anchor me to the place, I would have considered bolting.

This was more than I bargained for that day when we exchanged gold rings, cut white cake, and danced through the night. My carefree bride had kicked her shoes off and laughed as I pulled Mary Kline onto the dance floor. She wept a little when I did the same with Pearl, who giggled shyly as I took her for a spin through the dance hall while the night was still young.

I never was sure if Pearl understood the gravity of their situation, but in that moment, it felt like she deserved to enjoy some levity. She was, after all, the mother of the bride, too.

I swayed with bird-like Pearl under the lights as the singer crooned "You Send Me," and this seemed to delight her. Elizabeth had her mother's wispy frame and her bright eyes, and the way she cocked her head when she smiled confirmed that they were mother and daughter.

I could see out of the corner of my eye that my new wife was pleased with my gallant gestures. It seemed possible on that night that I was the knight in shining armor that this trio of girls needed. I was tolerant to a fault, willing to shore up all that was creaky and wacky and weird. I was up for it all, despite feeling weak in the knees much of the time.

I kept so much under wraps each time we drew our swords, or a new, unsettling truth poked its head into the light, that it probably didn't do either of us any good. I let Elizabeth get comfortable ordering me around, insisting that she win every battle.

Before Little Mary arrived, our skirmishes followed a predictable arc: rise to conflict, climax to fall, collapse, then sweet, frantic reconciliation. Rises could be a slow burn one day or a combustible burst the next. Conflicts ran caustic, then cutting, to be followed with climaxes that were spectacular in scale and scope.

Our four walls could hardly contain what we allowed to fill the space. What goes up must come down. Flared tempers reached their peak, then retreated. Weary and panting, we surveyed the collateral damage of each rift.

God Bless the Child

Elizabeth was bleary-eyed and sniffling, and I was battered and bruised, but determined to remain steady. She could cut deep. Her fangs were jagged, and she sharpened them on me, her willing whetstone.

What happened after every clash was as puzzling as it was thrilling. What she did to me during one of our throw downs felt worth it in the loving, just-as-desperate aftermath. While it was just the two of us, the merits of our highs justified the lows.

I was a big boy. I had chosen this, and I loved Elizabeth. What made the dance we did with one another less excusable burst into the world at seven pounds, six ounces. She was a hungry and helpless, miraculous bundle. At first, we were appropriately subdued by her arrival and we behaved ourselves. It seemed that motherhood moored Elizabeth. She settled into it, and we enjoyed the peace while it lasted. And then, our daughter could no longer be contained, which changed everything.

Little Mary no longer needed to be swaddled. Her tiny legs and arms stretched and flexed. Her neck grew strong enough to hold up a bobbling head. Her curious eyes took in every sight each day with growing, knowing clarity. Her baby hands grazed every surface and did what baby hands are designed to do: explore. She wobbled her way through our home, moving toys from one irrational place to another, leaving a tiny, adorable trail of clues to reveal her path.

Once she could pull herself up and toddle like a drunken sailor, she flung open kitchen cabinets, dumping out their contents with reckless, toddler abandon that was cute, but brought a new layer of uncontrolled complexity Elizabeth could not manage. She convinced herself that left unchecked, Little Mary's normal exploration was a portent of things to come. An avalanche would surely ensue. If left untended, our home would quickly decline into the worst state imaginable. It would be like the home Elizabeth had shared with Pearl and Mary Kline.

I'd been in that place more than once. It was a mess. I'd never seen anything like it. The living room alone was a shock to the system. There were few places to sit. Each surface was filled with knick knacks, reading materials, fabric, bills, mail, sewing patterns, old toys, cookbooks, and baskets of sewing tools.

The kitchen wasn't much better. Elizabeth's childhood home was a veritable archeological dig. I tried to assure her that we would be fine. Our home would never be like that.

"Honey, that's not going to happen."

"Mary Kline's house didn't get that way overnight, Elizabeth. Think about it."

"But it started somewhere, David. One mess started it all, when one day Mary Kline decided to let things go. That's not happening here. Not in my home! Not on my watch!"

I felt sorry for Elizabeth. I felt sorry for Mary Kline and Pearl, too. It was too late to rescue Pearl, and some days, it seemed too late to help anyone but my little girl.

One day, the dam was going to break. We might need to leave Elizabeth and that great big mother of hers to toil over their bubbling cauldron together, chanting nonsensical hexes at each other as they took turns putting salt in their soup and in one another's wounds.

Chapter Fifty-Two

Elizabeth

I'd begun to show only weeks before. Well into my sixth month, I was content about the life that had taken hold inside me. My body was ready. *I* was ready. This time, it was going to be different. I was going to relax, let the dishes sit a little longer in the sink, allow myself deep sleeps on the couch. I'd done all of that while carrying my Little Mary.

I was going to be vigilant this time so things would not slip into organized madness.

David was relieved to hear me say that out loud, but he knew better. The lucky man had the pleasure of staying up with me until midnight each night so we could stack the puzzles by size, arrange books, and inspect each furniture piece in our daughter's dollhouse.

This was such a comfort to me, so easily conquered. Each day, I removed the furniture and wiped out the inside with a damp cloth. Then, I'd polish tiny dressers, tables and even a miniature grandfather clock with furniture polish. I used Q-tips to get in between the spindles of the rocking chair. I even used a comb to brush out the thread-like fringe on a tiny living room rug that Mary Kline had stitched together. I couldn't rest until all of it was as it should be in the dollhouse and all the toys were sorted, down to the last cow in the silo.

One night, we turned the living room upside down to find a missing puzzle piece. We moved the couch and dumped out all the toys we'd just meticulously sorted.

Throughout the search, he was kind. He was also cowardly or wise enough to avoid mentioning my obsessive, compulsive tendencies. His willingness to offer relief left me unchecked and unquenched.

It was after midnight when David found the offending piece. Our child had stashed it in one of her little purses. She had a habit I found inconvenient, often using her toys beyond their intended purpose. This time, the puzzle piece was pretending to be a cookie. Maddening.

I lectured my four-year-old the next morning about how Daddy and I had stayed up half the night looking for it. I reminded her that she had an entire container of real play food, including a delicious-looking plastic chocolate chip cookie. Why would she want to put a cookie in her purse in the first place? What about the crumbs? David rarely displayed aggravation with me. He sorted books by size and author, even subject. Finally, I decided it was best to keep Dr. Seuss books together, followed by Little Golden Books. The to–do list went on and on.

Bless his patient heart. My husband endured the entire process with me every night, even when he was bleary eyed with exhaustion. The dear man never got angry when I rearranged what he'd already put into place as per my instructions. This happened often. I was in a constant quest to place each item we owned into a grand scheme that would make complete sense.

Chapter Fifty-Three

Little Mary

Mama loved me some of the time, but she wasn't steady like Dad or fun-loving like Gramma Mary. I could count on those two to make me feel soft and warm. Reading Mama's moods sapped all our energy.

I heard Dad and Gramma Mary whispering about that one night after I was tucked in tight and promised to not let the bedbugs bite.

Mama needed a mood ring. If she had one, the three of us could just grab her hand and consult the ring before we made our next move.

I was allowed to play in my room if Mama felt up to it, but the clean-up was a heavy price to pay. I was better off playing at a friend's house, or at Gramma's, where toys could be tossed around willy nilly into a giant toy box or even left on the floor, so they'd be easier to reach when I was ready to play again. When I stayed with Gramma, she loved me so much that there was never any clean up. Dishes soaked in the sink and our beds were never made.

"Oh, Sugar," Gramma would say, "let's not bother. Gramma Mary will get to that later. Now come here, sweet thing. We've got more important things to do."

Her list of important things was long, relaxing, and soft around the edges: making cookies or homemade donuts dusted with sugar, finger painting, stringing button necklaces, pouring cinnamon tea into a tiny teapot with even tinier matching teacups, then slurping it like two dainty ladies on the front porch. We colored and read books while snacking on bowls of pudding topped with whipped cream and sprinkles. Sometimes, Johnson joined us for supper and the three of us laughed while he and Gramma made a show of sassing each other.

"Mr. Kuhlman, it's time for you to go home now. We've got a lot to do before we hit the sack. Little Miss Thing and I are way too busy for the likes of you, so git!"

Johnson acted disgusted and headed for the front door. I watched from the kitchen as Gramma followed him. It made me feel all warm inside as he put his arms around her and kissed her right on the lips like they were in the movies. Then, the front door slapped shut and Gramma turned to me with a happy smile on her old face. She rustled me up to the bathroom for a bubble bath and let me drink a glass of chocolate milk right there in her tub while she washed my hair. I tilted my head back and let the warm water run through my hair and down my back.

Later, we snuggled under Gramma's covers, just the two of us. She rubbed my back and told me about when Mama was a little girl and the fancy dresses she made for her, and someone named Pearl.

"Which dress was Mama's favorite?"

"Hmm, let me think about that. It could have been the princess dress or maybe one I made for Easter when she was your age. I'll ask her."

Then I'd beg her to tell me every detail of those dresses.

"Well, Sugar, it's late. Pick one dress for tonight and I'll do my best to tell you every detail I can remember. We'll talk about another one in the morning. How about that?"

My eyes were usually drooping by then.

"That Easter dress was mighty special. It was pale yellow, with hundreds of tiny white dots. It's called dotted Swiss. If you remind me in the morning, I'll show you a picture of your mama wearing it. That yellow looked good with her pretty red hair. There were white ribbons sewn down the front and a yellow sash that tied in the back. But that wasn't the best part. The best part was the matching cape."

"Matching cape? Why did you make a matching cape?"

God Bless the Child

"I guess to keep her arms from getting chilly, and because Easter is special, and a girl can't wear any old dress for Easter Sunday. But oh, my little namesake, you should have seen the white gloves and purse that went with that outfit. They were something special."

By then, I was asleep, dreaming about Mama hunting Easter eggs in her fancy yellow dress, and eating jellybeans. I always woke up sorry that those happy dreams were over. I'd close my eyes as tight as I could, hoping I might slip back down the rabbit hole and find myself perched somewhere on the sidelines, watching my mother move through my dream, dressed to the nines and gathering sweet treats without a care in the world.

It was always hard to get back into those dreams because as soon as I smelled bacon and waffles or French toast on the griddle, I'd wish I could stay with Gramma forever. We were two peas in a pod, and I liked that pod of hers.

I always cried when it was time to go home. I was happy to see Dad at the front door, but we both knew there was nothing dreamy or creamy where we were headed.

"Oh, Sugar, don't get weepy on me," Gramma would whisper with a smile. "You've got to get back to your Mama. She'll need some of that sunshine you carry in your pocket."

Chapter Fifty-Four

Elizabeth

Once Little Mary got her first Barbie doll, I couldn't stop thinking about the best way to organize all the tiny outfits: formal and casual wear, Ken's clothes in one baggy, Barbie's in another? Tiny handbags in one container, shoes in another? Or would it be best to put each tiny outfit, complete with accessories and shoes, in its own tiny container?

Barbie's vehicles and pets introduced new levels of misery I could never satisfy, with packages of deceptive pinks, blues with the blahs and yellows that show dirt too easily. That plastic doll brought a warped world into our house, beckoning people like me to take on what became an impossible challenge.

One night, after Mary's sixth birthday party, when she'd received what seemed like hundreds of Barbie clothes, including some of Mary Kline's handmade tiny sweaters, hats, and mittens, David and I finally went to bed. He was kissing my shoulders and running his lips over my breasts, telling me how beautiful I was, but I felt restless.

Instead of enjoying his attention or reciprocating, I made a mental inventory of how Barbie's entire wardrobe would need to be rearranged to accommodate my daughter's new birthday stash of plastic hairbrushes, stilettos in every color, handbags, hats, scarves, boots, and those stupid hand-knitted sweaters. This doll's wardrobe had gotten out of hand. It became too big to fit in the tackle box I'd taken from David or a case we purchased as a gift.

As soon as David fell asleep, I ran down to the living room, where I stayed until three, hard at work at my ridiculous task. I was elated to remember some old ice cube trays we had in the garage. Each cube would hold a perfectly matched pair of shoes and handbags.

By the end of the night, I had ten trays stacked neatly on top of each other. One was labeled "red," another "blue" and so on. It took me half an hour to decide how Barbie would feel if I put her gold and silver footwear and handbags in the same tray. After a lengthy deliberation, I decided that it would be best to keep them separate, so nobody would be confused, not my Little Mary, not Barbie and most of all, not me.

Chapter Fifty-Five

David

Sometimes, it was easier to give in and let myself believe that what Elizabeth considered best *was* best. I mean, did it really hurt anything that my wife preferred order to chaos? For a while, her need for alignment was no more offensive to me than a nervous tick or a bad habit, like biting one's nails.

Some nail biters grow weary and dissatisfied with the crispy slivers of their own fingernails. When the nails are gone, these people start biting into the tough flesh at the tips of their fingers. Soon, they crave the blood that rises to the surface when they've gnawed and chewed into the nail bed. A person like this can hardly wait for new scabs to form so she can rip them off with her teeth, like they're a delicacy found only in specialty stores, right next to the caviar and pâté.

I wanted to please Elizabeth, so I played along, often unwittingly feeding her preferences. One afternoon, I spent $36.29 on 20 separate packages of hangers designed specifically for Barbie clothes. When I spotted them next to the Barbie shoes and purses, I grabbed them all to take home to Elizabeth.

She was pleased and flashed me a smile.

"David! I knew you'd come around!"

It wasn't until that evening, as I watched Elizabeth and Mary immersed on the living room floor, that I realized I'd just introduced an alcoholic to a new kind of drink.

"Baby, look what Daddy found for us!"

Elizabeth's eyes were glassy. She was excited by the idea of putting tiny sweaters on miniature plastic hangers. She was panting when it occurred to her to use tiny, gold–colored safety pins to secure the slacks and other coats and dresses that kept falling off.

Little Mary could see the same thing I saw from my perch on the couch. The woman feverishly putting tiny clothes on tiny hangers was someone neither of us wanted to be around.

Our child eventually walked away and read a book. Elizabeth didn't notice. She arranged Barbie clothes for hours, staying up long after we went to bed. If Barbie had come to life and walked into the living room, I'm not sure Elizabeth would have even noticed or cared.

After that night, Mary was allowed to play with the Barbie dolls, but only after taking a solemn oath to put the clothes back according to her mother's complicated system. But our daughter's little fingers weren't nimble enough to manipulate the buttons and zippers to her mother's liking. When clean-up time came around, after mere seconds of barely concealed impatience, Elizabeth would pounce on the child and take over the task.

At moments like that, I'd intercede, whisking Little Mary away so Mama could feed her beast, then collapse with exhaustion before we returned home. I wouldn't have minded so much, except that our little girl was paying a price for Elizabeth's nasty penchant for order.

Chapter Fifty-Six

Little Mary

I first realized how ordinary I was during third grade at Fripp Elementary School. It all started with my plainer–than–Jane name. I was a Mary, surrounded by girls with names that sounded like they'd been sprinkled with sugar and cinnamon or drizzled with honey: Krystal, Dawn, Janelle, Leslie and my favorite of favorites, Candy.

Candy Adams was the luckiest creature in the third grade, if not the entire world. She wore more whimsical clothes in one week than Mama had allowed me to wear my entire life. Candy's clothes were adorned with embroidered kittens, sequined tropical fish, ironed-on decals of puppies and strawberries. She even wore clogs, and sometimes, white go–go boots.

Mama said they were tacky. She preferred me to dress like I was living in a Buster Brown fashion catalog with lots of turtlenecks, slacks, and plaid jumpers, all in varying pigments of dark blue, white and an occasional red—when she felt like walking me on the wild side.

Just like my name, my clothes were solid, classic, and dependable, and as Mama revealed years later, easy to organize by color and season.

Every few weeks, Mrs. Whalen changed the seating arrangement in our class. Just when I thought the entire school year would pass, I got the chance to face the desk of the divine Candy Adams. That kind of proximity made me certain that her parents had given her that name because her skin smelled like the inside of a box of Sweet Tarts. I was never bold enough to lick her arm, but I was confident that if I had, she would have tasted like something darn close to powdered sugar.

Candy Adams had pierced ears. I looked forward to seeing which earrings she chose each morning. Would it be the tiny ladybugs, or the pink stars? Sometimes, it was gold studs, and even those sparkled. My favorites were a set of red strawberries with pink seeds. That pair looked so juicy, I wanted to pull them out of her ears and eat them.

"Tacky, tacky, tacky."

That was Mama's response after I informed her about Candy's beautiful ears. I'm not sure why I shared my observations because Mama was growing weary of what she called my "Candy reports."

"Candy this, Candy that. Mary, I'm sure that little girl isn't as perfect as you think. Just be grateful that your Mama has some sense. You'll thank me some day. You will."

I wasn't convinced, but I must have known that as far as Mama was concerned, to pierce or not to pierce was not a question worth asking. Nail polish, even the palest of pinks Candy Adams wore, would always be forbidden.

Mama wasn't cruel. In fact, I loved being near her. She always smelled like freshly washed skin. Her lips were painted to red perfection. But on occasion, she checked out of our family circle. Daddy and I both knew that despite appearances, Mama was far, far away, making her lists, and lists of those lists, all in a vain attempt to clean up things in her mind that were not tidy enough.

I was her new Barbie doll, fresh out of the box, a neutral toy for her to dress, feed and put away when I was no longer interesting. My desires didn't exist, and just like Barbie, I had no free will.

When she checked back in, or "engaged," as Daddy called it, Mama returned energized, willing to fight the good fight. To her, appearance was everything. She considered the clothing I wore to be her turf, and she approached her mission as a prepared, determined Mother Warrior. Armed with sensible plaids and darling sailor suits with white piping, she found me a defenseless opponent. I just stood there every morning while she dressed me like her doll. Mama looked satisfied as she smothered me in her choices, and I never put up a struggle. But by the time I sat across from Candy, I was becoming brazen and bold.

I wasn't exactly jealous, but I started hearing whispers in my unpierced ears that I'd never considered. When Candy wore little pink hearts that appeared to change colors as she moved her head, I started to doubt my mother's intentions. As winter wore on and my own ideas continued to form, I began to question a lot of the decisions Mama had made on my behalf.

With each pair of earrings Candy wore, I became more convinced that Mama had grand plans to suck every bit of joy out of my young life. I'd been allowing her to do it by never putting up a fight, always willing to please—that was me. It had always been easier that way.

But an act of defiance was bound to happen. My chance presented itself one Saturday afternoon, a few days after Valentine's Day.

Gramma Mary had sent me a card full of hearts and tucked inside was a new ten–dollar bill. For a nine-year-old, it might as well have been a million. The timing was perfect, too. I'd have my own private fortune to spend on our Brownies field trip to a local shopping center.

Troop #26 had big plans to organize in front of the dime store with our table full of Girl Scout cookies. After an hour of hopeful sales, we'd be free for 30 minutes to browse the dime store with our troop leader, Mrs. Blevins, standing by the cash register as we made our purchases.

After we'd peddled Scot Teas and Thin Mints for what seemed like the entire afternoon, it was finally time to shop! The dime store had so many choices: wax lips filled with flavored gel you could suck out and then chew the wax like gum, tiny Indian beaded fake leather purses with drawstrings, Tinker Bell talcum powder and cologne sets, yoyo's, rubber balls, even jewelry boxes with little ballerinas that spun around to music when you opened them. All of it was tempting, and with that crisp ten-dollar bill in my pocket, I could have made a haul. But none of it inspired me.

I was determined to leave that dime store with something I could wear. It would be my declaration of independence, the first time I'd ever chosen my own clothing.

Mrs. Blevins made an announcement in her most earnest voice.

"Girls, we have ten minutes left before we must leave the store. If you're going to buy something, please make your choices and head to the counter."

That's when I saw it, the piece of clothing that would send Mama a message loud and clear that my days of dressing like a cartoon sailor were over. I flipped over the price tag to determine if it was in my league, and it was!

The T-shirt was white with an oval-shaped stone sewn near the left breast. The stone was the same kind that some of my babysitters had been wearing: a mood ring stone! The writing next to it was in various colors, each corresponding with a mood. Blue was happy. Pink was excited. And black was angry.

I instantly thought of Mama mouthing the word, t–a–c–k–y.

I was sold, and for seven dollars and fifty cents, I'd even have money left over. I snatched up the shirt and headed for the counter. The clerk seemed amused that a Brownie would have that kind of money. She teased me about how wealthy I was after I'd fished the money out of my pocket, but I ignored her. This was serious business.

She put the shirt into a white paper sack and neatly folded it over in a crease at the top. I got my change and stood by Mrs. Blevins. My heart was thumping so hard inside the sensible, Mama–approved white shirt I was wearing that I felt like I might throw up.

What had I done? I was a good kid. I'd never been in trouble and buying the mood ring shirt was my first real act of personal rebellion. I was breaching new territory between Mama and myself.

Riding home in the back of Mrs. Blevins' van with my Brownie friends seemed to last an eternity. Finally, it was my turn to slide across the cool back seat and thank Mrs. Blevins for the ride. I knew that Mama would be waiting for me in the living room, probably sorting paper clips and rubber bands and thumbtacks into an empty egg carton. Perhaps she'd be in the kitchen with the junk drawer thrown open and a determined look on her face.

"Mama?"

"Mamaaaa!"

Odd. She was always interested to hear about my outings, although she never went along. I looked in the laundry room, her favorite sock-sorting haunt, but she wasn't there either.

As I tiptoed up the stairs, I heard her talking into the phone that rested on Daddy's nightstand by their bed. From the sound of her voice, something was awry. As the newest rebel in the house, I opted to put my risky purchase underneath my bed.

I stood in the hallway and listened to what sounded like an adult conversation, full of promise and secrets.

"You must be mistaken," she said. "I'm positive that I've felt the child move. Not once, not twice, but several times."

What child? Did Mama mean me? I strained to hear more.

"I insist on speaking directly with Dr. Hannigan as soon as possible. Don't tell me what I've felt or not felt. You don't know what I've felt. And it won't hurt to listen one more time."

I felt sorry for the person on the receiving end.

"Fine. Yes, I can be there. Perfect."

Mama hung up the phone. As she turned and saw me, her eyes gleamed with renewed, fresh focus that matched her determined voice.

Rebellion aborted. I knew it would be cruel and certainly not wise to spring the mood ring tee shirt just then. Mama was checked in all right, and she pulled me into her circle.

"Mary, did you have fun?"

She forced a smile and hugged me a little tighter than I liked.

Those tight hugs were significant. They almost felt like goodbye hugs. Mama was preparing to take one of her trips to some distant land where Daddy and I wouldn't be able to reach her. Together, we'd tiptoe around, roll our eyes, and give each other knowing glances.

"Here we go again."

Chapter Fifty-Seven

Elizabeth

On the same day Mary went on her Brownie outing, I was relieved she had something to do, and even more relieved that Rose Blevins, (I liked to call her "über Mother" behind her back) only honked when she picked her up.

Rose was okay, but she seemed to be enjoying motherhood an awful lot. She wasn't bothered in the least that her kitchen counter was covered with piles of permission slips, artwork, photos, birthday party invitations, newspaper clippings, and bills and coupons.

I can't think about it for too long, not without the steady stream of antidepressants coursing through my veins.

Once I went for coffee in Rose Blevins' home, and that's it. I could never accept another invitation. Her household might sink its happy teeth into my leg and never let go.

I crawled into our bed, crying uncontrollably yet again. I could not wrap my head around the message I'd received in the doctor's office the day before.

"No heartbeat?"

I protested to my doctor in disbelief. I was nauseated. My breasts had been painful to the touch. All the signs of a thriving pregnancy had been there all along.

"My stomach is huge. I'm showing. There's a child in me, a growing child. I'm sure of it."

The doctor nodded, confirming that he believed me.

"Could you listen again?"

God Bless the Child

A tear trickled down my cheek. I took the tissue Dr. Hannigan handed me. He placed the cold metal piece, slimy with gel, against my belly, moving it from side to side. His face was close enough that I could see the pores on his nose. I tried to read him, but his expression revealed nothing.

Pushing his wire rim glasses up higher onto his nose, he cleared his throat and wiped the gel from my tummy with a towel. He gently put my blue oxford shirt down over the bump and offered his hand to help me sit up.

"I'm so sorry. But there simply isn't a heartbeat."

He put his large, clean hands on mine.

"This kind of thing happens more often than you think. Go home and get some rest. Take it easy and stay close to home. Nature will take its course and when it does, just come to the hospital. We'll deliver this and get you home to recover. You'll be back here in no time to tell me another one's on the way. You'll see. But for now, I'm very sorry."

My doctor opened the door to the exam room and walked away. I shuddered, choking back big, sour-tasting sobs. I looked at my heavy, pregnant silhouette in the mirror across the room. I liked what I saw. No sucking in the gut, my breasts bursting out of my bra. David loved it, and so did I. This time, things were supposed to be different. I had willed it. Things would fall magically into place the moment I put that new and soft little mouth to my breast. It would be just as it was when we brought our Little Mary home: glorious! Some of that rapture would soften the sharp world and the featherless nest I'd created for us.

I don't remember the drive home. David was already there by the time I pulled into the drive. He looked at me and he knew. The man who knew most of my secrets and loved me anyway knew that something had gone horribly wrong.

That night, once Little Mary had fallen asleep and we'd put the toys in order, David spooned me, his arms resting on the tummy that had failed to produce a heartbeat. He was sad, but he hadn't reduced himself to a sobbing, sloppy mess like me.

The next day, a nurse called with instructions. If we could save some of the tissue in a jar, they'd send it to the lab. We pondered her choice of words.

"Tissue?"

"Honey, I think she's talking about the baby, Hon."

Tissue. *That* tissue.

I struggled to understand when a growing child becomes classified as medical waste.

"Okay, then go dump the jelly out of the jar in the fridge, so we can catch the tissue!"

I was spitting with fury.

"Calm down, Elizabeth. Calm. Down."

I could tell by the way David held his mouth that he felt like he was dealing with an irrational child. He was. At that moment, his chances of having an adult conversation would have been better had he gone to talk to our nine-year-old.

"When did the doctor say this might happen?"

I walked over to Mary's craft box and dumped the crayons from their container. Greens in one pile. Blues in another. Reds. Pinks.

"Maybe tonight. Maybe in the next few days."

Oranges. Browns. Blacks.

"Can't we just get this over with?"

David knew as well as I did that Dr. Hannigan liked to let things happen on their own. No unnecessary induced labors, no pill to dry up swollen breasts painfully. Nope. Mother Nature did things on her own brutal schedule.

I took a shower and climbed naked into our bed, squeezing the muscles down in my crotch as tightly as I could, willing that life to stay in my belly until it found the heartbeat it lost.

I chanted to myself.

"Poor little kittens, you've lost your mittens."

Chapter Fifty-Eight

David

"Why should my wife keep carrying around a dead baby?!?"

I was a bellowing Papa Bear who had come home to discover that nothing was just right. I waited for the voice on the other end to take me seriously. I needed a satisfactory answer, but all the nurse offered were factual, hollow assurances.

"Mr. Garner, I know this is distressing for you and your wife, but this really is the best course of action. Trust me. Mama's body knows what it's doing and if we let Mother Nature take over, Mrs. Garner will be healing in no time."

"It's cruel. Oh, Jesus! I don't give a damn about Mother Nature. I'm telling you she can't handle this. She! Can't! Do! It!"

Maybe a stronger woman could, but not Elizabeth. She wouldn't be able to withstand any well-meaning condolences.

"Well, it just wasn't meant to be" wouldn't fly—not from my mother, not from friends, not even from Dr. Hannigan, with his cheery predictions for the future. My high-strung wife was not equipped to accept her immediate future. We both knew it.

I hadn't been successful convincing anyone at the doctor's office or the hospital to put us out of our misery.

Elizabeth stayed curled in a fetal position on the couch and ignored the phone constantly ringing. It was probably Mary Kline—again—calling to see if anything natural had happened.

Maybe it was the pastor. Oh, Jesus. Not him. Elizabeth couldn't cope with that. The pastor's fairy tales would not be welcome.

Nope. I knew my wife. She was not impressed with God, and she wouldn't take kindly to hearing how much Jesus loved her.

Chapter Fifty-Nine

Elizabeth

I was cussing at God, blaming Him for my latest failure. I deserved a bolt of lightning, but I was rewarded instead with something else: a nudge from inside! And then another!

"Dr. Hannigan, maybe you ought to get your hearing checked, old man, because I just felt not one, but two thumps! And it's not gas!"

Thirty minutes later, I felt it again. Movement. I swear. Glorious, unmistakable movement.

I ran to our bedroom and closed the door. I dialed Dr. Hannigan's office and spoke with a nurse, who had the nerve to tell me that it was common for a woman well into her sixth month to feel involuntary movements of the fetus, but that did not mean it had a pulse.

"Oh, Hon. I'm sure you did. Okay, now. I'll page Dr. Hannigan to see what he thinks. Okay? Okay, Hon."

I wondered if this patronizing bitch had ever enjoyed physical contact with another person, aside from taking people's blood pressure and helping pregnant women heave themselves onto the scale. She could "Hon" me all she wanted and give the "cuckoo" sign to her fellow nurses in the office. So what? What did this stranger know about me or my stability, and the baby I was going to have?

Going to have.

I felt confident that Dr. Hannigan and Nurse What's-Her-Name were as wrong as they could be. My baby was letting me know that everything was okay.

Mama's here, Baby. I can feel you. That's it. Come to Mama.

I was already forgiving Dr. Hannigan for his mistake. He was only human. I started rehearsing what I'd say to make him feel better about his blunder.

"Well, maybe at the time, you *didn't* hear a heartbeat. I know. Things like that happen."

I was forgiving my baby for playing hide-and-seek. I had even begun to forgive Mother Nature and her good friend, God Almighty.

After I hung up, I saw Little Mary in the doorway. I quickly daubed my eyes and wiped my nose. She looked so sweet with her brown hair cut in its perfect little bob, with her liquid brown eyes watching me. I hugged my guinea pig child, my first chance that I'd damn near blown with my stacks and containers and tidy expectations.

Everybody can make mistakes, right? Doctors do it all the time. And so do busy mamas.

I had a ton of tasks to complete. Straighten the fringe on the living room rug. Stack the soup cans. Make sure all things were tucked away, properly sorted, and resorted again. Our home was bursting with urgent matters that needed resolving, and I was ready to do this over and over again until they were just right.

Chapter Sixty

David

As humbled and frightened as I had been during the hours it took for our Little Mary to work her way into the world, at least the ordeal had a promising outcome.

Nine years later, our second visit to a delivery room felt the same, with its clinical greens and blues and the clanking of metal birthing tools. We waited for Mother Nature to take over and let Elizabeth's womb know its job was done. My poor sweetheart was so distressed that she imagined she could feel the baby moving.

"David, I'm serious! Come here. Put your hand here. There it is. Can you feel that?"

I felt nothing, not the first, second or third time she insisted I try, pressing my hand against hers.

Finally, several days later, Mother Nature put us out of our misery. We drove in silence to the hospital, where Elizabeth reluctantly pushed out a tiny, nearly translucent baby who could not take a single breath. But he was our son, a tiny, perfectly formed boy.

The nurse cut the worthless cord and wrapped up this would-be human being in a blanket that smelled like talcum. I never realized that the same little blankets that bundle a living newborn could also swaddle a dead one.

I sat there with my tiny son as the medical team clicked instruments and sanitized the sad surroundings. His perfect face reminded me of a baby bird that falls from the nest while its mama goes looking for food.

This little bird's mama was far away in a drug-induced sleep. She was hunting in her dreams for something more nourishing than food. I wondered how she would react when she came back to our nest.

Elizabeth had been correct about one thing. What I held in my hands was not tissue. No. Tissue doesn't have a face with delicate ears, miniature hands and fully formed feet.

Chapter Sixty-One

Elizabeth

I woke up drowsy and confused. My left hand felt stiff and was mottled with purplish and yellow bruises where I'd been connected to an IV. The white tape that kept the line in place had been stretched too tightly across my puckered skin.

A heavy, blood-soaked pad was wedged in my throbbing crotch. My thighs had been stretched and my hips were sore. My neck ached. My sweaty hair was matted and smashed against my cheek.

"Hey, Lady."

It was David, always-to-be-counted-on David, sitting in a chair next to my bed. As he leaned in to kiss me, his breath smelled like fresh coffee. Why was this man still here? Lately, I'd been as much fun as an old-fashioned gum scraping. At that moment, it wasn't my winning personality or dazzling good looks that drew him to my bedside.

I was missing what could be called "sparkle" over the last few years. My mother-in-law was always commenting about how tired I looked. I probably *was* because sorting pencils all night by color and size and making sure they were sharpened to the exact same length will tire anyone out, right?

It wasn't the mind-blowing sex that once tethered us so tightly. I hardly had a pulse most of the time, and it was hard to focus on anything but straight lines, sharp angles, clear glass, and ensuring alignment. Sex had too many blurred lines and sensations, with its uneven breathing and unpredictable outcomes. It was nothing short of a miracle that this baby had been conceived in the first place.

The circles under my husband's eyes were dark enough to be bruises. His eyes didn't sparkle, and I could see he was struggling to speak.

"Elizabeth, Honey. How are you feeling?"

I didn't respond. David and I were the proud parents of a what? I was sure I felt movement. Nurse What's-Her-Name must have been right. Were those flutters just this baby waving goodbye?

I heard Cowgirl Barbie, dressed in jeans and a crisp gingham shirt, squeak her ugly message into my ear:

"What a fortunate little fetus! He must have caught wind that his mama was a bundle of trouble. Better get out while the getting's good, little one. Look at your sister!"

David finally got the words out.

"You delivered the baby, Honey. Remember, we drove to the hospital? But there was no heartbeat, Babe. They were right about that. But it's going to be okay."

David choked on his words. He tried to believe them. I touched his hand and caressed his smooth cheek. He was surprised that I didn't lash out to blame the doctor. His response was standard David: pats and hand squeezes while spoon-feeding me with gulps of hope. That kind of petting used to work. But on that day, my womb had emptied out its precious contents, and my husband's touch was irritating.

I should have known that something was wrong before the heart stopped beating. Maybe I didn't notice because I was busy organizing the house inside my head.

God confirmed what I already knew—that I didn't deserve another child. The one I had was not transforming me, so why would another? My first little waif, the one we'd so casually discarded, had been my first squander. I was being punished. That's it. It was best to place this nightmare into two mental files: angry God and chastised mother, in no special order.

My grief left no room for David's. This was not the first time I'd neglected his needs. My heart was full of nasty secrets I shared with God and Mary Kline. She and I deserved to be punished, but not poor David. He did not deserve to stand with us in our sorry corner. After he went home, I didn't resist the Percocet the nurse offered, and I soon floated into a deep sleep, sans dreams, sans baby, sans anything.

In the middle of the night, a tired mother was rolled into the bed next to mine. My side of the room was dark, and as the nurses tended her behind a curtain that separated us, I could tell that my new neighbor had just given birth to a child that came complete with a beating heart.

The word *bitch* stuck to the roof of my mouth, and I sucked on it like a bitter lozenge. I turned my exposed backside toward her side of the room. I hoped she had endured hours of hard labor. I wanted her to have gained more weight during pregnancy than her doctor approved and for her middle to be nothing but a fleshy, stretch-marked blob. I wished that her piles would be larger than marbles, the kind that made her fight the urge to scoot around on the carpet like a dog. I hoped that it would take weeks before that new mother could take a dump for fear of ripping out the tight stitches that separated her ass from her crotch. I prayed her dope of a husband would have to wait months to make love to her. I wanted no new child coming to her.

My jealous dreams were dashed a few hours later, when the infant was rolled into the room in a bassinet—a bundle of red, delicate flesh, wrapped expertly in a perfectly pink blanket.

This new mama was receiving her perfectly made girl. I listened as she fumbled to get her breast out of the hospital gown. I could hear the baby's muffled grunts as she rooted for her mother. Finally, contented sucking. Mother's milk was flowing.

I closed my eyes, trying to block that beautiful tableau from my mind. Those first sucks hurt, tiny gums pulling at delicate flesh that's never had such a vigorous workout. It takes your breath away at first. Excruciating. I remembered Little Mary's tiny fingers resting on my breast, her transparent fingernails a faint purple, her eyes squinting to take in this Big Mama Stranger.

Salty tears streaked down my cheeks, and I didn't bother to wipe them away. They flowed, as did the reddish–black clots from my womb, and I swear I could feel my own breasts swelling with something. Was it milk?

Who thought it was a good idea to put a happy new mother and her perfect fucking baby next to me?

A few pain pills later, the curtain was drawn. The happy side of the room was brimming with pink carnations and roses, nestled in baby's breath and gingham ribbons. Pink balloons exclaiming "It's a Girl!" bobbed against the ceiling.

Kind David sent a flower arrangement for me full of bright yellow daisies with velvet brown centers, along with a card.

Everything will be all right.

Love you —— David.

As usual, David looked at the bright side. He could filter out the bad stuff and focus on the sunlight streaming through a window, but I could see the smudges and smears on the glass and the tiny particles of dust, millions of them, swarming in the air before me.

I tossed the card across the room and slept some more. Soon, they would make me go home. But I wouldn't find comfort there, not with the forks and spoons and knives calling me to master them. The fringe on the rugs would taunt me with its tangles, along with Little Mary's toys, which had dared to venture from their assigned posts while I'd been away.

God Bless the Child

I was about to come home without a second chance. Without my little redeemer, I'd become a slave again to my obsessions, which meant my innocent child would be stuck with the same old Mama, not the new one I had hoped would save us all.

Chapter Sixty-Two

Little Mary

While Daddy was away at work, I went to school, and when I got home, Gramma Mary was there waiting for me. Daddy said that Mama would need to stay in the hospital a few more days, and that I could go with him one evening to visit her.

I missed Mama and her riddles, and the bright red lipstick kisses she planted on my cheek each morning before I went to school. What I missed most were the rare times she brushed the hair off my face as I fell asleep.

"Well, Honey, it wasn't meant to be, that's all," Gramma Mary said.

She patted my hand, assuming I knew what had happened to Mama.

"Your mother will be fine. Maybe another baby will come along. It's probably for the best, anyway. Let's just be good to her, okay?"

The baby. Mama and Daddy had just recently revealed this news to me. Something exciting was coming our way, and before I could even taste it, it was snatched away.

During the first days Gramma Mary ruled the kitchen, there was always something in the oven: a bubbling pan of lasagna, roasted chicken, blueberry muffins, peanut butter cookies, even cupcakes.

Her idea of tidying up was as delicious as her cooking. She let the kitchen sink's growing pile of pots and pans and spatulas and wooden spoons and whisks mount higher and higher until they blocked out the window. Plates were left stacked on the counter.

The mess made me feel like I was a bad girl, but I'd been given permission by an adult to be that way. I was also a good girl. A grown-up in the room wasn't concerned with the chaos at all. Most of all, I was a nervous girl who cowered at the thought of Mama standing in the middle of it. Gramma Mary could read my mind.

"We'll get to that later. Your mama would have a fit! We won't tell her though, will we?" She pushed my school papers aside so we could cut out some paper dolls she'd found. We were too busy with matters more serious than a dirty kitchen.

Gramma Mary smelled like cold cream, and I loved it. She rubbed a little of it on my cheeks the night before and it felt like smashed pearls and whipped cream.

Her hands were soft and capable. They worked efficiently as she deftly cut out each paper doll and outfit. By the time I'd finished one paper dress, she had completed a full page. Gramma Mary cut and cut, letting the excess paper outlines fall like flimsy skeletons on the table, on the chairs, or on the floor. We cut for a good hour and then she suggested we have a bubble bath.

I was happy to oblige, soaking in the warm bubbles until my skin felt like a giant prune.

We decided I'd sleep in my underpants and an undershirt because we couldn't find my nightgowns. I knew that Mama kept them in the bathroom closet since that's where I usually got dressed after my bath. I didn't tell Gramma Mary that there were probably ten identical, white cotton nightgowns stacked right next to a glass jar of Q-tips and Mama's hot rollers. The chance to wear something else to bed was too exciting to ruin.

Gramma Mary wore an amazing aqua nightcap to bed, with netting gathered up in a bunch at the top of her head. I laughed and pointed and laughed some more, but the next night, when she pulled a pink version of the bonnet out, I snatched it and put it on my head. We were two ridiculous birds, nestled in the guest bed together.

Before we settled in, Gramma Mary suggested that I set out some clothes to wear in the morning, because Daddy was taking me to the hospital to pick up Mama and bring her home. I yanked a pair of navy slacks out of my dresser and then remembered the package I'd shoved under my bed. Gramma Mary loved my shirt, and she was impressed that I'd bought it with my own money.

"I bet your mood will be happy tomorrow, my little namesake. Your mama will be home, and we're going to take really good care of her!"

I fell asleep on my tummy that night. Gramma Mary gently rubbed my back. I dreamt of the dime store and the clerk who commented about how wealthy I was when I made my risky purchase. She asked if she could borrow it.

The hospital people called to tell us that Mama needed more rest, that she couldn't come home for a few more days. I missed her, but Gramma Mary could stay longer, which was fine with me. With her in charge, there were fewer flat surfaces and more gentle hills—nothing sharp or abrupt, and I liked it that way.

Mama's lipstick kisses would have to wait. There were pancakes on the table, and Gramma Mary didn't mind if I covered them with my own syrup and chocolate chips.

Daddy and Gramma Mary whispered about Mama late at night, but I couldn't make out any details. They seemed worried about Mama staying in the hospital, and just as worried about her coming home.

Chapter Sixty-Three

David

Dr. Hannigan was a brave, wise man. I wanted to kiss him right on the lips when he suggested that Elizabeth wasn't ready to come home.

She was exhausted, for sure. I reminded myself that my wife had essentially just given birth. Her body had gone through all the motions in a marathon with no victory lap. Her body deserved rest. But I knew this woman's face better than the doctor. I could see how she controlled her angular chin and how the dark circles under her eyes were in sync with the tone of her voice. Her soul was battening down its hatches, preparing for a dark and swirling storm. It was churning up something black and nasty that would frighten her as much as it might me, or Little Mary or Mary Kline.

When I walked inside our house, the kitchen was buzzing with happy vibes. Peanut butter cookies and ginger snaps were cooling on the counter. Something savory bubbled on the stove, and the sink was piled high with mixing bowls, cookie sheets, and coffee cups.

The chef and her adorable sous chef were still in their robes. They'd been taste-testing batter, and the short one had a thick milk moustache. They were hunched over an Easy Bake Oven that Mary Kline had snuck into the house a few days earlier. Elizabeth would never have allowed it, but those two merry makers had that baby fired up.

"Dad! Wait until you try my chocolate cake! It's almost done!"

I picked up Little Mary and hugged her. She was a sticky, glorious mess and smelled like a sugar cookie.

"Yum! I can't wait, Honey. I cannot wait!"

I watched them peer into the tiny oven's window to see how the miniature treat was doing under the glare of a light bulb.

"Still looks a little soupy in the middle, Sugar," Gramma Mary said. "Let's check it again in three minutes!"

"Do I have time to tinkle?"

"Yes, and there's time to wash those hands, too. Don't forget that."

Mary Kline chuckled and put her hand on my shoulder. Her touch felt good, as if my own mother was comforting me.

"Oh, David. I sure am sorry about the baby. I sure am. What can Mary Kline do for you?"

I've never been much of a crier, and I was sure that I'd never caved that way in front of Mary, but I felt my lip quiver. Before I knew it, I was sobbing like a baby, which was surely not a manly thing to do, but I didn't care. It felt like such a long time since an adult had asked me what I needed.

It had been less than 48 hours since I'd handed over our teeny tiny boy to the nurse. Elizabeth had refused to look at him. I felt I owed our son something sweet. I let my lips land tentatively on his forehead. The skin was translucent, too fragile to withstand a full kiss. A tender graze was all I could muster. The sadness and loss took me by surprise. I'd been so busy being stoic and strong while tending to Elizabeth that I hadn't really let go and said goodbye.

Before I said a word, Mary Kline's giant arms wrapped around me. She smelled like a sugar cookie, too.

"Oh, David. I think it's good that Elizabeth is resting for a few more days, don't you?"

She patted my back.

"You're going to have a big bowl of my jambalaya. We made it today from scratch. And then you need to get yourself to bed, Sir. You've been through plenty. You need a good night's sleep, David."

God Bless the Child

I nodded like a tired child. Mary Kline knew best. The jambalaya was life changing. I had two bowls and a single bite of Little Mary's chocolate cake, which tasted like it had been cooked by the glow of a low-watt lightbulb. The kitchen was a disaster, but none of us cared.

I heard Little Mary and Mary Kline giggling in the guest bedroom. As their sleepy chatter subsided, I let myself cry some more and wondered if Elizabeth had fallen asleep yet in her hospital bed. I wondered if she was thinking about us, settled in for the night without her. We three were unfettered without her, free to listen to our own hearts. The happy and the sad blended into one big mess, but it was ours.

Chapter Sixty-Four

Elizabeth

Remaining longer in the oasis of my hospital room came as a welcome respite. The mother in the bed next to me was gone, with her happy little family intact. I was glad to see them pack up their balloons and go home with their bundle of joy. From what I could see, she wasn't that adorable anyway.

Those fools had no idea that this new person would take over their home. Over the coming years, her belongings multiplied and consumed more and more space. They would have little to no control about what came in, but they would be completely responsible for keeping it all sorted, stacked, folded, and tucked.

I was glad it would happen to them, too. I didn't bother to tell them about the joy they had in store. I didn't want to give them anything to look forward to. I wanted those people to head off with their babe into the abyss.

Once they were gone, and I had the room to myself, I resisted the urge to let my thoughts stray too close to the baby boy who eluded me. That was too sad and would have required more of those tiny white pills that the nurse brought me every six hours. Between doses, I drifted instead toward higher, happier ground with thoughts of our Little Mary.

Chapter Sixty-Five

David

Mary Kline and I sat exhausted at the kitchen table, beers in hand, long after Little Mary had been tucked in and kissed goodnight. Elizabeth would be coming home in a few days, and my makeshift mother–in–law and I were worried about her landing.

Our home had gone to hell, and we weren't even close to bringing it back to the standards my wife demanded. I cleared the living room to a degree, and Mary washed and dried all the dishes, but the kitchen floor was sticky, and a basket of unmatched socks blocked the way to the back door. There were three baskets of clothes to fold and put away, and Little Mary's room was a sea of spilled toys and rumpled clothes. I did not have the energy to go through the ridiculous rigors Elizabeth usually demanded.

"David, how long do you think Elizabeth will want me to stay?"

"I don't know."

The next few days promised to be tense. We were sure to be chided like children for allowing ourselves to be so sloppy in a home that was usually so tightly wound. Little Mary would not be spared, either.

"David, be good to my Elizabeth."

She pointed at me with the neck of her beer bottle.

"She is the way she is for a lot of good reasons. Elizabeth just wanted to be as different from me as she could. That's all. If I could do things over again, I would, David. I sure would. I'm not so sure I did Elizabeth and Pearl much good. Maybe I should have run as far away as I could from Pearl. She and Elizabeth would have been better off, I'm sure."

Mary Kline was fishing for a compliment, and I didn't have the heart to leave her with an empty hook.

"Don't say that, Mary. It's not true. You know Elizabeth loves you like a mother. You *are* her mother. And Pearl would have been worse off without you. You know that. We couldn't be here without you."

Mary Kline let my kind words wash over her. She smiled softly and took another swig of her beer.

"Thank you, David. That's kind for you to say. But, oh, Honey, no, no, no. There's so much more you don't know. I'll share it with you another time if Elizabeth will let me."

We sat a while in the semi-dark kitchen, sipping our beers. The quiet air between us buzzed with a tipsy but trusting new territory we'd never allowed.

"None of this is Elizabeth's fault. Not one bit. And she's lost a baby. She's going to need a lot of care. Maybe it would be best if I wasn't here when she gets home. Maybe the two of you need some time."

She wasn't wrong about that. We *would* need some time. As much as I appreciated having help with Little Mary, I was grateful that Mary Kline realized that extending her stay could complicate Elizabeth's homecoming. The two would start sparring within minutes of their hello hug. It was how they sent smoke signals back and forth.

Their sass with one another took some getting used to. Sometimes, a referee was needed to ensure that neither party sustained an injury as they exchanged their brand of love. Elizabeth and her Mary Kline were not related by blood, but they shared something deep and enduring that kept their barbs sharp when it was convenient for either one of them.

I nodded.

Maybe it would be better if I took this next round on my own. But Mary had another idea.

"Let me take that lump of sugar home with me for a while. We'll have ourselves a fine time, David. You know we will. That will get me out of your way and neither of you will have to worry about our Little Mary. You can come get her in a few days after the two of you have rested up a bit."

It was settled. We'd pack two bags the next morning, one for Mary Kline and one for Little Mary, who was beside herself with joy to be headed off to her grandmother's house of fun.

Chapter Sixty-Six

Mary Kline

That little thing is nothing but a lump of pure sugar. When I saw her for the first time that afternoon at the hospital, armed with a huge pink teddy bear tucked underneath my arm, I was determined to do it right this time. This baby was Elizabeth's, not mine.

My Johnson, holding a big bouquet of pink roses nestled in baby's breath, greenery, and a satin bow, had coached me in the elevator as we approached the maternity ward.

"Sweetheart, you can do this. Remember what we talked about. Elizabeth loves you. You are her mother, Honey. For every practical purpose, you are her mother, and you did a wonderful job. A wonderful job, Mary. But now, it's her turn to be the mother. Right? You are the grandma, Honey. You get to do all the fun stuff this time around. You can do this."

I laughed to myself. He was cheering me on as if I was birthing a child. I nodded and squeezed his hand to let him know I heard him and appreciated him and needed him whispering in my ear. Johnson knew me. He understood what parts of me needed filling and he did not recoil at the raw, throbbing growl that never left my body or the heart it held.

This new child was not mine to raise, but I could love her in ways that were less reckless and grasping than what I displayed with Elizabeth and Pearl. I owed the two of them and this new little girl far less than I could give, but more than the spotty affections my own mother tossed at me like breadcrumbs to a hungry, desperate little bird.

Elizabeth and I spatted and sparred, but I knew one day she might need me measured and steady. That day had come. I could catch that call of hers as it whistled on the wind toward me and do her plenty proud without choking on my own needs.

I would love this new child without smothering her. That's not what Elizabeth needed from me. This child of hers, the one she named after me, was my chance to redeem myself for all the wrongs that stood between me and her mother. If I could do that just right, perhaps Pearl would see it all from her perch in Heaven, and she, too, would forgive me for taking advantage of the misfortunes of her life.

I hoped so, and that feeling brought with it a pure, acceptable, and appropriate love I would shower on Little Mary when she needed it. This would be the kind of loving I could be proud of, with bubble baths, paper dolls, and powdered sugar, Barbie clothes and sleepovers and snuggles and hugs that needed nothing in return.

I loved Little Mary, but I did not need her. I could give Pearl's grandchild everything she craved. I could and I would, and that would be enough.

Chapter Sixty-Seven

David

The Elizabeth I brought home was weak and diminished. I expected angry outbursts but found her profoundly sad and defeated.

She acknowledged my pats on her leg as we drove home, but that was more out of habit. I tried to deliver a message by patting her hand.

Pat — Pat — Pat.

"I — Love — You."

My lover and wife, this girl who could be so wonderful, would usually pat me back her response in our own Morse code.

"I — Love — You — Too."

Four pats. During our early days, I would have panicked at the lack of responding pats, but I'd evolved. Elizabeth and I had lived through enough rough moments that I knew we were fine. My wife loved me. She loved me more than she'd ever loved anybody, perhaps even more than she loved our daughter. One of the things she loved most about me was that I didn't demand constant assurances and affirmations.

Elizabeth didn't even ask about Little Mary's whereabouts when we walked in the front door. She could be an aloof mother, a distant mama bear, but she always liked to know where our little cub was situated. She didn't even head up the stairs to our bedroom, as she usually did, to plunge into one of her dark funks.

This wasn't a funk or one of my wife's rituals driven by her usual depression. For once, Elizabeth was just deflated, and understandably so. It was as if some force had pulled the plug on her OCD battery pack.

We'd just lost a child.

She entered the living room and lay face down, prostrate on the carpet and sobbed.

"David, I can't bear this. I can't."

She asked for me and I didn't disappoint. I covered the two of us with an afghan from our sofa. Usually, Elizabeth preferred to be spooned with her back curled inside my torso. But this time, we held each other face–to–face and openly wept, comforting each other. She was my kitten. I stroked her red hair until we both fell into a deep, sad sleep. She smelled so good. How could these heartbreaking, awful events also feel so good?

Chapter Sixty-Eight

Elizabeth

David and I woke up on the floor at nine in the evening. My whole body ached. I felt like I'd just given birth, and as the sleep wore off, I remembered that I had. I'd given birth all right, but came home with empty arms.

"Hey, we really conked out, didn't we?"

David was resting his head on his hand.

"Don't poke your fingers through that," I said.

Mary Kline had made the afghan that covered us, and David had a bad habit of poking his fingers through the holes, stretching out the pattern. Little Mary liked to do the same thing.

"Where's our girl?"

I hadn't seen her since the night I went into labor and David rushed me to the hospital.

"Have you already put her to bed?"

"Elizabeth, we thought it would be better to let you rest when you came home, so our girl is with Mary Kline for a few days. We'll drive down later to get her."

Mary Kline had been in our house. Goody. I should have remembered that. Just what I needed to come home to. I dreaded making my way through the house, where signs of her presence would jump out at me. It was like she marked her territory whenever she had the chance. She lifted her leg and sprayed her stinky funk all over my house.

I was exhausted just thinking about the mess. Mess after mess, with messes on top of messes. I'd spend hours cleaning up after Miss Good Times. And David let it happen.

God Bless the Child

My absence was like a vacation for my husband and young daughter. I knew if I went into the kitchen, I'd find dried out peach pits on the windowsill above the sink. Empty soup cans would be stacked next to empty toilet paper rolls and 20 other pieces of trash that Mary Kline might be able to use for who knows what.

The truth is, Mary Kline had the makings of a wonderful preschool teacher or scout leader. I tried to imagine my fat mother and Rose Blevins duking it out neck and neck to be the first to earn their coveted "Can't Throw Shit Away" badges.

My husband could read my tidy mind.

"Listen. Mary Kline was a huge help and Little Mary loved having her here. Just relax. We'll get this place whipped back into shape."

Why yes, we would because I'd be the especially crabby overseer, holding the whip. Disorder bothered me, but the way Mary Kline took over turf that wasn't hers bothered me more.

I was Pearl's daughter, not hers. That aborted baby was my problem, not hers. Little Mary was my little girl to pet and love, not hers. This house was my house, not hers.

"David, go look in the kitchen. Go. Go look. I bet that bitch has at least ten peach pits on the windowsill."

He laughed at me. I was ridiculous.

"Honey, come on. She took care of Little Mary while you were in the hospital, and I was at the office. The woman, your mother, was here helping us. Jesus! Be grateful. Can you just be grateful?"

"Don't speak to me like I'm a child and she's some normal adult, David. Don't go there."

He was never going to understand.

"Elizabeth. Look at me. Mary Kline's a lot. I understand that. But she is our family. So, things are a little messy. Big fucking deal. She really helped me out. Having her here was good for Little Mary.

Maybe, just maybe, it's not only about you. There's a concept, huh? Something that isn't *all* about Elizabeth."

David didn't usually speak to me that way. I was usually the one erupting while he played the soothing agent. Now, he was erupting, and I didn't know how to soothe.

"Throw the damn peach pits in the garbage when she leaves, Elizabeth. Problem solved."

Aha. David needed to be educated.

"Honey, this is so much bigger than peach pits! Can't you see that? Jesus Christ! Can't you see that? Mary Kline manipulates everything to suit her. She'll help you to death, David. Don't get sucked in by Mary Kline's loving martyr act. Can't you see it? Mary loves to excess. She loves us to *death*. Everything is her way. And in case you've forgotten, I just lost a baby! If I don't want any goddamned peach pits on my sink, they shouldn't be there. She knows I don't want them there, but there they are! And why? I'll tell you why. Because Mary Kline takes what she wants. This is my house, not hers!"

David was quiet as he shifted into adult mode. I was an irrational child, and he was preparing himself mentally to placate. He was digging out his infuriatingly even tones and his "feeling-friendly" words. My husband was raising the bar for himself, I was sure of it.

I was wrong.

"Elizabeth, I know this is hard for you to fathom, but this house is also mine. And another person lives here: our daughter. Remember her? Our home will not be the battleground any longer for your hang–ups. If you and Mary Kline have stuff to work out, then do it, but don't do it here! And don't expect our nine–year–old and me to stand here and watch you and your fat mother throw peach pits at each other."

I tried to interject.

"I object to your tone, David."

God Bless the Child

I had to point out that Mary Kline and I didn't have hang-ups. We were on the verge of an earthquake, and it was her fault for taking over, while pretending she only wanted to help. To the untrained eye, Mary Kline appeared to be a harmless, squishy granny, cooing and patting her way to sainthood.

"David, you don't . . ."

"Let me finish. I am going to finish."

"We lost a baby. *We.* That baby was mine, too, Elizabeth. I'm sad, too. Do you think I enjoyed the last week? I've lost something, too!"

We weren't going to fuck our way out of this argument.

"While you were popping pain pills and some of that excess self-pity you keep on hand to numb yourself, I held our dead son. I rocked him until the nurses insisted I go home."

David pressed on, holding my gaze with his glare.

"Do you want to know the saddest part? Do you?"

He was going to make me ask for it.

"The saddest part wasn't that our child was dead. It was what I said to myself as I drove home after I handed him back to the nurse. I was thinking that our boy was better off dead. I knew this baby was better off dead!"

I'd had the same thoughts myself, but hearing David say them like that especially stung. Weren't those my thoughts to have? I was the mother. If the mother says that, isn't she within her rights? If the father says something like that, isn't he just a bastard?

I allowed another question to stir within me. It was dark and lived in my bitter heart for Mary Kline alone. Just how much say should she have had that morning when we took our drive? We had some trash to take out that morning. We headed for the open road with a tiny load and pulled back into Poulson by nightfall, one heartbeat lighter.

Chapter Sixty-Nine

David

My wife was right. There were seven peach pits lined up in a precise row on the ledge. I picked one up. It must have come from a recently devoured peach. Its pockets were still filled with slimy pulp. Saving peach pits *was* a disgusting habit, but it wasn't dangerous or harmful or perverse. Still, it was enough to elicit venom from Elizabeth.

She was willing to sink her teeth into her mother over peach pits, but she didn't argue with me when I suggested that our stillborn son was better off dead. What did this sad fact mean for us?

As I cleaned the dishes from the day before, I watched Elizabeth go into the bathroom and heard the shower begin to hiss hot water.

I was cruel to my wife, who had just lost a baby. I said terrible things to her. What was the matter with me? She needed something I wasn't giving her. I wasn't sure I was strong enough to be with this version of Elizabeth.

I wanted to wrap the truth about her into a neat little package and return it to the store. I wasn't sure I could subject my daughter to her craziness any longer.

Elizabeth could beat me up with her glares. She could throw me against a brick wall or knock my head into the ground. I could probably take it all and come back for more. But holding our tiny, dead son had jolted me out of denial. Little Mary was just as vulnerable as an unborn baby around her mother. If I didn't protect my daughter from whatever was haunting my wife, I could be rocking her in a dead sleep, too.

Elizabeth was dripping wet. When her hair was wet and slicked back, it looked black, not red. She wrapped herself in my robe and came to me at the sink. Her silence told me that she knew she'd pushed me far enough. I was angry and sad, afraid that if I didn't get through to her, we couldn't be together anymore.

She wrapped her arms around me and rested her cheek on my back.

"I need to know that this isn't about peach pits or keeping Barbie's clothes arranged just so. Tell me this is bigger than our fucking spice rack. Tell me what will fix all of this."

I started to cry and turned to her. I took her hands from my waist and pressed them to her chest.

"I deserve to know, don't I?"

Elizabeth was deciding if I deserved to know the secret handshake, and if I should be granted the password into her complicated inner life.

"David, it's hard to explain. You'll never get it. You just won't get it. What I've got is heavy."

"Babe, it's time to unload it. If you're coming with me and our little girl, you're going to unload it right now. I mean it, Elizabeth."

She looked scared.

"Maybe I don't want you to know about it, David. It's ugly and shameful."

I shook my head vigorously.

"Nope. That's not going to work. I've been loving you and wanting to wring your neck for years. I've already seen parts of you that aren't nice to look at. You're going to have to give me some credit."

She sighed and chewed the inside of her cheek.

"You know a lot already."

"Obviously, that's not enough because I don't get it, Honey. Tell me what I need to know."

"Okay. Okay."

She decided to try stalling.

"Mary Kline and I have some really unpleasant secrets between us."

She spoke calmly, like that was going to be sufficient for me.

"Well, you can choke on your nasty secrets, or you can spit them out right here."

"David, this boy, this baby son of ours . . . he isn't the only child I've lost."

"I know, Honey. I know. You need to find our Little Mary again, before it's too late. Find her, Honey. Find her and keep her."

"No, I'm not just talking about Little Mary. I've lost two children."

"Two? What are you talking about?"

"It was way before you. I was seventeen, and I got pregnant. Mary Kline and I went to an abortion clinic. We scraped that baby out and threw it in the trash."

I envisioned our dead son, the one I'd cradled and kissed, his face injured with cuts and bruises, his mangled body tossed in the trash, next to coffee grounds and banana peels. I turned away from Elizabeth.

"Hey! Don't you judge me, David! Don't you dare! You wanted the whole story, and I've given it to you. I told you that you wouldn't want this. I've lived with this, not you."

I remained still. Was I judging her? It was her body, wasn't it? It was her baby, her choice to make, right? That baby wasn't mine. It didn't change anything about us, did it? Was what she did as a stupid teenager, before she even knew me, any of my business?

I decided it was. She had promised to give me "all she had, and all she was." That was our vow to each other. But Elizabeth gave me just a piece of her. I was the victim of a sneaky round of bait and switch.

"What else is there?"

"I don't like your tone, David. You *are* judging me!"

"Maybe I am, but you can't control how I respond. Regardless of how I feel about abortion, you made a conscious choice to deceive me. Every day you chose to keep this from me was a fresh, new lie. Every day we've shared together looks different to me now. We've been together for twelve years! I'm in this marriage too. When are you going to let me all the way in?"

"Are you angry with me?"

"Yes, I am. I'm furious. I don't know how I feel about the abortion, but I'm angry that you've deceived me. You didn't trust me enough with your story, Elizabeth."

"Would knowing this part of my story really change anything?"

"If I'd known, maybe I would have looked at you differently. Maybe I wouldn't have wanted to kill you every time you acted like a distant bitch to our daughter."

I was hurting her feelings, and I was ashamed of myself because I didn't care.

"What else have you got for me, Babe?"

"Forget it, David. I don't need this shit."

She turned to leave.

"If you leave this room, Elizabeth, I'm getting in the car and I'm driving to get Little Mary. I'll take her with me to my folks. You can sit here in this fucking house and play Barbie by yourself for as long as you like."

She stopped in her tracks.

"I mean it."

What Elizabeth shared with me next was chilling, but it was also a relief. She had been carrying a big load. She wasn't a total nut job. Armed now with the missing pieces of her puzzle, I could see my wife clearly for the first time.

Another moment of clarity hit. After what I'd just learned, I wasn't so sure I was comfortable leaving my daughter in the care of Mary Kline.

Chapter Seventy

Elizabeth

Mary Kline wasn't going to hurt Little Mary. I knew that. But I wasn't sure if this mother of mine could be trusted to protect her properly, either. She hadn't protected me or Pearl.

In the night, for so long, we had no guardians. When I finally told her about the intruder, she seemed appropriately indignant, ashamed, and enraged. But she responded by moving us back with the Klines, where she thought we were out of danger. In fact, we were pushed closer to the horror. Pearl and I knew we were sleeping under the same roof with a vile and dangerous man. She cried at bedtime each night. She couldn't be soothed, and she wet the bed like a child.

"Pearl, Honey," Mary would say. "What is the matter, Honey? You're okay, now. Everything's okay. Nobody's gonna getcha. Mary Kline's here. I've got ya, Honey."

My dim–witted mother knew that everything was not okay, but she was incapable of telling anyone about the dragon who left the Kline house by day and returned at night. I don't think he would have ever risked approaching either of us in the Kline home. It was too risky. Pearl wasn't smart enough to think beyond the terror of that possibility, but I was.

One night, I prayed that our intruder would die a horrible death, which would fix this problem. But he came home for supper every night, safe as ever. He glared at me, a deep, nasty glare, meant to let me know what a nuisance we were. He didn't want us there in his home anymore. We were like tempting candy that could talk. He could feel safe that Pearl would never spill, but he couldn't be so sure about me.

"That girl needs to be in a home, somewhere," I heard Mr. Kline say one night.

"Pearl *is* in a home, Daddy," said Mary Kline. "And I'm telling you, she wasn't safe in that apartment. You don't know how dangerous that was. Leaving those girls alone in that apartment at night was the worst thing we could have done. I'm not even going to tell you what went on, Daddy. You wouldn't believe it if I did."

"Oh, yes he would!" I thought to myself. "He could tell you a thing or two about what happened."

How many times I wish I had piped up. There was a big disconnect going on, but I wasn't sophisticated enough to sort it out. Mary Kline was certain about who the intruder was, *so* sure that it made *me* unsure of what I knew to be true.

Edward Kline was our visitor in the night.

If I'd asked her about her version, things might have been different between us. Mary Kline would still have been needy, but I would have looked upon her with more confidence. I would have been sure of the adult charged with my care. As it stood, I wasn't sure what Mary Kline knew or didn't know, but one thing was clear: she didn't have what it took to protect us from harm. Pearl and I were fair game.

And then, blessedly, Mr. and Mrs. Kline were killed in a car accident. My prayer had been answered. That week after the wreck, people brought food and flowers. Pearl and I watched Mary Kline's heavy body shudder as she wept. I felt relieved that nasty old Mr. Kline was gone, but kind of guilty that I'd prayed for it to happen.

Pearl sat hunched in the corner and soon stopped wetting her bed.

Chapter Seventy-One

Louise Kline

When the telephone rings after ten in the evening, it's usually bad news. Someone has died, there's been an accident, or some other calamity must be communicated. You can answer that call for help if you like, but you can also let the phone ring and ring. It's your call.

However, when your doorbell rings late at night, after you've turned out the lights, wiped the cold cream from your face, and set your alarm clock to rise and shine the next morning, you have fewer choices.

It could be the police looking for a robber on the loose, or kids down the street playing a prank. It could be your husband coming home late from the store (again) and he's forgotten his keys. He'll probably be angry because it's taking you too long to come downstairs. You won't care because you've not spoken a word to one another in days, and if he's going to be out night after night without even placing a common courtesy call to his wife or remember his house key, he deserves to stand out there in the chill a few minutes longer. He might even need to ring the bell twice.

If you are in my family, one that has made trades with the Devil, that ringing bell will one night announce a red-headed little girl you know too well. She's come in her pajamas from two houses away. Her hair is wet, and her lips are blue. She's not wearing a robe or a coat because there's nobody there to tend to such a detail.

You'll open that door, and you won't even pretend to be shocked that she's standing there on your front porch. You knew it would come to this. You look both ways, hoping to God that nobody saw her coming down the sidewalk alone like that in the dark. You pull her inside. She needs to be brought in from the cold and warmed up.

It's essential that you keep the commotion to a minimum. You knew this would happen. You just knew it. The situation you'd allowed to happen has finally unraveled. Surprise! You didn't start this mess, but you didn't stop it, either.

Shame on you, Louise Kline.

I hollered for Mary. My giant girl lumbered her way to the top of the staircase and looked down on us with sleepy eyes. She moved faster than I expected to the bottom and took over. The look of distress on her face hurt my heart. She was a better mother than I'd ever been as she swept into Mama Bear action. There was no stopping her.

I could have made a scene, but I wasn't about to get in her way. I stood on the porch in the cold and watched my daughter pull the child of the Davis girl behind her to the apartment where we'd planted them right after the little girl turned two.

The decision to move Pearl and Elizabeth to a place of their own was a calculated one on Edward's part. My good sense knew better. It did. But I let myself believe that this move would provide a much-needed release for Mary.

We never should have taken on the Davis girl and the baby she carried. Mary was a child, herself. She had no business raising a child. I told her it wouldn't be like babysitting. There would be no breaks and she wouldn't be able to leave her friend in the lurch. That girl needed attention, too.

Mary belonged in college. She needed to get out of this town, away from the cruel taunts and far away from Edward. But she wouldn't have it. She'd grown accustomed to having her way, and we obliged. We needed to keep that big girl of ours satisfied.

If she had a slice of happy, our Mary Ann might not think too much about her size, about why she slept upstairs with me, and why her daddy had his own room downstairs.

I knew this plan he'd hatched would fall apart. As soon as little Elizabeth started school and innocently spouted about the odd arrangement we'd come to, common sense and concern would come calling. It wouldn't matter how nice our house was, or that we owned the only department store in town. Kline's was a great big smokescreen, but it wouldn't serve us forever.

We did not see much of Mary during the week. She was up before the sun each morning to go to her girls and didn't come back home until after dusk. She took care of Pearl and Elizabeth admirably. Bathing them, cooking, cleaning, sewing, and loving.

She'd bring them over to sit in the parlor while she used my sewing machine. After a few months of that, I had Edward take the machine to the apartment. I wasn't doing any sewing at that point.

One day each week, we made an official appearance, all five of us. Each Sunday, Edward and I pulled the car up to the apartment to find Mary standing there with Pearl on one side and Elizabeth on the other, both dolled up with something frilly and pretty she had made. What wonderful, generous people we were.

Edward was not going to like it that Mary was bringing those girls back home with her for good. He was disinterested in finding out more about the night intruder. Mary wanted to call the police, but Edward insisted that we not make such a call. Not everyone would understand, like we did, how much sense it made to leave the slow Davis girl and that little girl all by themselves at night. It would be bad for business.

Edward didn't like having those girls back under our roof, either. He was crankier than usual at the prospect of it, and even more irritable when they were right there at the dinner table.

God Bless the Child

I expected my husband's late nights at the store to become even later and more frequent, but that's not what happened at all. Edward ate at the office most nights, preferring that Mary, the girls and I had dinner without him, but he usually came home right after we'd all settled in for the night. His late nights at the office had come to an end.

Chapter Seventy-Two

Mary Kline

David called Saturday afternoon to say that he and Elizabeth would be fetching Little Mary that night. Rats! I wouldn't get the chance to show her off at church. David sounded clipped on the phone. Abrupt. Maybe things weren't going well. Elizabeth probably wasn't too happy to see the house in such a state.

I'd yet to console Elizabeth since she lost the baby. Poor thing. I'd have to give her a big hug when they got here. And a meal. I'd need to make a meal. I threw open the freezer to find some meat. Aha! Pork steaks. Perfect.

Elizabeth looked pale as she stepped onto the front porch.

"Baby, Honey . . . oh, I'm so sorry, Elizabeth."

She stiffened, but I was used to that. She wasn't generous with her hugs and kisses, so I took what I could from this girl of mine. Even if it felt awkward and forced, it was better than nothing.

"Where's Little Mary?" Elizabeth said.

"Mama! Mama!"

Little Mary came running into her mother's arms. David stayed on the sidewalk. Odd. He usually had a hug for old Mary Kline. Perhaps he was tired from the drive.

"Daddy! Daddy!"

Little Mary jumped into his arms.

"Mama, I want to hold you both. Both of you at one time!"

Little Mary pulled her mother in tight. I knew I'd never be invited into that circle.

"Baby, Daddy's going to take you to the park for a while, and Mama and Gramma Mary are going to visit, okay?"

The child didn't like the idea, but she went in the car with David, and they drove away.

"I need to check the pork steaks."

Elizabeth followed me into the kitchen.

"Elizabeth, I was hoping I'd get to have that little imp one more day, so I could take her to church with me."

I could feel Elizabeth's tension rearing its ugly head.

"You've had her long enough, Mary. I didn't think we'd have to drive all the way over here to see her when I got out of the hospital!"

"Just wanted to help . . ."

"Well, you're good at that, aren't you? Helping is what you do best, isn't it?"

"Honey, I thought so. I just thought you needed the extra rest, and David agreed."

I felt like she was attacking me.

"Elizabeth, I just want what's best for you, that's all. That's all I've ever wanted."

I was pretty sure I meant that.

"Mary, that sounds nice. Really. It looks good on paper, but it's not true. That has never been true."

"Elizabeth! Of course, it's true. I'm not perfect, but I tried my best with you and Pearl. I did the best I could."

"Mary, how can you say that? You left us alone in the apartment. Alone, Mary Kline."

"Elizabeth. It's not that simple, Honey. Not that simple at all. Mother and Daddy insisted on that for a while. They did. And I didn't know better. I was just a kid myself. I'm so sorry about that. As soon as I knew something was wrong, I got you and Pearl out of there, didn't I? The very next day, you were back home with me."

I'd fixed that, hadn't I? I remembered that night clearly. As soon as they were settled, I let James Pullman have it. He'd never try that again. To protect my Pearl, we didn't even bring her to church that often. She could stay a few hours by herself. On some Sundays, Daddy would stay home to keep her company.

"Elizabeth, Honey. I need you to tell me that you understand me, that as soon as I knew that bastard was coming around, I got you out of there. Didn't I? Didn't I do that, Elizabeth?"

I'd never shared the attacker's identity with Elizabeth. I didn't want her to have to deal with that. Elizabeth had a creepy father who preyed on a slow girl and came back for more. I never wanted to share that part with her, and I didn't. I realized now that I might have to tell her the truth to get her off my back.

"No, Mary. You didn't protect us at all!"

Elizabeth was heading toward another rage, with extra hormones running amuck from the pregnancy.

"Yes, I did! Honey, your father was the one who came back to see Pearl in the night. It was your own father. He was trying to get back at me! As soon as I knew what was going on, I stopped it. I moved you girls out of there and in with us. As soon as I knew that was happening!"

Elizabeth would never appreciate what I did for her and her mother. I'd started to accept that fact. Even blood mothers and daughters have tension. From the beginning, Elizabeth and I had nailed down that part of our parent-child bond. Perhaps we were related after all.

"Mary! My, God! How can you say that? You didn't protect us! You moved us right in with the monster! Pearl was so terrified and started wetting the bed! Can't you remember that?"

God Bless the Child

I moved them in with the monster? What did she mean by that? I got them away from James Pullman. He was the one who came back to get Pearl. It was his nasty way of shutting me up, and it worked. He was dangerous. He scared the shit out of me. I'd played with fire and been scorched. What did she mean, I moved them in with the monster?

"Elizabeth, did you see the man who attacked your mother? Do you remember his face?"

I was expecting her to describe James Pullman and his smooth, handsome face.

"Yes, I did, Mary Kline."

"Well, Honey, that man is your father."

I never wanted to tell her that. It wasn't necessary. James and I had agreed we'd leave it.

"No, Mary, that's not what happened. It *didn't* happen that way. The man who came to us night after night was *your* father. Your daddy! He was the one who hurt Pearl! And you moved us right back into his house, Mary Kline! He was right there!"

Elizabeth looked earnest. Without her makeup, she looked just like she had when she was a child, full of freckles. Tears streamed down her cheeks, and they didn't leave a mascara trail like they had ever since she was a teen.

I'd seen that beautiful face cry many times. Elizabeth cried out of anger or frustration. I'd seen her cry because she was afraid, and I'd seen tears of pain.

I'd never seen tears of relief until then. Elizabeth, my daughter, was unloading a heavy, cumbersome burden, and she was doing everything in her power not to drop it right into my lap. She had enough heart to lay the nasty truth on the floor between us and allow me to take it in on my own.

Chapter Seventy-Three

Elizabeth

I told Mary that her father had attacked Pearl, and all she could do was check the meat in the oven. The woman's priorities fascinated me. I'd finally revealed to her why I was so angry with her and why I never trusted her. She responded by making sure that the food wasn't going to burn while we had our crisis.

"Mary, did you hear me?"

She was quiet, but I saw her shoulders shake. She turned toward me, and as if in a trance, picked up two potholders. Mary lifted the greasy pan of pork steaks as high over her head as her arms would allow and flung the hot splattering mess into the wall. Sizzling meat flew everywhere and streaked down the wallpaper. The pan landed on top of the old highchair. Mary's knees buckled under her, and she collapsed to the floor.

I wanted to rush to her, but I stopped myself. She looked so oddly tiny. It seemed disrespectful to stand over her. The grease dripped slowly toward the floor. That wallpaper would need to be replaced.

Mary's breathing usually filled a room when she exerted herself, but she was still. She must have been holding her breath, weighing the pros and cons of taking another.

A deep, painful scream forced its way through her clenched teeth. I pushed a chair out of the way to rush to her, and as Mary Kline looked up at me, she could hardly speak. Finally, she pushed her words out.

"Elizabeth, that is a lie. That cannot be. That simply *cannot* be."

God Bless the Child

She begged me to change what I'd said, as if I could take it back. I couldn't do that. We'd come too far and suffered enough. I shook my head, feeling sorry for all of us: Mary and Pearl and me.

Once again, I'd wounded the woman who raised me. I wanted to withdraw the arrow, but I didn't know how. Mary was trembling, but her eyes were bright and pretty. Even as drenched in anguish as she was, they sparkled. I felt ashamed I'd never noticed the beautiful parts of this woman.

She had more to say.

"Elizabeth. I didn't know. You must know I didn't know! Oh, my God, I thought I was protecting you and Pearl. How could I have known? Tell me you believe me, Elizabeth. Please. If you don't believe that I never knew it was Daddy . . ."

She faltered, choking, and moaned so intensely it made me shudder. I put my arms around her as far as they would go. I wasn't holding a fat, old woman. I was patting the back of a terrified little girl.

Chapter Seventy-Four

Louise Kline

My mother and grandmother liked to remind me how grateful I should be that I had a husband at all.

"You're not the prettiest thing in the world, Louise," my mother often said. "You should be thrilled with any man, and here you've got yourself one with money. Just suck it up and do whatever he asks. You're a lucky, lucky girl."

Grandmother would nod until I agreed. Edward wasn't that bad. Our life was nice. I had new furniture and a big house. Anything I wanted, really.

And I had our Mary Ann. As a newborn, she was delicate. Even my mother and grandmother agreed that she was.

"Must take after Edward's family," said my grandmother.

I was an ugly girl with a good, solid husband and a baby girl lucky enough to not look like me. What more could I ask? For a while, I was content. Edward was busy building Kline's Department Store, but when he came home, he was ours. On Sunday afternoons, unlike so many fathers I knew, he would let me go for a long walk by myself. He'd shoo me away for a nap or take Mary Ann to the store with him for the afternoon.

But the child soon became clingy. She didn't want to leave my side. She'd cry and carry on if Edward reached for her. She'd weep if he suggested they go to the store after supper. I thought this was normal toddler behavior and felt sorry for my husband. How hurt he must have been to be rejected by our daughter.

But the terrible twos became even worse threes, and when Mary turned four and got a little chunky, our child said something to me I knew was true the minute the foul words left her little mouth. I froze. Little girls didn't make up stuff like that. It wasn't possible for a child to piece together images and words like that unless they had experienced something terrible for real. I chided her, despite knowing better.

"Mary Ann Kline! What kind of talk is that?"

Before I knew what I was doing, I slapped my child. She didn't cry. She absorbed the blow and looked at me, confused, as the little wheels in her mind tried to process the slap and the sting on her cheek.

"Uh, oh. Mama, are you angry I told a secret?"

Tears pooled in her eyes. My knees buckled and I hit the floor.

"Yes, I'm angry because that's not a secret, Mary Ann. Secrets are true. What you told me is a lie. That was a dirty, ugly thing to say, young lady."

I tried to sound calm, like a mother who was sure of herself. But I wasn't, so I sent Mary to her room and went to my own bed. If I closed my eyes tightly enough, maybe the nasty truth would slink away and scurry down to the gutter where it belonged.

I rushed to the bathroom and dry heaved in the toilet. When Edward came home, he was alarmed to discover me standing at the top of the stairs. My chest was still heaving, heavy with outrage.

"Louise, Honey, I told you not to wait up for me tonight, didn't I? A late shipment of men's shirts and suits arrived, and I wanted them on the floor for morning. What's the matter? Are you not feeling well?"

He came to the top of the stairs.

"No, Edward. I'm not feeling well. I'm not feeling well at all."

"Well, get back to bed, then. I'll check on Mary Ann."

"No! No! You will not check on Mary Ann, not ever again, you sick bastard."

I moved quickly to block his way to Mary's room.

"Let me assure you, Edward, that you will never touch a hair on that child's head again. Do you understand me? Do you?"

I felt my rage spray over my husband's face. I considered pushing him down the stairs until a look of understanding registered on his face. Edward knew that I knew, and he didn't insult me with a denial.

"It's not what you think, Louise."

I followed him downstairs. We stayed up all night, arguing, negotiating, explaining, pushing, and pushing back. I cried, and he tried to stop me. I cried more. I was ready to walk out the door. I started up the stairs for our suitcases: one for me and one for Mary Ann. I'd call a cab. We'd stay in a hotel. I'd call my parents in the morning. Maybe call the police, too. This was not sustainable. I needed to leave. I needed to get our child out of there.

Each time I made it halfway up the stairs, Edward pulled me back down, pleading with me to stay and hear him out.

My folks would let us stay for a few days, but they would encourage me to go back home to my husband. Fewer mouths to feed that way. Less gossip stirred up about why Louise was home with that new baby of hers. They liked the discounts at Kline's. Exhausted, I knew I would have to stay, but not without terms, not without conditions.

"Edward, I'm not interested in talking about this anymore. Not for one more second. I like this house, and this nice life we have here. But if you touch our daughter ever again, even once, I will leave you and tell everyone. Everyone, Edward. I will tell everyone I meet about the pig you are."

For the first time ever, my husband had nothing to say.

"You can camp your sorry ass on the sofa tonight. Tomorrow, we're rearranging the furniture. You will need to find a new place to sleep. Mary Ann will sleep with me."

"Louise, wait."

"Wait for what, Edward? Wait, so you can tell me more details? Our little girl told me quite enough, and I've punished her for it. You and I better hope and pray that she keeps her mouth shut. You never know what a child might say, do you, Mr. Kline?"

As he looked at me, his eyes and shoulders pleaded guilty.

I wasn't finished. I pushed against his chest and pulled the wire-rimmed glasses from his face and threw them at him. In that moment, I felt courageous and strong. But I was neither. I was a cowardly keeper of secrets.

Edward retreated to the store. I sought comfort in our nice house and with my nice clothes and my equally nice reputation. Mary Ann sought comfort in food.

From then on, the three of us tiptoed around the truth.

Chapter Seventy-Five

Mary Kline

Daddy said everything was fine, and something lulled me into believing him. It was easier to be reckless and forgetful, so that's who I became as I grew up.

It wasn't the first time I tuned out my gut and stuffed my feelings inside my emerging body. I arrived in this world as small and dainty as anyone. My hands and feet were once as tiny as my Elizabeth's and Little Mary's, too. At first, I ate because I was hungry, and food tasted good. Later, I came to the table with no appetite, but I stuffed myself anyway. I'm not sure I could recognize hunger, especially not the kind that rumbles for attention.

As my body expanded, I knew I was becoming repulsive. I made myself into a horrible-looking toad. Mother tended to me anyway. Daddy just looked away and spent more and more time at the store. I survived by instinct, by burying myself in fat. Nobody could find Mary Ann Kline. That little girl went into hiding and never emerged.

Chapter Seventy-Six

David

After playing at the park, Little Mary and I stopped for an ice cream on our way back to Mary Kline's house. As I watched my daughter lick the sprinkles off her vanilla cone, I looked her over for signs of abuse or neglect and saw none. She was eager to see her mama.

As we entered the hallway, I heard sobbing in the kitchen. I told Little Mary to stay put as I inched toward the back of the house.

"Why is Gramma Mary crying? What's wrong?"

"I'm not sure, Honey. Daddy's going to go check. You stay right here. I'll be back in a second. I need to make sure everything's okay."

The sobs sounded almost melodic, so I knew they weren't coming from my wife. I'd never seen Mary Kline cry, let alone sob.

"Oh, Mary, I'm sorry. I'm so, so sorry," said Elizabeth. "Shh. It's alright. Oh, my Mary Kline . . . oh, my honey."

My wife was comforting her surrogate mother, rubbing her giant back and cooing to her. I was surprised how she assumed the role of comforter so easily. I was dumbfounded. This wasn't what I expected. I thought I'd find Elizabeth on the porch, arms crossed, angry we'd been gone so long, and more than ready to leave her mother. Instead, I found two women holding on to one another for dear life.

"Elizabeth? Mary? Is everything alright?"

Elizabeth looked up and shook her head. I could tell by how Mary Kline trembled that nothing was right for her. Nothing. I left the two women rocking together on the floor right next to a pile of pork steaks. We weren't staying for supper.

A small hand grabbed my leg, and before I could stop her, our Little Mary dashed past me to her mother and gramma.

"Mama! Mama! What did you do to my Gramma Mary?"

As she tried to pry Elizabeth away from Mary Kline, my wife looked anguished as she realized our daughter instinctively championed her grandmother, not her.

"Gramma Mary, what's wrong? Are you hurt?"

Little Mary tried again to wedge her little body between these two grown women. Mary Kline looked up, pale and overwhelmed, as if she'd been made completely vulnerable.

"No, Baby. Your Mama hasn't hurt me."

She touched Elizabeth's red hair. Little Mary was confused, and I knew I needed to help them get through this crisis. I convinced my daughter to leave the kitchen and watch some television. Once I got her nestled on the couch, I returned to the kitchen and offered to take Little Mary home with me and come back in a few days.

"No," said Mary Kline. "I won't have that. That child needs to be with her mama. It's been too long. You go on home. I'll be fine."

"I don't like that," said Elizabeth. "I don't like that at all. You come home with us. Come with us for a while."

What the hell had happened? What about the peach pits? What about Mary Kline taking over? I missed something, and it had to be big.

"Elizabeth, I'll be fine. I will. In fact, I think I *need* to be alone tonight. I've got some thinking to do, and some more crying, too."

"Let me call Johnson. I don't want to leave you alone tonight."

Mary slumped her shoulders and shook as she quietly cried. The kitchen, normally so busy with lots of action, was still as we put our collective minds together to put Mary Kline back in one piece again.

"Yes, call Johnson," she said. "I want you to call him, please, and stay with me until he can get here."

God Bless the Child

Elizabeth walked her mother down the hallway into the bedroom and shut the door. I heard her talking quietly into the telephone as I cleaned up the greasy carnage.

Little Mary had fallen asleep on the couch. Fifteen minutes later, I heard the front door swing open and slam shut.

"Johnson! We're back here."

He made his way to the hallway.

"What's going on? Where's Mary?"

I nodded toward the bedroom. He walked gently to the door and knocked softly.

"Mary? Mary, Honey, it's Johnson. Let me in. Mary Kline. You need to let me in, Sweetheart. Come on, you can do it."

The door squeaked open slowly and Elizabeth emerged from the dark room. She turned and blew a kiss toward her mother.

"I love you, Mary."

She made way for Johnson. As he entered the room, he waved the two of us away, smiling grimly as he closed the door.

I picked up Little Mary and got her into our car. As we drove home in silence, I didn't press Elizabeth for details. I'd done enough of that the day before. Our time for secrets was over, and I knew my wife would tell me what I needed to know once she understood it herself.

Late in the night, I spooned Elizabeth in our bed, and she spooned our daughter. As I held my wife's body next to mine, her posture felt different. The tightness that had always been there had lost its grip. Her neck was relaxed, and her breathing was even and deep. As I drifted asleep, I heard Elizabeth and Little Mary breathing in sync, perhaps for the first time ever.

Chapter Seventy-Seven

Mary Kline

Without Pearl and Elizabeth, I am nothing.

I didn't take them because I wanted to. I took them because they were a lifeline, and without them, I would have sunk to the bottom of a lagoon. I was too big to hoist myself out, and nobody else would have been able to do it, either.

Needing a girl like Pearl might have been pathetic for anyone else, but it wasn't for me. Pearl didn't have any choice or the wits to fend me off, so I forced myself on her, and she accepted. I was a parasite with big, powerful suckers, draining the life out of her. That's what I did. I drained Pearl of her youth. I was no better than James Pullman.

Elizabeth, Pearl, and I were held together by many emotions, including love. But the love would always be eclipsed by something bigger. In the beginning, baby Elizabeth needed me as badly as I needed her. But she soon grew into a goddess who recognized her pathetic surroundings and her skewered circumstances.

What I gave Elizabeth could be called love, but it was complicated and conditional, tangled up with traps. My love offerings looked like acts of worship, but we both knew they were peace offerings meant to appease her, to atone for my most grievous sin: I needed her.

Chapter Seventy-Eight

Elizabeth

I wasn't sure how to store the information from my recent exchange with Mary Kline. My largest file, one labeled, "anger," no longer seemed logical. What I thought to be true—that Mary Kline knew her father was coming to Pearl at night—and that she'd solved the problem by bringing us even closer to the danger—belonged in a pending file, to be looked at repeatedly until I could understand it. This was a cross-referencing nightmare. I hadn't given Mary Kline much credit.

I had to be angry with someone for leaving Pearl and me alone in the night, but Mary Kline did not deserve the bulk of the blame. How could she have recognized that Mr. Kline had devised a plan to clear the way for his nasty, unnatural urges for vulnerable little girls? Pearl and I had become part of a twisted compensation package the Klines threw at their daughter. Pearl and I were rescued by predators.

Once I learned that Mr. Kline had also abused Mary, I could see that she and Pearl were sisters in a sick sorority, stuck at the bottom of a nightmarish food chain. Mary was certain that the attacks on Pearl came from the same man who was my father. I learned how she thought she'd provoked the whole thing with some heavy-handed taunting. Finally, I understood my father. Knowing his identity didn't make me feel like dashing off a greeting card. Not at all.

Once again, I started questioning God. What kind of deity created me? I was sired in the house of God—by a man of God. I'd been conceived in what must have been a confusing and frightening experience for my mother. Why had God allowed me—a cruel mistake—to take root in Pearl's womb?

I stumbled upon a reason one afternoon, looking through old photos at Mary's house. She was holding me, her cheek pressed to mine. In year after year of birthday photographs, there I was, wearing a fancy dress and ready to blow out candles on an even fancier cake, made painstakingly for me by Mary Kline.

Pearl was there, too, on the sidelines, wearing a cardboard party hat, smiling faintly for the camera. We celebrated my birthdays with gusto and meticulous preparation. As I grew, I came to love, then like, then tolerate, then abhor these celebrations. But Mary always insisted on marking the day of my birth with great fanfare.

Then, it hit me. My birthdays enabled her to crawl out of the hole she'd been thrown into by her awful parents. Perhaps I'd been born for one purpose: to save Mary Kline. And perhaps God told her that she'd been born, abused, and survived for one purpose: to save me. And, in her own quiet way, Pearl saved us both.

At last, I came to an astonishing, liberating conclusion that could free me from the love and hate grip I shared with Mary Kline.

It was no longer just about me. This stopped the minute my Little Mary was pulled from my body and placed on my chest. I began to understand that my birth allowed Mary Kline that same kind of release. With me to hold and love and clothe and feed, she didn't have to think about herself anymore, and for someone like Mary Kline, that was a soothing and welcome alternative.

Chapter Seventy-Nine

Mary Kline

There have been many times I longed for a conversation with Pearl. I wanted to know what went on in that empty head. Did she understand the gruesome truths of our friendship and what bound us together?

Did she? Could she? And if so, how could anybody forgive the Klines for the way we used her to satisfy ourselves? Where should an apology even begin? Everyone abandoned her in some way or another. Her parents died. Her brothers, satisfied to stuff their pockets with Mother and Daddy's cash, left her behind. James Pullman had done the unspeakable many times over. Even Elizabeth, especially as a teen, looked upon her mother as a burden.

I remember being fascinated learning about how early Native American Indian tribes used every part of the buffalo they slayed for their survival—the skins, meat, bones, marrow, hooves, and even the testicles. Wasn't it with the same efficiency that Pearl Davis was stripped to nothing? Her ripe and luscious body was used again and again by young James Pullman. And my father.

We snatched her offspring for our purposes, and later, my father took whatever shred of dignity she had left. When we were through with her, when I was too overwhelmed to keep my promises, I put her in a place where strangers might do it. She had served her purpose.

I had abandoned Pearl. I was a Kline alright, through and through.

I decided to sift through the piles to unearth the piano in my living room. My Elizabeth would have been delighted to see me in action. Some of the papers had a furry sheen of dust. Many had yellowed and even stuck together, bound by mildew and inertia.

I filled two trash bags with grocery receipts and unopened bank statements dating back at least 15 years. Without ceremony, I dumped hundreds of glossy catalogs and magazines and parted with electric bills and coupons for products that were no longer on the market. I tossed cards of all kinds—birthday greetings, children's Valentines, business cards and appointment reminders, too.

I showed no mercy, until I reached Elizabeth's things: photos of Little Mary, wedding shots of her and David, and newspaper clippings, announcing their engagement and the wedding. Another announced her college graduation. I threw all those things in a grocery sack. Maybe Elizabeth would want that stuff, but probably not.

I dug and sorted until I reached another layer, one that should have felt like sacred ground: the hundreds of sympathy cards we received when Mother and Daddy died.

I sat on the couch and tried to remember opening them for the first time, but none of the designs or signatures helped. Some of them had well-intentioned notes scrawled beneath one trite ditty or another about time healing all wounds and the comfort of memories.

Mary, our thoughts are with you during this difficult time.
We're so sorry for your tremendous loss.
Edward and Louise were such wonderful people.

Tremendous loss. Wonderful people. Hmm. How many people had observed the three of us thoroughly enough to see that something was seriously wrong with the Kline tribe?

Chief and Squaw have big, big problem, oh Observant One—even bigger than Chafes When Walking.

Mother, did I embarrass you? Were you ashamed of your great, big girl? Did you wish you could thread a needle and use whipstitches to sew my gaping, cavernous mouth shut to keep food from going in and the wrong words from coming out?

God Bless the Child

Daddy, did you find what you were looking for when you explored me in the dark? Once you undid me from myself, what kept you coming back? Could there possibly be more to drag into the sunlight? Did going where no grown man, no father, should ever, ever go, turn you into a trailblazer?

What kind of pact did you make with Mother? Did you shake her hand, the one that slapped my confessing mouth? Did you slither back to the store while she let the seams out of all my dresses?

You blazed a trail of shame for us, didn't you?

Chapter Eighty

Elizabeth

Weeks later, as Mary Kline and I sat in therapy, I heard the saddest, sickest story I ever imagined could be possible. I realized how fortunate I'd been that those attacks in the night had been absorbed by Pearl.

She bore the abuse that could have been heaped on me. Edward Kline liked little girls, too. In her denial or ignorance, whatever you want to call it, I guess Mary Kline saved me after all. Her daddy would have never tried to reach me under his own roof. The risk of being caught was too great.

Mary Kline started to look different. So many times, I'd wanted to ask her, "Mary, do you know how it feels to be left alone in the night with a predator at your door? Do you know what it feels like to know there's nobody there to catch you? Do you? Do you know, Mary?"

She did know, all too well, how it felt to be left alone in the night with a predator at her door. She didn't have anyone to catch her. But I did. I had Pearl. On that cold night so long ago, when Pearl kicked Mary's father in the face, she saved me from a monster she and Mary knew was real.

All this time, I believed *I* was the one who didn't have a mother worth a shit. With my two misfit mommies, I was in relatively good shape compared to Mary Kline. The only mother she had *knew* what had been done to her daughter and had chosen to stick around.

Even my father was better than Mary's. I now understood why she was so fat. I could even see why she blocked her early experiences with her own father out of her mind. Mary was a victim in her own right. I even began to understand her never-ending smothering.

Chapter Eighty-One

Mary Kline

I knew what I had to do, and I didn't like it one bit. There were many things I couldn't make right. It was too late to apologize to Pearl. For the rest of my life, I would apologize to Elizabeth in as many ways as I knew how. I finally figured out that the most appreciated gift I could give the child I raised was to stop needing her so much. And when I did need her, all I had to do was just say so.

"Mary, it's enough. Don't give me one of your crap lines about having something for Little Mary or call me to ask my size," Elizabeth said. "Just say you miss us and you want to see us. That's all you need to do. You don't need to invent a reason to make contact. We're family. Just say you're lonely, and then come to us or we'll come to you."

Why was that so hard for this fat old girl to do? Had I been so lonely and pathetic while I played mama to Elizabeth and Pearl? And what did James Pullman think of me? The notes and taunts were something I could address with an apology. I didn't like the reverend, and he'd done terrible things to Pearl, but I had behaved like an insane person.

"Mary, you can plead insanity if you like, and you'd probably be justified," Johnson said. "But Reverend Pullman is hardly without flaws. You can point that out to him. Don't let him off the hook for his part in this. You can tell him you are sorry for what you did, but that's it. Just tell him you're sorry, and leave."

My Johnson. He'd seen all of me—my wobbly thighs, my sloppy house and even the darkest corners of my emotional life—and still, he wanted to hang around. He was in my corner.

"Why on Earth would you want to be my friend, Johnson Kuhlman? Look at me! Just look at how fat I am!"

"I don't care, Honey. I *don't*. I love every inch of you, Mary Kline. Every inch. Don't lose one pound, because all those beautiful pounds finally belong to me."

At least he wasn't throwing me lies about not being able to see my fat. He didn't dare tell me he was blinded by love. Some women might appreciate that kind of deceit, but not me. I had a man who saw my size, admitted he saw it and embraced me with his whole heart. Johnson made me feel like a real woman. What did I do to deserve this man?

Sometimes, I tested him, just to clear the air and make sure I wasn't being used. I wasn't interested in being someone's mother figure.

"This isn't some weird fetish you have for fat chicks, is it? If just any fat gal will do, I'm outta here, Johnson."

When I said something like that, he put his hands on his hips and shook his head in disgust.

"Mary Kline, please. Could you give me some credit? Geez. I love and want *this* fat chick. You!"

Then he'd hug me as best he could. He'd wrap his arms around me and kiss me on the back of my neck. Johnson Kuhlman could sure make me feel good. He was just as good at insisting that I do the things that were hard but valuable.

"You need to just do this, Honey. You'll feel much better. Do you want me to go with you? I will."

He would have gone to the parsonage and stood right there with me while I apologized to James Pullman, but I needed to do it by myself. It was time I squared away what I could. I didn't have to like the reverend, but I did have something to say to him.

Chapter Eighty-Two

James Pullman

When the doorbell rang, I wondered what problem had cropped up this time over at the church. I looked through the window and saw it was Mary Kline.

We'd agreed many years before to drop our pissing match over Pearl and Elizabeth. After Louise and Edward Kline passed away, Mary stopped showing up for church. She wasn't the only one who refused to allow me to just get my punishment over with. Even my own mother refused to let me confess to anyone what burdened my heart, especially not my father.

"James! No. Just no. That will *kill him.* Kill *us*!"

That's what my tiny, freckled, redheaded mother bellowed at me every time I brought up the subject. She was going to let me endure something far worse than a beating, or public shame. I was sentenced to having no visible consequences at all. Instead, I would struggle on a private cross.

What did Mary Kline want? I opened the door.

"Mary."

"James."

"What can I do for you, Mary?"

"I have something to say to you, James."

I sighed.

"I'll be brief."

She placed her plump hand on the door.

I did not want to be with her, but I ushered her into the living room.

"Please sit down."

She shook her head.

"James, I owe you an apology. That's why I'm here."

This wasn't what I expected, but I still wasn't interested.

"Mary, this isn't necessary. Really, we've hurt one another enough, haven't we?"

As far as I was concerned, we'd hashed this out years ago. I'd held up my end of the agreement, and so had she. This was a done deal. What else was there to say? Years of pastoring hadn't improved my patience. If anything, I was short with everyone who wanted something from me. I was bitter, and resentment bubbled under the surface of my nice smile and smooth talk.

"Alright, Mary. What is it?"

This woman knew I had a dark side. There was no need to hide who I was with her.

"I know you weren't the one who hurt Pearl in the apartment."

This was it? This was what she wanted to say? Of course, I hadn't come back to Pearl again. I'd told her that.

"It was someone else. I know that now. Someone else hurt Pearl. I was sure it had to be you, that you were getting back at me for the taunts and the letters. I was sure it had to be you. I'm sorry. I was mistaken."

We stood there in awkward silence. Any idle chatter would have been better than the quiet.

"Okay, fine, Mary. Fine. I accept your apology."

"No, James, there's more."

"Mary, look, let's not do this, okay? Really, let's not."

I headed toward the door to usher her out. I just wanted her to leave.

"James, shut up, okay? Just shut up and let me do this."

I'd seen Mary Kline mad, and I wasn't interested in seeing it again. Big women are scary when mad, but not as frightening as angry little women. I'd rather face Mary Kline than my tiny, redheaded mother. Maybe this was God's plan, to defer and prolong my punishment.

"Reverend, I need to do this. Please allow me. You don't know what it's like to not be able to fix all the things you've broken."

I bit my tongue. That's right. I didn't know a thing about watching my sins fester and come to a head, not a thing. God must have been enjoying the irony.

"James, you were wrong to be with Pearl. We know that, but what you don't know is that the person you and Pearl made—Elizabeth—saved my life. You and Pearl and your daughter saved my life."

I think she meant what she was saying.

"Don't you see, James? Can't you see?"

She was barely able to contain her emotion.

"Without Elizabeth, I would have had nothing. Nothing at all."

I didn't exactly get it, but what she said triggered a thought, that the woman standing in front of me may have saved *my* life, too. It certainly could have been a whole lot worse. If the Klines and their daughter hadn't snatched up the mess I'd made with Pearl, things could have turned out very differently for me, and not for the better.

"Mary, I told you long ago that taking in Pearl and Elizabeth was a good thing. I believe I even thanked you for it."

"No, James. Stop. You don't understand. Stop and listen to me. On the surface, what Mother, Daddy and I did may have looked good, but it wasn't. It was not good at all."

I tried to interrupt her, but she held out her hand to shush me.

"Let me finish, James."

"Mary, if you're here to thank me for my stupid, youthful past, you're welcome, okay? I'm glad I could be of service to you."

"It was my father!"

"What?"

"I said it was my father. He was the one who went to the apartment to hurt Pearl."

Edward Kline. *The* Edward Kline? The Kline's Department Store Edward Kline?

During the next few hours, I was able to counsel Mary Kline, a woman I'd detested for years. With the truth, God let me see this person in an entirely new way. She was no longer a great, big nuisance. She wasn't a needy cross I'd have to bear anymore. She was a person in pain, a woman fighting for her life. That afternoon was the first time in my entire stint as a pastor that I felt genuine, like my robes finally fit.

We'd both suffered enough. We were two hurt animals, scratching and biting for territory of our own. One day, we'd both have to answer to God for poor Pearl. For many years, I hoped she was the prettiest, smartest, most beloved angel in Heaven.

Elizabeth was still on Earth. God made a daughter with our bodies one summer afternoon. I didn't want to take advantage of the neutral ground Mary and I had finally reached, but so much time had already been wasted.

"Mary, I must thank you."

I took her hand in mine.

"By coming here today, you have saved *my* life."

I asked her a question I first asked a long time ago. This time, I was sincere.

"Do you want me to take my place as Elizabeth's father?"

"James, that's not my decision to make. Don't you imagine I've twisted and manipulated your little family tree enough? Elizabeth will always be my daughter. I didn't do much right, but I did the best I could, with what I had. Don't you think, Reverend Pullman, that God would want you to have the same kind of chance?"

God Bless the Child

That night, I found a quiet sanctuary inside the church as I locked the door and lay face down in front of the altar, my arms stretched as far as they would go. I prayed and wept. Finally, I'd been forgiven, and I could forgive myself.

Chapter Eighty-Three

Elizabeth

Mary Kline had already shared with me the identity of my father. It was no wonder she'd kept that to herself. I was grateful to her for that. Next to making my perfect wedding gown, keeping my father's identity from me was probably one of the better decisions she'd made on my behalf. I wasn't even angry with her for insisting that he stay away from me when I was a child. Chock another one up for Mary Kline. Maybe the old girl's maternal instincts weren't so bad after all.

When Reverend Pullman called to see if we could meet for coffee, I didn't see why not. I hadn't had a mommy, not in the traditional sense, and Mary Kline was more than enough of a mother for me. I certainly didn't need a daddy. But I was curious. I had questions only this man could answer.

We met a few times for coffee and idle chitchat. It wasn't exactly your typical, long lost, father–and–daughter reunion. Finally, I just asked him what I wanted to know.

"Reverend, did you hurt Pearl?"

That was the impression I'd gotten from Mary Kline. Pearl was raped. To Mary, it was a fact. The sky was blue. The Earth was round. Slow girls had sex one way: rape. Pearl wasn't capable of any type of consensual sex.

The man sitting across the table from me seemed surprised I would ask him such a direct question, but he didn't falter.

"Elizabeth, I hurt Pearl. I did. There's no question about that. I hurt your mother, but not in the way you might think. I didn't hurt Pearl the way Mary Kline thought I did."

He brushed his hand through his thinning hair, embarrassed.

"Did you rape her?"

It was my right to know, wasn't it?

"I tried to once, but I couldn't go through with it. I couldn't be rough with Pearl, like I'd been with other girls. Pearl and I had pleasant experiences. They were wrong, very wrong, but they were pleasant. I should never have been with Pearl in the way I was."

I must not have looked convinced.

"The truth is, Pearl was a wonderful kisser. We could kiss for hours and hours."

He turned a bit red in the face. After all, he was a father having a talk about sex with his daughter. I suppose he was entitled to feeling a little light-headed. He'd missed so many father–daughter moments.

I smiled because I found it hard to believe that Pearl, slobbery Pearl, could have been much of a kisser.

"What makes you and Mary Kline and the whole world so sure that slow people can't enjoy what their bodies and hearts have to offer, just like anyone else? We were both kids, but our bodies did some amazing things. I'm not going to sit here and tell you that what happened with Pearl didn't feel good. I've told enough lies. It felt good to me, and I'm pretty sure she felt something, too. I think Pearl enjoyed herself."

"Did Pearl think you loved her?"

He needed to think about that.

"Elizabeth, I'm not sure what she was thinking. She wanted to be with me. I should never have allowed it to happen. It was wrong for me to take advantage of Pearl. I knew that, but she didn't. It's possible that she felt loved. It's possible."

"Did you love her?"

"No, Elizabeth, it was not love. She deserved that, but it wasn't in me at the time."

My father smiled at me. He knew what I needed.

"Pearl might have believed that she loved me that summer. That is possible. In her limited way, she might have considered what happened between us to be love."

"Are you sorry, Reverend? For what you did to my mother?"

He nodded. I watched him manage the tears that threatened to spill down his cheeks. This man's blood pumped through my heart. I wished that I loved him.

"Yes, I'm *very* sorry. I have been sorry for a long time. It was a terrible mistake."

"Would you say I am a mistake?"

He put his hand on mine and squeezed gently.

"Elizabeth, look at me. The answer to that is no. You are no mistake. You are a lovely outcome. You are proof of God's wonderful way of transforming things that are ugly into something beautiful. You blessed Mary Kline, you know. You are beautiful. Pearl was beautiful, too. She was."

For the first time ever, I wanted to think deeply about Pearl. It was too late to touch her, inspect her hands, or look more closely at her features. She'd passed away just a few years after the wedding.

I wanted to go to Mary Kline's house and find Pearl's things. I wanted to get out photos and pore over them with fresh eyes and a fresh heart.

I felt sad for Pearl, and hopeful. She didn't have much to hold onto in her life, but at least she'd experienced what she thought was love. Maybe for a few brief moments that summer when I'd come into being, Pearl felt wanted and desired. I hoped she was so naïve that she never detected the wrongness of it all.

God Bless the Child

Maybe she felt like a princess. I remembered the way her face glowed as we held hands and spun around and around in the pink princess gowns Mary Kline made for us.

Maybe Pearl wasn't thinking about the gown at all. I liked to think that somewhere deep in her mind she was recalling those few spiraling moments she had shared with James. Maybe a tiny voice inside Pearl reminded her in a gentle way that I wasn't her sister, but her daughter—somebody God had allowed to come into being with two bodies blending and believing, even for a moment, that they belong together.

Chapter Eighty-Four

James Pullman

As an ignorant youth, I wished I wasn't Protestant. I preferred the Catholic notion of keeping my uglier deeds between myself, a priest, and God.

With a screen between us, and a curtain drawn around us, I wouldn't even have to look God or his agent in the face as I spilled my guts. As I matured, I came to understand that it was more complicated than that. The essential component to forgiveness was sincere remorse, not just raw confession. My entreaties to God were always half-baked and my penance half-hearted. Luther and God weren't about to excuse me with a good set of rosary beads and a feeble promise to do better.

My father, and his father before him, believed in a God who demanded public confessions from sinners who couldn't be cleansed without paying a steep and painful price. God sent his son Jesus to save us all, but a nod from a crucified man who lived in the past had little to do with the public outrage of mere mortals in the here and now. Those who were hurting from my transgressions deserved a pound of my flesh, but I was too frightened to bare my chest for the first cut.

I was a sinner of the hair–splitting variety. I felt genuine remorse for the urges I unleashed on the girls I'd brutalized, but I was not the kind of boy or man who would go to the trouble of finding each victim to come clean and apologize.

I owed Pearl a different kind of apology, but one never formed on my lips. I let myself believe that the tender nature of our subsequent meetings was a good enough demonstration of my remorse.

As time passed, I landed on a complex and uncomfortable truth: my less forgivable affront to Pearl happened during our sweetest moments together. I was the smarter, more savvy of the two, and I should have stopped what was happening. My gentle and unprotected moments with this girl were more damaging than any of my usual rough overtures.

Pearl Davis might have been better off had I bloodied her nose or dislocated her jaw. The tin taste of blood might have scared her away. A good, hard slap on her face might have protected this girl from my self-satisfying plunges.

I was willing to take my lumps, but I wanted to do it in private. In some ways, Mary Kline was right about me. I never came back to Pearl for more, not like Mary thought. But I let many years pass, so apologies would be too late, and a daughter of mine went without a father. I was firmly fixed to fiction. I was just familiar enough with the Bible to make myself sound like an authority. I was charming enough to sound like I had just returned from a mission trip to a remote, pagan land.

My selective memory gave me permission to bury the parts of myself I didn't like anymore. Mary Kline called me a fucker, and she was dead on. I was a total fraud.

What Mary, Pearl, and my mother could not know was that I *did* stop hurting women. That summer with Pearl, though an outrage, was my last plunder. Something about those exchanges changed me. I did not pursue encounters while in seminary or after. God must have been working on me. I was a project that would require miraculous powers of grace and patience.

There was no one with whom I could unburden myself of my guilt. I was forced to reckon with my hypocrisy and sit in my sin. It was a humbling journey that I had to take. My blunder was expecting the path to be linear and without points of pain. I expected forgiveness to wash over me before I made dutiful visits to every station of the cross.

Chapter Eighty-Five

Mary Kline

Johnson and I spent weeks cutting up old dresses. Most of the time, my darling was patient and didn't ask questions. But sometimes, his inner seamstress would come out and he couldn't resist.

"Mary, are you sure you want this?"

He held up a dark brown corduroy jumper that Mother must have made for me back when I was nine or ten years old.

"I know. It's ugly, but I want some of it."

Johnson sucked in his breath and started cutting. When we were half-way through, he took a break to have some iced tea. I kept cutting.

"Why are we cutting all of this fabric into crescents?"

"Johnson, please trust me. I know what I'm doing."

"Alright, Mary Kline. Whatever you say."

Our excavation project was a trip down memory lane for both of us. Johnson remembered a lot of the fabric. After all, he'd measured and sold us most of it, first to Mother, and later to me as I sewed things for Elizabeth as she grew up. He recognized the broadcloth material used for my shirts and many of the plaids Mother selected for my enormous skirts. We both laughed as we cut into the dark green graduation gown Mother had to make special for me. He held up one of the pink jumpers I'd worn as a little girl.

"I remember seeing you in that dress."

"Oh, Johnson. You do not."

"No, no, Mary. I do. You were wearing this dress one day when Mrs. Phelps sent me here to deliver fabric. You came to the door, and then disappeared down the hallway. I think it must have been the first time I ever saw you. You were so cute."

He had such a sweet look on his face as he remembered me as a little girl that it made me cry.

"Mary, Honey . . ."

He rushed over to me.

"What? Did I say something that hurt you?"

I let my head rest against his chest, and I wept.

"No, no. It's just that I don't think anyone ever thought of me in a nice way when I was a child. Nobody ever said I was cute."

Johnson and I held one another for a good long time, and he never questioned my plan for Elizabeth's quilt again.

I pieced together hundreds of different crescents of fabric, starting in the middle of the quilt with the dark, scratchy, heavy, uncomfortable fabrics that defined my youth. I worked each crescent into a circular pattern, making the design look like an enormous whirl.

As it grew larger, the colors lightened. It was here that Pearl's dresses and the light, billowing, shimmering fabrics I used to create Elizabeth's clothes, blended into a swirling blaze of hot pinks, rich reds, wild rainbow prints, sparkling teals, daffodil yellows, dotted Swiss and deep tangerines.

Just as Pearl and Elizabeth, my two darlings, had pulled me out of the dark and into the light, so did the remnants of their dresses, now sewn into an everlasting quilt.

All along the edge of the quilt, I added a white border made of the smoothest, cleanest satin I could find in Johnson's store.

"Mary Kline, this is just incredible, Sweets. Elizabeth is going to love this. She's going to *love* it!"

"I hope so, my dear. I sure hope you are right."

Chapter Eighty-Six

Little Mary

We started visiting Gramma Mary a whole lot more after Mama came home from the hospital. She smiled more and didn't seem to mind as much if there was a mess in the house. She even let me wear my mood ring shirt and didn't care if we dumped all the Barbie outfits into a great big rubber tub.

By the time I started fourth grade, Mama and Dad had some news for me. We were going to have a baby! By summer, I'd be a big sister. We decided we should let Gramma Mary know, and right away.

"Should I dial the phone, Mama?"

"No. No, I think we're going to deliver this message in person."

Mama rubbed her tummy and smiled.

Gramma Mary and Johnson were sitting on the front porch swing when we pulled up in the driveway. Gramma Mary stood up and stretched her arms out for me.

Mama let me be the one to share our news. Johnson and Gramma Mary whooped and hollered and squealed with joy.

"Oh, Elizabeth, this is perfect," said Gramma Mary. "Just perfect. Come here. I've got something to show you."

I followed the two of them into the dining room, where a great big, crazy-looking quilt was hanging on the wall at the far end of the room. Mama drew in her breath as Gramma Mary turned on the light.

"Oh, Mom, it's, it's incredible," Mama said.

She reached up to touch the colorful design. Then, the two of them moved in closer, touching and pointing to each patch.

"Look! There's the fabric from my kitten pajamas and I see my confirmation dress. Oh! There's my pink fairy princess costume."

"Yes, and see this? It was the dress I made for your senior prom. And this was from a big dress my mother made for me the summer before you were born. Johnson remembers selling us the fabric. Here's Pearl's little green dress I made for her to wear to your wedding."

They whispered and pointed at the quilt for the longest time. Gramma Mary's eyes were glistening, and so were Mama's. The two of them hugged each other. Mama's arms could hardly reach around Gramma, but it didn't matter. She gave her the best hug she could, and they both held on tight, just like a mama and her girl should do.

After that day, Mama planted lots of lipstick kisses on my face and was willing to leave them there for the whole day. Mama was more fun than I could ever remember.

I'm not sure what happened during those weeks Mama was away, but it must have been important. When she came back, things had changed. We were better. All of us. We were finally a family.

About the Author

Since she first fell in love with writing in high school, Anne Shaw Heinrich has been a journalist, columnist, blogger and communications professional. Her first article appeared in *Rockford Magazine* in 1987. She's interviewed and written features on Beverly Sills, Judy Collins, Gene Siskel, and Debbie Reynolds.

Anne's writing has been featured in *The New York Times* bestseller *The Right Words at the Right Time, Volume 2: Your Turn* (Atria) and Chicken Soup for the Soul's *The Cancer Book: 101 Stories of Courage, Support and Love*.

Her debut novel, *God Bless the Child,* is the first in a three-book series. She and her husband are parents to three adult children. Anne is passionate about her family, mental health advocacy and the intrepid power of storytelling.

Upcoming New Release!

ANNE SHAW HEINRICH

VIOLET IS BLUE
The Women of Paradise County Series
Book Two

Violet is a teenager, sporting a hideous tattoo on her pelvis. She started calling her parents, Skip and Gloria, by their first names. Her new friend, Jules Marks, is unsuitable for more reasons than Gloria can count. He's from Shakey's Half, just outside Poulson's city limits, where the poor folks live.... Gloria and Skip have no idea just how thick their daughter is with her unsavory friend, but they will learn soon enough and realize they owe that kid some respect. Once they discover why Violet has turned so sullen and difficult, they have a problem much bigger than her tattoo…

Gloria pays a visit to her sister, Ruth. The two were at odds growing up, but that seemed mostly behind them until Gloria springs an accusation about Ruth's only son, James. Ruth must do some fancy footwork to keep her husband, Rev. Richard Pullman, in the dark about that boy of theirs…

**For more information
visit: www.SpeakingVolumes.us**

Upcoming New Release!

GERI SPIELER

REGINA OF WARSAW
LOVE, LOSS AND LIBERATION
Regina of Warsaw Series
Book One

Regina Anuszewicz looked forward to visiting her sister in Bialystok for a late afternoon stroll along the Bialy River. It was June 1906, and it should have been an exciting time to stay overnight in the women's boarding house. However, a violent pogrom blasted those plans as a rage of violence shook the town and Regina's hopes. Stormtroopers swarmed the streets and homes, stomping up to her sister's boarding house, forcing Regina to hide inside the wardrobe, barely able to breathe as she heard screams and people begging for their lives. The trauma of that day shaped Regina's life and every decision she made as she moved through the days and years, coloring her approach to every event that took her from Poland to the United States and the four children she sought to protect.

For more information
visit: www.SpeakingVolumes.us

Now Available!

JACQUE ROSMAN

MURDER IN GEORGETOWN
The Academic Mom Mysteries
Book One

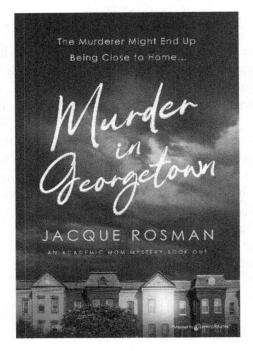

**For more information
visit: www.SpeakingVolumes.us**

Made in the USA
Monee, IL
08 July 2024

61509260R00173